A CONSPIRATORIAL COURTING

A CONSPIRATORIAL COURTING

A Conspiratorial Courting © 2023 by Martha Keyes. All Rights Reserved. 2nd edition. Previously published as My Wild Heart. All rights reserved. No part of this book may be reproduced in any form or by any electronic or mechanical means including information storage and retrieval systems, without permission in writing from the author. The only exception is by a reviewer, who may quote short excerpts in a review.

This book is a work of fiction. Names, characters, places, and incidents are either products of the author's imagination or are used fictitiously. Any resemblance to actual persons, living or dead, events, or locales, is entirely coincidental.

Martha Keyes
http://www.marthakeyes.com
First Printing: February 2020

Dedicated to Mom, the woman who taught me—and seventeen years' worth of sixth graders—to love and appreciate Shakespeare.

Preface

"Contempt, farewell, and maiden pride, adieu!
No glory lives behind the back of such.
And Benedick, love on; I will requite thee,
Taming *my wild heart* to thy loving hand.
If thou dost love, my kindness shall incite thee
To bind our loves up in a holy band.
For others say thou dost deserve, and I
Believe it better than reportingly."
—Beatrice
Much Ado About Nothing by William Shakespeare

Creating a retelling is a challenging task. Deciding how closely to keep to the original while also bringing a fresh take on a story is no small task, and certainly not less so for being one of Shakespeare's beloved plays.

I have long enjoyed Shakespeare's *Much Ado About Nothing.* When I set out to evaluate which of his plays I wanted to use as inspiration in a series of Regency era romances, it was the only one I *knew* I wanted to do. But when I contemplated the play, I found myself more drawn to the humorous situation and

PREFACE

engaging relationship of Beatrice and Benedick than to the fairly melodramatic story of Hero and Claudio. So, I decided to flesh out what takes up a relatively small part of the original play and to reimagine the events resulting from it. Hence, this is more of an inspired-by romance than it is a retelling.

Whether you are a lifelong Shakespeare lover or have never read one of his plays, I hope that you find *A Conspiratorial Courting* to your liking.

Chapter One

No doubt, the best thing to do was to ignore her cousins. But Edith Donne had never been good at holding her tongue, and certainly not when the topic of conversation was love and marriage.

"Edith thinks herself quite above falling in love." Her cousin, Mercy Kennett, shot Edith a provoking glance, eyebrow tipped up and a hint of mischief in her eye. "But that was also the case for Sarah Brailey, and look at *her* now."

Edith satisfied herself with a slight roll of the eyes, letting the periodical in her hand fall open and tipping it so that the candlelight fell upon it. She knew Sarah Brailey—or rather Sarah Pickard since her surrender—and knew her well enough to take issue with the comparison. She kept her eyes on the periodical as she responded with a bite to her tone, "Yes, Sarah was very vocal in her supposed protestations against love."

"*Supposed* protestations?" Mercy said with a laugh.

Edith looked up, meeting her cousin's skepticism with a clear gaze. "Certainly."

"They sounded very convincing to *me*." Edith's cousin, Viola Pawnce, was curled up in the window seat, the customary book open in her lap. Her finger was poised on the page, keeping her place. The curtains were pulled back from the window behind her, revealing an evening landscape washed in twilight's soft blues and the deeper shades of rainclouds.

Edith let out a little scoff, nodding at the book in Viola's lap. "You are reading *Hamlet*, are you not? Can you not tell an Osric when you see one, then? All affectation and pretense? Sarah's act was nothing but ill-disguised despair of ever finding love. Those protestations were a manipulative way to garner attention—they were a cry *for* love, not a determination against it. Only look how quickly she submitted to Mr. Pickard's attentions and with what haste she agreed to marry him once he began fawning over her."

She returned to her perusal of the periodical, content that she had made her point. How her cousins managed to doubt her sincerity—comparing her even to Sarah Pickard, of all people—was beyond Edith's understanding. No matter how firm and steady she was in her opinions, they seemed to think she simply hadn't yet found the right gentleman to pique her interest.

With time, they would know better, but Edith couldn't help wishing that they would simply believe her.

The two men were lingering over their port, and Edith would have been content for them to do so for some time yet. She had nothing against Mercy's husband Solomon—indeed, she liked him very well—but she preferred spending time with Mercy without the displays of mutual affection that the couple was wont to engage in. In a few short weeks, Mercy and Solomon would sail for Jamaica, and Edith didn't know when she would see her cousin again.

"But you have truly *never* fallen in love?" Viola looked puzzled as she asked the question.

Edith smiled widely and shook her head. "Terribly

provoking of me, isn't it?" She came up beside Viola, a hand on the curtain as she watched raindrops speckling the window.

"Provoking? No." Viola's frown deepened. "It is just that..."

"It offends your sensibilities. I quite understand." Edith gave Viola a teasing pat on the shoulder. "But don't let it trouble you, love. I am an anomaly, you know."

"Only because you *choose* to be." Mercy perused the music sheets on top of the piano.

"What's this now?" Edith said in a rallying tone, folding her arms. "I had thought that at least *you* understood me."

Mercy smiled and set down the page she held, tilting her head to the side in thought. "Yes, well, that was before I was married. *Now* I know what you are missing by holding so tightly to your cynicism."

Edith didn't respond. She couldn't deny that Mercy was at her happiest since marrying. And Edith wasn't so steeped in her cynicism, so determined to make others miserable, that she had any intention of saying what dissatisfaction she foresaw. Indeed, she hoped for Mercy's sake that she would be proven wrong. But she had watched it happen too many times to believe that even two such decent people as Mercy and Solomon would be immune to it. Edith lived in a house where it was evidenced daily in the interactions of her own parents.

Even those marriages that started out happily—and Edith suspected there were fewer of them than people wished her to believe—invariably became less so with time. She had come to the conclusion that this was a result of people misunderstanding their own motivations in marrying. Marriage in the name of love sounded much more noble than marriage in the name of convenience, but the truth was, they were both selfish —both an act of union between two people hopeful of extracting every last ounce of happiness from one another.

The initial haze of novelty and excitement invariably wore off in time—Edith had seen it happen shockingly fast—leaving the two souls to reflect upon the truth of the phrase that William Congreve had so aptly coined: "Married in haste, we may repent at leisure."

Edith did not take for granted how fortunate she was in having no obligation to marry. Her aunt's deathbed bequest could certainly not have been bestowed upon someone more grateful. The bequest was poetic—from a confirmed spinster to one in the making. It made Edith smile.

But Viola was not satisfied. "Perhaps you need only find someone who shares your—your—your—"

"Pessimism?" Edith offered. "Skepticism? Misanthropy?" She well knew how she was viewed by others.

Viola's brows came together. "I was going to say your wit."

Mercy let out a laugh as she seated herself on the piano bench. "What? And have them at each other's throats all night and day? What a frightening prospect you paint."

"Then perhaps someone more docile? Quiet and meek?" Viola sounded skeptical of her own idea.

"A church mouse, perhaps?" Edith suggested, feigning interest.

"And have her frighten the poor man to death?" Mercy said with a grin.

Viola let out a disappointed sigh. "No, it wouldn't do, would it? But then who?"

Mercy lifted her shoulders, and Edith laughed. "I am pleased you have come to the conclusion—quite inevitably, I might add—at which I arrived years ago. And now not only can I pursue my path of determined spinsterhood in peace, but we can move on to more interesting topics of conversation. Don't make me regret having invited you." She winked. Even if she had to endure this same conversation every day of their two weeks at Shipton House, Edith would be glad of her cousins' presence.

Mercy opened the lid of the piano. "Very well. We shall be on our very best behavior. Is Lydia to come?"

Edith thought of her sister, cooped up in her small house with her children. Edith had written to invite them, but she had known it a lost cause from the beginning. "No. You know how she frets over the health of her youngest—James has never done well on carriage rides."

Mercy nodded with a sympathetic frown.

There was more to it than that, but Edith didn't trust herself to say it without sounding embittered. She was fairly sure Lydia would have chanced the journey if she'd had a trustworthy escort. Her husband was entirely useless for something so chivalrous—or for anything other than making Lydia's life miserable—and Edith's father had excused himself from the task with the familiar justification that he was too busy with his latest political venture to take three or four days racketing about the countryside. Indeed, he and Edith's mother were even now dining with a family in hopes of garnering support for the vote. It was a singularly united gesture by a couple normally divided in their politics. Edith mistrusted it.

She only hoped that the peace would last the duration of the house party. At least her brother Matthew would be there to help her diffuse any awkward moments that might crop up during evenings when they were all together.

Edith considered herself fortunate that Matthew had even agreed to join the spontaneous group—he generally spent his summers bouncing from house to house among his friends. But in order for Mercy's husband Solomon to feel at home in the group of women, they had needed Matthew. In the end, the house party would just comprise Edith, Matthew, their parents, Viola, and the Kennetts. It was small and very familial, certainly, but far preferable to spending the two weeks alone with her parents. And there was something to be said about spending time with a gathering of people who already considered themselves such close friends.

The door to the drawing room opened, and Edith let out an audible sigh. "Good heavens. Who invited *you*?"

Elias Abram stepped into the room, grinning widely at her. "I considered declining your brother's invitation, but he assured me that you would be in a state of the mopes for the duration of the house party if I didn't come, so"—he held his hands out, palms up— "*me voilà*, as the French say."

Edith directed a raised brow at her brother Matthew, who followed Elias into the room. Solomon Kennett trailed behind them, his eyes finding his wife Mercy's immediately.

Edith looked away from the unmistakable warmth that passed between the couple, directing her attention to her brother. "You might have warned me he was coming along."

"I told you I wanted to invite him." Matthew said. "I just thought he couldn't come."

"Yes, and I was lulled into a false sense of security when you never brought it up again."

"Oldest trick in the book," Elias said, disposing of his person in the chair Edith's father normally occupied—a grand, imposing piece of furniture, with far too many tufts and a tendency to resemble a throne. It was just the sort of chair that would appeal to Elias's bravado.

"Yes," Edith said, putting her reading material down and making her way to the door. "I suppose someone with your penchant for repelling people *must* resort to such tricks, taking people unawares—the element of surprise is essential, isn't it?" Before he could respond, she bid the company a good evening, gave a quick dip of the head, and shut the door behind her, a satisfied smile on her face.

Elias Abram's gaze lingered on the door Edith had shut, his eyes narrowed but the corner of his mouth turned up in acknowledgment of his having come off the worse in that particular battle. "Does she never exhaust her wit?" He stretched out his legs a bit farther and tucked one ankle under the other.

"If she does, I have yet to observe it," Matthew said. "You'd do well to take a page out of my book, Eli."

"What? And let her trammel me underfoot?"

"No." Matthew shot him an annoyed glance. "Simply refrain from provoking her. And if you can't manage that, don't engage with her at all. It is that simple."

Elias shook his head. It wasn't that simple at all. He and Edith had been engaging in this type of warfare for longer than Elias could remember, and to back down now would be tantamount to offering her his pride on a silver platter. "A woman like your sister will wither away if no one provokes her. I am providing a service, in fact—a kindness and a condescension."

Matthew shot him a skeptical glance. "You merely can't forgo an opportunity to cross swords when it's presented to you. But even if what you say *were* true, you do the rest of us an *unkindness*, for we are caught in the cross hairs of your supposed service to Edith. I think that the good of the whole must supersede whatever imagined good you think you are doing my sister. Do you not agree?" He looked to the others for confirmation.

Elias waited for the others to throw in their lot with Matthew. He didn't anticipate anyone in the room would side with him in such an argument. It made people uncomfortable to witness Elias and Edith engaging as they just had. But he could never help himself. There was too much satisfaction in it. Edith was overconfident, and no one else seemed the least bit interested in helping her realize it.

"I certainly agree." Solomon seated himself next to his wife on the piano bench. It was far too small to allow for two, but they didn't seem to mind in the least. He pressed a kiss onto his wife's forehead. "If she truly enjoys such encounters, it seems strange indeed that she would choose to retire so immediately after your arrival."

Confound the man. Elias smiled genially. "Perhaps she was feeling less mentally astute than usual—not having had enough time to prepare for my arrival, I mean, for I am convinced she must rehearse these quips—and wished to make her escape before she could be bested?"

A laugh escaped Mercy. "An unlikely hypothesis, I'm afraid. Like you, Edith cannot resist an opportunity to showcase her wit—unless she feels victory is too easy."

"Ha!" Elias said, shaking his head. "I stand with my own interpretation of her departure—a cowardly escape."

Matthew let out a dramatic sigh. "It is merely a sad case—certainly not without precedent—of you not understanding women, Eli."

Elias let out a scoffing laugh. "On the contrary. I understand them all too well!"

Matthew grasped his shoulder and pinched his lips together pityingly. "If that were true, you would be married, wouldn't you?"

"*Or*"—he removed Matthew's hand from his shoulder unceremoniously—"perhaps that is precisely why I am *not* married. I know women too well to trust them. What is *your* excuse?"

Matthew gave Elias's shoulder another squeeze, much tighter than the first, and rose to his feet. "Take a damper! Are we to play a game of whist or sit here forever discussing your lack of address?"

"Address I lack not. It is value for their affection that I lack, rather. But by all means, let us sit down for a rubber."

Chapter Two

Edith was the last to join the other five in the echoing entry hall late the next morning, having spent the prior hours in her corner of the library.

Elias was the first to notice her approach. "Ah. So, the recluse deigned to grace us with her presence, did she?"

Edith flashed him a mocking smile. "I try to reserve unpleasant interactions until *after* I have breakfasted."

Matthew set his hat firmly atop his head. "Oh, enough already. If you two intend to bicker the entirety of the expedition, please at least walk behind the rest of us a few yards. Come, Vi. Let us go see some ruins." He tugged Viola with him, and Mercy shot Edith a laughing glance before taking her husband's arm.

Edith looked at Elias, who grinned at her with his arm out in invitation. Her lips pinched together, and she took it. "Let us not ruin this for the others, shall we?"

"I'm afraid the object of the expedition is *already* ruined." He kept his gaze forward, but the corner of his mouth twitched. He was obviously quite pleased with his pun.

"Oh, for heaven's sake," Edith said, pulling her arm free of his. "If my choice is between listening to your awful jokes and returning to the house, there really is no choice at all." She turned back toward Shipton, but Elias grabbed her arm, drawing her back toward him. A dash of sandalwood enveloped her briefly. He might make terrible jokes, but at least he smelled decent.

"Very well," he said, tucking her arm back into his. "No more puns. But I could hardly let that opportunity pass by when you set it up so beautifully, could I?"

"If you insist on making a fool of yourself, I certainly shan't be the one to prevent you," she said cheerfully. "I doubt I *could*, in truth. Some forces are simply unstoppable—too strong to be resisted." She stole a glance at him and couldn't suppress a satisfied smile when he threw his head back and laughed. Though she would never admit it, she was glad he hadn't let her return to the house.

He cocked a brow at her. "You are hardly the first woman to tell me I'm irresistible."

She let out a shout of laughter that was hardly feminine. "If *that* is what you gathered from my words, then it is no wonder you conduct yourself with so much confidence. If Midas's touch turns everything to gold, it seems your sense of hearing turns everything to a compliment. Perhaps you should consider employing a translator to help you understand what women mean when they insult you."

"Are you offering yourself for the position?" he asked.

"I think I might be overqualified."

"So certain?" he said, his mouth pulled up in its characteristic, self-assured half-smile. "If I were to unleash the full power of my charm upon you, Edith Donne, you would be helpless against it. Yes, even *you*."

"I wait with bated breath," she said dryly, slowing as they approached the others, who had come to a stop. Before them, a blanket of yellow wildflowers carpeted the area surrounding what remained of an old priory. Vines crept around the ruins, hiding some of the areas where stone had broken away from the original structure.

Solomon looked back at Edith and Elias, his expression turning to one of surprise. He nudged Mercy. "You were right. They *haven't* killed each other. Bravo, you two." He gave a small clap.

"Killed each other?" Elias said. "Surely not. In fact, Edith was just telling me how very irresistible she finds me." He looked down at her with his teasing grin.

"Behold me enraptured." Edith tugged her arm away from him and used her hand to stifle a feigned yawn, then made her way toward the priory.

Elias's top boots shuffled through the long grass that had grown up around the rear of the priory. Two broken stones lay on the ground, and he turned one over with his foot. "This place is more ruined each time I come." He shaded his eyes as he looked up at one particularly jagged wall. "I remember the first time we came here, this wall was nearly intact."

Matthew picked up one of the stones, turning it over in his hand. "Yes, well, fifteen years of desperate villagers filching stone takes its toll on a place. Not to mention the time you scaled the wall. I seem to remember two or three stones coming loose then, too."

Elias smiled, picturing his boyish form trying to find footholds. "But I *did* make it to the top."

Matthew scoffed through his nose. "Just before toppling onto me and spraining my wrist. Do you remember that, Mercy?"

Mercy turned to face them, and her husband followed suit.

Having her attention, Matthew repeated the question. "When Elias sprained my wrist while you were visiting that summer?"

"Come now," Elias protested. "You can't place all the blame on me! You were the one foolish enough to stand directly below me. Besides, I saw a snake, and the surprise caused me to lose my footing. I can hardly be blamed."

"A snake?" Viola curled her arms inward and looked down at the ground below, as Solomon drew back a bit, eyes searching the tall grass.

Edith stepped toward Viola, setting a reassuring hand on her arm. "A likely excuse from Elias. And indeed, even if there *were* any snakes here, they would have long since been frightened away by all of us traipsing around."

"She is right, Vi." Mercy pulled at her husband's arm, bringing them closer to the group. "I remember that day, though, Matthew—you with a sprained wrist and Elias with a twisted ankle, if my memory serves. And the both of you crying miserably, blaming each other."

Both Elias and Matthew opened their mouths to protest.

"I don't remember *that*," Elias said.

"Surely not *crying miserably*," Matthew objected.

"Your memory *does* serve," Edith said, stepping into the grass and tugging the hem of her dress free from a weed. "Mercy and I didn't feel the least bit sorry for either of you, though, seeing as only that morning, you had snuck ink into our tea."

Elias exchanged a conspiratorial glance with Matthew, then schooled his expression into one of innocence. "I haven't any idea what you're referring to."

"The ink smudges on your fingers begged to differ," Edith replied saucily. "I hope they took as long to fade as the ink stains on our lips."

Solomon folded his arms with a small smile and leaned

against the ruined wall, where Matthew reclined on a shoulder, fingers toying absently with a blade of grass. "Was that when all this" —Solomon gestured between Edith and Elias— "began?"

"Oh, no," Edith said, crossing her arms with a challenging smile at Elias. "*That* was when he put a frog in my bath."

"Baseless accusations," Elias said, though he couldn't keep from grinning. He could still recall the sound of her girlish scream reverberating down the corridor. "Besides, the trick was more than repaid when I slipped my feet into my boots the next morning."

Solomon's mouth pulled into a curious half-smile. "What, then?"

"Slugs," Elias said.

Solomon looked to Edith in surprise, and she shrugged, shielding her eyes as she glanced up at the sky. "I have always tried to give as good as I get. I have checked my bathwater ever since, and *you* still check your boots, don't you?"

Elias's toes wiggled, and he gave a reluctant nod. He couldn't deny that he *did* indeed check his boots, despite the fact that his valet also checked them. He suppressed a shudder as he remembered how it had felt the last time he hadn't.

It had been some time since they'd played those sorts of tricks—in the beginning it had been Mercy and Edith pitted against Matthew and Elias, but Edith and Elias had always been the driving force behind the rivalry, and as they had grown and matured, such pranks had slowly given way to verbal battles.

Elias looked down at his boots, hidden in the tall grass, and frowned. A long piece of rope sat a few inches from the toe of his black boot, winding through the amber and green blades, well hidden by its dull color. He glanced through the paneless window of the priory wall to where the rectory stood, fresh laundry hanging from a similar rope in the garden. No doubt the rope had come from whoever inhabited the home.

The conversation had turned, and Elias kneeled with the pretense of brushing some dirt from his boot, covertly taking the end of the rope and standing with his hands clasped at his back so that the rest of it trailed behind him.

He composed his face in an expression of polite interest and then, when the time seemed most propitious, yelled out, "Snake!" and jumped away from the group, making the rope rustle the grass.

Chaos erupted: two screams—indistinguishable in pitch—from Solomon and Viola, yelps and a dancing of feet from the others, while Elias teased the rope and feigned terror.

Two insistent hands wrapped around his arm, and Edith pressed her hunched form into him. Matthew and Solomon were huddled together against the wall, their wide eyes trained on the ground, while Mercy and Viola had both run to the shorter, wildflower-speckled grass.

Elias raised the rope in the air, giving in to his laughter, and wiping at his eyes.

Edith immediately stepped away from him. "I might have known."

He wagged his brows at her. "*Irresistibly* drawn to me, were you? You might have taken refuge in any number of places, but you chose me."

His words elicited a disgusted snort from her. "It speaks volumes that your *irresistibility* depends upon your ability to terrorize your victims." She looked to Matthew and Solomon with a raised brow. "Though I *do* find it very interesting that Mercy and Viola were left to fend for themselves while the two of you flew to each other for protection. Did you not promise to comfort Mercy and forsake all others, Solomon?"

Solomon acknowledged the hit with a humorous glare, though his chest was still heaving from the fright. Mercy rustled through the grass to take his arm. "Solomon hates snakes more than almost anything."

"Are there no snakes in Jamaica?" Viola asked, still stepping cautiously through the grass, as though she still didn't believe that it had all been a prank.

"None that are venomous," Solomon said, taking in a deep breath. "One of the island's many attractions."

Elias held up the end of the rope, smiling. "Neither was this snake venomous."

"No." Edith was gathering up the rest of the rope in her arms. She tossed the bundle toward him, and Elias scrambled to catch it. "Merely a nuisance."

Matthew glanced at Edith and Elias up ahead. Rather than trailing behind the group, they had taken the lead on the return to Shipton House, and their pace matched the quick-moving debate they were engaged in, putting them far out of earshot, while the remaining four walked abreast.

"Not much has changed in the past fifteen years, then, has it?" Solomon said.

Matthew laughed. "No. Though it *has* been some time since Elias subjected us to one of his larks, and even then, he always involved me in them." His eyes narrowed, and his mouth pulled into a smile. "I have a mind to take revenge."

"You can count on my full support," Solomon replied. "It would be refreshing to see the tables turned upon someone like him for a change."

Matthew glanced at him thoughtfully. "Between the two of us, I'm sure we can come up with something satisfying."

"Why not the four of us, then?" Mercy said. "We were *all* subjected to his prank, after all. It seems only fair that we should have a hand in the retribution—in serving him some humble pie."

Matthew chuckled, kicking at a tuft of grass. "It is not as

easy as it sounds. I have tried to serve entire humble pies to Elias on any number of occasions and have yet to hit upon just the thing. He's dashed difficult to outsmart or catch unawares."

"We must come up with something entirely original, then," Viola said prosaically. "A prank unlike any you have employed before. The element of surprise is essential."

Matthew nodded. "A fake love letter, perhaps?" He snapped his fingers. "From Miss Jenkins! For he cannot abide the wiles and lures she sets out for him."

Mercy shook her head, frowning. "I cannot like Miss Jenkins, either, but I should hate it if word were to reach her of the prank. It might well put Elias in a difficult position, for she is certain to capitalize on it in whatever way she can."

"A woman, then, whom we can trust *not* to do so," Solomon said. "A prank we can sustain just long enough to throw him off balance."

A particularly heated part of Elias and Edith's debate brought their muffled, intermixed voices sailing back to the group, and Matthew jumped out ahead of the others, putting his hands out to stop them.

A smile grew on his lips as he considered the possibilities. "Edith," he said.

"What?" Mercy frowned.

Matthew shrugged. "Why not use Edith? What could throw Eli off balance more than discovering Edith was in love with him?"

Solomon shook his head. "He would never believe it. Really, only a fool would."

"People can be brought to believe anything with enough reason," Viola said. "Only think of Malvolio in *Twelfth Night*. He is quick to believe that Olivia loves him when *he* receives a falsified letter from her." She tapped a finger to her lips. "What if Edith was made to believe that Elias was in love with her, as well?"

Her words were met with silence as Matthew and the others digested the suggestion.

"The pranksters become the pranked," Matthew said slowly. He pointed a finger at her. "I think you are onto something, Vi. It would throw the both of them off kilter if we can manage it right." He slapped his leg. "Ah, what fun! What better way to play a trick on them than to convince them of something so entirely contrary to what they believe? The perfect way to take down their pride a notch or two! What say you, Mercy? Can it be done?"

She looked unconvinced. "It seems...cruel."

"Come, my dear," Solomon said in a rallying tone. "Do you truly think either of them would be hurt by such a thing?"

Mercy's mouth twisted to the side. "I suppose not. In fact, I would be surprised if she even believed it."

"Which is why we must plan things," Matthew said.

"They will not begrudge us a bit of fun," Solomon said. "And it will be but temporary—only long enough to see how they react. Neither of them is too rigid to enjoy a well-played trick, surely."

Matthew watched as Mercy regarded her husband with indecision.

"Edith will think it the best of jokes," Matthew said encouragingly, "as will Eli. I assure you."

Mercy glanced at Matthew, lips twisting to the side. She sighed, and her mouth broke into a reluctant smile. "Very well. What exactly shall we do?"

Chapter Three

Elias's eyelids fluttered, and he winced with discomfort as he shifted on the chaise longue in the library. He hadn't come there with the intention of falling asleep, but the book he had been reading lay on the floor, open but upside down, and his boots dangled over the edge of the chaise. It was the quiet corner of the library—quite obviously made to feel secluded, tucked as it was in the back rim of the room and hidden by a large screen. The faintest hint of vanilla hovered in the corner, reminding him of something familiar he couldn't put his finger on.

He made to reach for the book on the floor but stopped short at the sound of voices.

"Mercy herself told me, you know. You mustn't tell anyone else, though, for she would wring my neck if she knew I'd said anything." It was Solomon, and he likely was unaware of Elias's presence in the room. It would be best to make some sort of sound to alert Solomon and whoever he was talking to to Elias's presence.

"So it *must* be true, then." There was awe in Matthew's voice as he responded. "One thinks one knows one's own sister!"

Solomon chuckled. "Yes, well, I'm afraid there's no doubting the truth of it—she's in love with him. Quite enamored, from what Mercy said."

Curiosity made Elias's skin prickle, but now was the time to act. He swung one leg over the side of the chaise, bringing the other behind it. It stopped mid-air.

"Heaven only knows why!" Matthew said. "Eli's my closest friend—more like a brother, really—but he's the deuce of a fellow to Edith. And she is even worse to him! I can't begin to understand it." He let out a strange noise. "In *love* with him? I say, it's enough to strike one dumb."

Elias sat cemented to the chaise longue, his breathing slow, body leaning forward, leg suspended just above the floor.

"You know her better than I, of course," said Solomon, "but Mercy says she is nothing if not prideful—"

"An understatement if I ever heard one!"

"—not to mention she despairs of his returning her regard, so she has vowed never to say a word or give him any indication of the true state of her feelings."

Elias's eyes grew large, his heart thrumming against his ribs.

Matthew blew out a breath. "Women are strange creatures, are they not? Certainly beyond my ability to comprehend. Ah, here's the book. And don't bother returning it—if I never have to set eyes on it again, I'll be the happiest of fellows."

"Very good," Solomon said. "I shall gladly take it off your hands. You've spared me the trouble of locating a copy for myself."

The footsteps of the two men drew farther from Elias, followed by the opening and the soft thudding of the door closing.

Only the crescendoing ache in his thigh, suspended in the air, brought Elias to his senses. He lowered it slowly, eyes wide, heart beating like a chorus of drums.

What—what had just...? He blinked rapidly and rubbed at

his eyes, wondering if perhaps he was still sleeping, experiencing some sort of strange dream. But the library looked very much like it had before he'd dropped off to sleep.

He slapped his cheek, wincing.

Nothing.

What in heaven's name was he to do with what he had just heard? Matthew had said it was enough to strike one dumb—and that is precisely how Elias felt. Speechless.

Edith Donne *in love* with him? She despised him! Took pleasure in tearing him down! And yet....

He stood, picking up the book from the floor and tossing it carelessly on the chaise. He strode past the screen so that he had more room to pace.

Perhaps he had simply been missing the signs. It seemed unlikely, but he certainly hadn't been on the lookout for them. Stranger things had happened in history—or things nearly as strange, at least?

He had the sudden, overpowering desire to seek Edith out—to search for the evidence he had apparently been missing these past...how long exactly *had* she been in love with him? Weeks? Years?

But, even then, what did it change that Edith was in love with him?

She was undeniably alluring, and never more so than when she felt she had bested him in one of their battles of wit— more frequently than he cared to admit. Her dark eyes gleamed, and the smile she clearly thought she was suppressing tugged at her lips.

And yet, no. Love him or no, she was still the arrogant, aggravating woman he had known for years. He was intrigued at the thought of her love for him, but only because it was so very far from the truth he had accepted: Edith Donne disdained him.

There was nothing more to his shock than that. It was only natural, and it certainly was no indicator at all that he had misjudged his *own* feelings. After all, how could one possibly mistake love for spite?

Chapter Four

Edith shaded in the stem of the rose she was sketching in the gardens of Shipton House, stepping back to inspect her work. Her mouth twisted to the side. She was out of practice. It had been years, in fact, since she had last taken out her sketchbook. But she was happy to do so now, if only for an excuse to get away from the house for an hour.

It wasn't that she disliked having company at her childhood home; she was merely unaccustomed to having all her nooks and crannies—the ones she had used since childhood to avoid whatever quarrel her parents were currently engaged in—invaded by others.

And, though she would die before she admitted it, the constant back and forth with Elias required a great deal of her energy. She needed to gather her faculties. He was quick to sense any weakness.

A breeze blew into the garden, rustling the leaves on the rose stems and causing a few red petals to drop from the blooms she was sketching. The ground was littered with the petals, giving the gardens an almost morbid appearance, like the scene of some bloody—and strangely located—battle.

Footsteps sounded in the walking path behind Edith, but the intruders were hidden from view by the tall boxwoods that surrounded the rose garden.

"...but how very unexpected!" Viola's enraptured voice pierced through the hedges easily.

"Yes," came the resigned voice of Mercy, "but nothing to rejoice over, I'm afraid, for nothing can come of it. He is too proud to make a clean breast of his feelings for her, and *she* is prouder still—far too proud to do anything but scorn him even if he did confess his love." She sighed. "No, things will go on as they always have. Edith will never know herself beloved of Elias, and he will continue meeting her disdain with his teasing."

Edith's pencil dropped to the ground, and she clenched her eyes shut, cringing at the loud clatter it made on the gravel-specked dirt. But the slow footsteps continued.

"It is such a terrible shame, though," Viola said. "I am of a mind to tell her myself."

"Oh no, you mustn't do any such thing," Mercy was quick to reply, and distance was beginning to make their voices harder to hear. "Elias would be mortified. Or livid, perhaps. One can hardly blame him, for it would be very much like Edith to lord it over him. Besides, Solomon told me in the strictest confidence, and *he* had been told in confidence by Matthew. Indeed, I wouldn't have said anything if you hadn't brought up the subject."

"Very well," Viola said in a resigned voice. "I shan't say anything."

"It is for the best, I think. You had better direct your energies toward nudging Elias's affection in a more promising direction."

Edith shot a hand out to the nearest bush as she realized that she was teetering on the edge of her chair, trying to hear the last snippets of Viola and Mercy's conversation as their walk took them to other parts of the labyrinth.

She found that her breath was coming quickly and that she had a sudden need to move. She set her sketchbook upon the chair, grasping at her skirts and blinking in confusion. It was nonsensical. And yet she could not deny what she had heard. Elias Abram in love with her?

But why? She had never said a kind word to the man. If any person on the earth had a reason to hate her, it was Elias Abram. She had been a veritable minx to him for the past decade and more, and well she knew it. And yet, it was like a well-worn track in the road. Try as she might to urge her words into a more polite and civil route, they *would* insist upon taking the path they knew best.

And certainly Elias bore some of the blame for this, for there was no denying he took great pleasure in provoking her. Why a man would so relish being verbally flogged, she couldn't understand—particularly if he truly harbored some affection for her.

She didn't know whether to feel encouraged or disappointed.

The latter. It must certainly be the latter. She couldn't *unhear* her cousins' words, and those words changed everything.

She might despise Elias's unearned confidence and his obvious misunderstanding of women, but she had no desire for their repartees to come to an end—little though she wished to admit it.

And even less did she revel in the prospect of rebuffing him were he to express his apparent feelings for her, though evidently Mercy thought there was no risk of that. Even if there were, Edith was not so terribly insufferable as Mercy had said. She took no joy in someone else's pain—even if that someone stood in sore need of a knock to his pride, as Elias did.

She brushed a finger along the outer petals of the nearest

rose, fanned out in a full and perfect cascade. She frowned at the realization of just how unsatisfactory her sketch was. There was so much more depth and range of color at this close distance than she had captured from her seat. She leaned in so that her nose nearly touched the bloom. Closing her eyes, she inhaled.

The scent was sweet, but not cloying, and the fragrance somehow enhanced the perfection of the flower. Surely nothing deserved to be so perfect.

She opened her eyes, then ran a finger along the tip of one thorn and then another. The second thorn pricked her finger, and she smiled. The rose was perfect, and yet ready to do battle—to protect itself, to draw blood. It wasn't some helpless thing for the taking. One must understand the thorns in order to properly benefit from the bloom.

She placed her fingers carefully between the thorns and bent the stem until it yielded with a snapping sound. Setting it atop her sketch, she brushed off the frustration at the contrast between her immature depiction and the transcendent reality that nature created again and again—so effortlessly.

The sun was dipping down toward the horizon, and she needed to dress for dinner. Her heart quickened as she picked up her belongings, and she hated the reaction. She was never nervous to see Elias. And she didn't wish to remark anything approaching love in his eyes when he looked at her. She merely wished for things to continue on as they had been.

Chapter Five

Edith put a hand to her coiffure as she took the staircase down to the drawing room in preparation for dinner. She had chosen the dress that made her look her most formidable, as well as asking that her hair be arranged a bit differently than usual. The dark waves had been slicked back with pomade and then arranged high on top of her head in a way that, frankly, looked quite silly. But she wanted to appear tall and imposing.

Perhaps if she looked intimidating and unapproachable, Elias would come to his senses. Whatever image he had created of her in his head, she was not that, and the sooner he realized it—preferably without her needing to say anything on the matter—the better it would be for all of them. They could go on as they had been.

Or at least she sincerely hoped so. For her part, she would act no differently. She would not curtail her wit or treat him with kid gloves. He was a full-grown man who obviously knew how to protect himself, just as she did herself. And while she had a sliver of curiosity that begged to be indulged about what exactly was the nature of Elias's sentiments and how long it had been since he had convinced himself that he was in love with her, she would not surrender to such a silly impulse.

The thought of his regard still mystified her. It somehow made her feel unworthy, which she detested.

The company was all gathered in the drawing room, save Edith's parents, who had only returned from their short journey to Keldhome two hours earlier. She was still surprised that they had gone together at all. Her parents agreed on nothing when it came to politics, and her mother was not one to hold her tongue on the matter. Edith had inherited her boldness and her spirit—a sore trial and a constant provocation to her father, whose beliefs on the place of women's opinions was widely known.

She forced herself to breathe evenly, scanning the room without allowing her eyes to dwell on Elias, yet aware of the fact that he had stopped talking upon her entrance. She clenched her teeth slightly, disappointment settling into the pit of her stomach at his reaction. She would rather he launch some cutting quip at her—teasing her hair, even—than train his eyes upon her as he was now.

"Mother and Father aren't down yet?" Edith asked Matthew, though it was obvious that they weren't.

He shook his head. "But I heard Father barking orders at Rigby about the state of his boots as I was coming down, so I think it shan't be much longer."

Edith let her eyes travel to Elias, her heart lurching at the unfamiliar glint in them. Would she not have noticed such a thing before? Had she been so blind?

She let her gaze linger on him a moment longer, then moved it back to her brother. "I see you've brought your loyal puppy with you. Have you managed to train him yet?"

There was only the merest hesitation—and perhaps she was making it seem more than it was—but it was there, all the same.

"Trained to bark and bite," Elias said, baring his teeth slightly. The familiar twinkle reappeared in his eyes—the one that told Edith he was ready to do battle.

A little wave of relief flooded her at his response, and she cocked an eyebrow at him. "You had better keep your boasting to yourself. Barking and biting *should* come naturally to canines. Only the most deficient of dogs would require training for such things."

The door opened, and Edith's parents entered. Her mother looked poised, as always, and her father? He always entered a room as though it was meant to be dominated and controlled. His graying hair curled tightly, providing a contrast to his wife's dark, sleek locks.

"How was Keldhome?" Edith asked as her mother touched cheeks with her. It wasn't a warm embrace, but Edith's mother had never been particularly warm. She was far more interested in discussing ideas than in exploring emotion. Indeed, Edith's father displayed enough emotion to more than compensate for her mother's lack—though his emotion was generally of the explosive type.

"I believe we made some headway," her father replied. "But only time will tell! If the borough boundaries are rearranged as I wish, the voters of Keldhome will be *vital* to my reelection."

Her mother sighed. "There is far too much resistance to the cause—too much to lose for too many men. But the time for the change is far past."

"What cause is this you speak of?" Solomon asked.

Edith could have kicked him. Her muscles were tense, just the way they always were when politics came up with both of her parents in the room. It found its way into every conversation, somehow.

"There is talk of rearranging the borough boundaries in an attempt to balance out the power," Matthew said. "Boroughs like ours have precious few voters but just as much say in the House of Commons as the more highly populated boroughs."

Solomon nodded thoughtfully. "Forgive me, Mr. Donne, but is not that a Whig cause? I was under the impression that you were a firm Tory."

"I am!" Edith's father wagged his finger at Solomon. "Never doubt it. But some causes should have the support of both parties, and this is one of them. Come. I am starved." He turned to lead the way into the dining room.

Edith listened as Matthew leaned in toward Solomon with a wry smile. "Father always thinks Tory support should align with his own interests."

"What do you mean?"

Matthew shrugged. "If the vote passes muster—which would be a miracle, mind you—and the boundaries are changed, our borough is likely to lose a seat in Commons. The other seat is held by a man my father heartily despises, and the proposed boundaries would force him into Whig territory, leaving Father to win the sole seat here—handily."

Edith came abreast of them. "Inspiring, isn't it?" she said sarcastically. "I beg you will not bring up the subject during dinner, though. I have had enough talk of boroughs and boundaries to last me three lifetimes." For some reason, the prospect of having her parents debate in front of the others filled her with a sense of dread. There was still plenty of fodder for debating, even regarding a cause they were united in.

Perhaps she was being silly, though. Causing tension in a room was not something foreign to Edith, after all. But there was something quite different from the playful banter she engaged in and the fraught exchanges her parents had—full to brimming with history and deeper significance. They were not above embarrassing each other—or themselves—in company, and Edith would never wish for anyone else to witness what she had grown up experiencing on a daily basis—the glaring brokenness of it: of her father, of her mother, and, as a result, of herself. Indeed, how could she be anything but broken after such a childhood?

Chapter Six

Elias couldn't keep his eyes from Edith the entirety of the meal. That is, he *did* keep his eyes from her—he was no greenhorn, after all—but he had found that, absent his intervention, his gaze insisted upon returning to her again and again, as if it was being compelled there. And yet he was certainly not doing the compelling.

He simply found himself intrigued. It seemed impossible that any woman as deeply in love as Solomon and Matthew had described would look like Edith. She seemed hardly to notice Elias, in fact—aside from that barbed comment about his being an inferior breed of canine.

His lip tugged up at the corner. She had a fiery tongue, and no doubt about it.

But whether she looked like a woman in love or no, he could hardly doubt someone as near to Edith as Mercy. If anyone were to know the state of Edith's heart—apparently she *was* possessed of one—it would be Mercy.

Throughout dinner, Elias looked for any sign at all that what really lay behind the hundreds upon hundreds of mocking remarks was, in reality, something besides disdain.

Only once was he rewarded for his efforts. It was the most fleeting of glances, but he hadn't missed it. Her gaze, breaking contact with Matthew's, had flitted straight to Elias during the second course, only to return to Matthew as quickly as it had left him. Elias could have sworn the pink in her cheeks hadn't been there before.

And what did he make of such an insignificant moment? He hardly knew. Did it change his own feelings? Why should it? He'd had any number of women throw out lures to him over the years, and the mere knowledge of their regard for him had done nothing to spark reciprocity. Nor did he think that it was doing so now—and Edith was hardly *throwing out lures*.

Elias was merely curious, as if he had been seeing Edith Donne in the shade his entire life, and now the smallest shaft of light was presenting her to him in a new way. He had always known she was beautiful, but he now had to wonder if perhaps she had something of a heart, too, behind the stony façade.

He stepped into the drawing room beside Matthew, his eyes immediately finding her. If she *was* hiding a heart behind those walls, it was somewhere deep within. He thought she had never looked so unapproachable as she did that evening. Her hair—normally pinned back in a wavy knot near the crown of her head, with escaped wisps framing her face—was swept back tightly and piled atop her head this evening, with a large riband circling the glossy tresses.

Elias absently followed Matthew, then, realizing he *did* look somewhat like a puppy following on its master's heels, dropped back to a more reasonable distance and sat himself in the chair at the far end of the settee upon which Edith sat. Her gaze flitted to him and, as if to discourage his saying anything to her, she reached into the basket beside the settee and pulled from it a stocking and a threaded needle.

Matthew took the place immediately beside her, squinting over at the stocking she held. "What are you doing? You can't darn that without a candle, silly. You'll poke holes through your fingers."

"Nonsense," she said. "I can see just fine." Her eyes squinted slightly, but she seemed to catch the contradiction to her words and blinked them open wider.

Matthew only shrugged, leaning toward her more closely. "Not terribly keen on Mum and Father's newfound alliance, are you?" He spoke in a low voice, but not low enough to keep Elias from hearing.

Edith didn't look up. "I hesitate to apply the word *alliance* to something so doomed to fail."

"Fail? They are for once in agreement on something! Even if the vote doesn't pass—and I don't think it shall, mind you—that has to count for something, surely."

She gave her brother an almost pitying look—one Elias knew well. "Perhaps I would rejoice in that if I weren't aware how widely diverging are their reasons for seeking the same end. Mama has long wished to rid England of its rotten boroughs. For her it is a matter of justice and progress. But for Father...."

"A way to solidify his continuing reelection," Matthew said, leaning back with a sigh. "But can we not still rejoice in the temporary peace?"

"Of course you may," she replied, applying herself to the stocking again with lips that pursed in concentration. "You must merely prepare yourself for the *grande bataille* that will surely follow when what is clear to us becomes clear to them: they are *not* fighting for the same thing. Father is fighting for more personal power; Mother is fighting for equal distribution of power."

"Ah," Matthew said with a smile and a glance at Elias. "When that battle happens, I shall simply take myself off for a visit to Elias at Wooldon. Besides, I have witnessed too many *grandes batailles* between the two of *you* to quake in my boots at the prospect." He looked at his sister and then to Elias significantly.

Edith glanced at Elias, whose mouth pulled up into a half-smile. "I hope," he said, "that the victories in your parents' encounters are more equally divided than those between your sister and me."

She raised her brows, and he saw the familiar glint—both engaged and engaging—enter them. "Indeed. You have certainly gained a deep and personal understanding of those who are forever losing in such encounters."

"Ha! If I have ever lost such a battle—which I cannot agree with—it can only be ascribed to my chivalrous desire not to humiliate a lady every time I meet her."

The light in Edith's eyes flamed brighter, and she dropped her hands to her lap, letting out a small cry when the needle poked her. She tossed the stocking and needle into the basket in frustration and stood, rubbing at the injury. She smiled at him. "I assure you I require no such *chivalrous* gestures. You may bring your full artillery when you engage with me, Elias. Indeed, I shall take offense at anything less." She gave a slight curtsy. "Now, if you'll excuse me."

Elias clenched his jaw as he watched her make her way toward the piano, but his mouth pulled up into a smile.

"'Fraid she had you in that one, Eli," Matthew said, folding his arms and watching him.

It was true. She had beat him handily. He would have to sharpen his wits if he wished to prevent her from becoming bored of him—as Mercy had said, one hardly battled opponents one was confident of routing with no effort at all.

And for some reason, the idea of Edith Donne thinking him an unworthy opponent was more agitating than the prospect of her humiliating him in front of everyone he knew.

Chapter Seven

The candles blazed from the chandelier hanging in the large drawing room of Guildbury Park, and the room hummed with chatting and laughter as the musicians prepared their instruments. Everyone in the county seemed to be in attendance at the Haynes' ball, and the amount of covert flirtation happening underneath the noses of chaperones made Edith smile with a hint of derision.

A couple tucked away in the corner, almost entirely concealed by a large plant and the thick brocade curtains at the window beside it, stood perilously close to one another. Edith was certain that Miss Dyer's mother wouldn't approve of her proximity to a rake like Mr. Marke. He leaned in to whisper something into Miss Dyer's ear, and her cheeks blushed rosily as she looked up at him through her lashes.

People made such grand fools of themselves in love—or whatever it was Miss Dyer and Mr. Marke thought they were feeling.

Edith's father scoffed beside her. "I might have known Stratton would use the opportunity here to persuade Haynes to his point of view. Well, he is too late! I already spoke with Haynes, and he assured me of his support."

Edith said nothing. If her father insisted upon maintaining a constant monologue of political talk, she might have to go join the couple in the corner. For her father, there was nothing but politics. Every social engagement was but an opportunity to ensure that he stood in no danger of losing the next election, or that his fellow MPs were of his same mind on whatever bill was currently being debated.

"The fool stands to lose everything if this bill passes." Her father could hardly have sounded more pleased with that fact.

Edith followed his gaze to the two men holding drinks in their hands at the long edge of the ballroom. She avoided talk of politics whenever she could, but she would have had to be entirely deaf not to know that her father considered John Stratton his archenemy.

Edith held her father in cordial dislike, but she couldn't deny that Mr. Stratton was even less likeable. Her father was at least straightforward—one knew precisely what he was thinking at all times—even when one didn't *wish* to know. Mr. Stratton, on the other hand, seemed a more slippery fellow— the kind to use silky words when they served his purposes. Edith's father wouldn't know how to make himself more palatable if his life depended upon it. And that was what his constituents liked—they knew what they were getting when they voted for Leonard Donne.

As the two sole MPs in their borough, her father and Mr. Stratton both lived in fear of being challenged by a new, third party with the power to unseat either of them. And with just two other landed gentry in the district whose votes decided who represented them in the House of Commons, it was entirely possible for them to be persuaded against either Stratton or Edith's father. At times, Edith wished for it.

"...I have it on good authority that, if the bill passes, the boundary should be drawn at Dalton, which is just shy of Stratton's estate. And if that were the case, not only would I be rid of him, *he* would be forced to contend for—and assuredly lose—his place in Commons, for there are upwards of fifty voters in the proposed borough, and the grand majority of them Whigs."

Edith's father never seemed to need any input from her—indeed, it only served to anger him—but he expected her to stand with at least a pretense of paying attention. Whether he was aware of how heartily she disliked politics and simply didn't care, or was entirely oblivious, she didn't know, but it was all she could do to stay where she was as he so remorselessly betrayed how selfish he was in his desires for the act to pass.

Edith's mother had been attempting to draw attention to the issue for years, but it was only now that it served her father's personal interests that he endorsed such a reform.

"...will increase the number of voters in my district as well, of course, but I shan't have any trouble at all keeping my seat. Of course, Stratton would dearly like to find something to use against me, but" —her father chuckled— "I dare him to try! I haven't lived the life of a saint for nothing."

Edith suppressed the scoff that rose in her throat. A saint? Only if a saint's chosen method to ensure obedience was to browbeat and harass.

Her father had always been a stickler about the Donne family image. Their behavior was to be above reproach. It was why his wife's political activity and opinions angered him so violently. And, for a saint, he certainly had the temper of a devil.

Edith tried to breathe deeply to release the annoyance and anger building inside her. At her father's first drawing of breath, she would make an escape.

But they were interrupted when Elias appeared before them. "May I have the pleasure of this dance?" He bowed politely, bringing his gaze to hers with a knowing glint in them.

Her father had stopped mid-sentence. "Oh, yes, yes. By all means, go dance, Edith."

Edith didn't particularly enjoy dancing. And for some reason, she felt like taking Elias's arm would be a sort of surrender—for he seemed to perceive that she heartily wished herself anywhere but at her father's side.

But dancing and regaining the upper hand in her ongoing battle with Elias was certainly preferable to consigning herself to more of her father's one-sided conversation, so she swallowed her pride, curtsied, and took Elias's arm.

"You are welcome." He nudged her with his elbow as he led her to the ballroom floor.

"For what?" she asked with pretended ignorance, returning the nudge with more force than he had used.

He grunted at the jab and put his free hand to his side. "For rescuing you."

"I hardly required rescuing. I am very capable of looking after myself." She dipped her head to indicate the spot he was rubbing on his torso.

"I disagree." He looked down at her with the most maddening of smiles. It was full of victory and teasing—and perhaps the smallest bit of sympathy. "You looked a veritable damsel in distress."

She chuckled. "I am even less a damsel in distress than you are a knight in shining armor."

They took their place amongst the set, and Edith felt her anger and tension seeping away as it was replaced by the allure of crossing swords with Elias. She would never admit that he had rescued her—her father wasn't a villain, after all—but she was certainly grateful for any distraction from listening to her father.

Now she had only to remind Elias that whatever love he felt for her was entirely misguided. It was something she felt quite confident of achieving.

Chapter Eight

❦

Elias hadn't been able to resist stepping in when he saw Edith looking for all the world as though she wished to strangle someone—her father, most likely.

Elias had been coming off the worse in their recent encounters—that tongue of hers was fast as lightning, and just as dangerous—and he wanted to remind her that he was a worthy opponent. And nothing would irritate her more—or make her eyes come more alive with challenge—than feeling obliged to him.

He met her gaze across the set, narrowing his eyes. "Something has just occurred to me. Have we ever danced together before?"

The corner of her mouth tugged up at the side, and Elias wondered what error he had made in asking his question. "No. I make it a point never to dance with someone I dislike."

He grinned, and his heart skipped a beat at the implication of her words. She seemed to realize her slip of the tongue, though.

"Only the greatest desperation persuaded me to violate my strict policy this evening," she said.

"Ah, I see," he said. It seemed strange that, in all the years they'd known each other, they would never have been partnered for a dance. But Edith didn't tend to do much dancing—she had no compunction in refusing, and it had garnered her somewhat of a reputation amongst the gentlemen.

The music began, and they came together in the space between the couples. It was obvious that Edith's history of declining to dance was not a function of her lack of grace or capability. "You claim to dislike dancing," he said. "I find that to be an excuse made almost exclusively by those who have no talent for it. Shall I prepare my toes for annihilation?"

The merest dimple appeared at the corner of her mouth for a moment. If Elias hadn't had so much experience watching Edith's expressions, he wouldn't have noticed it. She was skilled at maintaining an impassive expression. "Allow me to reassure you. If I step on your toes, it shan't be for any inadequacy in my dancing skill."

"Out of an unadulterated desire to do me harm, then?"

She merely raised a brow and smiled. Her eyes moved to a point somewhere behind him, and her smile flickered.

"What is it?"

She took in a breath and shook her head. "Nothing."

They rotated around in a circle, and Elias searched out what might have bothered her. His gaze scanned the groups of attendees, finally landing upon Miss Pawnce, who was speaking with Mr. Marke.

"So the rake has found the romantic, has he?" Elias said.

"It was only a matter of time." Her eyes sought the two out again.

"You think her vulnerable to his charms?"

"Charms? It is a wonder he has ever convinced a woman to look at him twice, much less entertain any of his insipid conversation or look upon him with any interest."

"Not everyone has a heart encased in steel, Edith."

Her gaze flew to his, and he could have sworn he saw a flash of hurt in them. But she blinked, and it was gone. "No, few are so fortunate," she said. "But it only requires the merest vestige of common sense to recognize Mr. Marke for what he is."

"And Miss Pawnce is lacking just such a vestige of common sense?"

She gave a light shrug. "Do you deny it?"

His eyes found Miss Pawnce again, watching how she looked up at the tall, dark figure of Mr. Marke without the least bit of guile. "No, I don't deny it. She is easy prey for someone with as much world experience as Marke. But what can one do?"

Edith looked at him in amusement. "I imagine Viola would expect you to challenge him to a duel or some such thing if you were fearful for her."

Elias chuckled. "No doubt. But I am hardly the person to take on such an unenviable task." The dance brought them together, giving him the closest view of her eyes he'd ever had —and a resulting flapping of the heart.

"Are you incompetent with all types of weapons, then? Or is it merely pistols and your wit that are lacking?"

She really *did* find joy in trying to provoke him. Her cheeks had an attractive flush to them, and her eyes shone with energy in the candlelit ballroom.

"I do very well with pistols, I thank you," he said on a laugh. "And as for my wit, well, I believe it speaks for itself. But no, I imagine Miss Pawnce's father or brother would be a better candidate to challenge Marke."

"That she has neither brother nor father to do so is part of her allure to him, I'm sure." She lifted her head to look over Elias shoulder, leaning nearer to him as she squinted. A rush of vanilla wafted under his nose. So *that* was why the scent had been familiar in the library. He found himself wanting more.

He blinked, giving himself a shake. He was acting like a fool since overhearing that conversation between Solomon and Matthew. Women like Edith Donne took pleasure in giving set downs to gentlemen. And even if she *did* fancy herself in love with him, she was still a woman. Their affections were fleeting and changeable. Whatever she was feeling toward him, she would think better of it soon.

She seemed preoccupied with monitoring the movements of Viola, though she managed to keep up a formidable repartee despite it. He found himself surprised—and even touched—by her concern for Viola. Every interaction he had seen between the two cousins was marked by the obvious awe in which Viola stood of Edith, while the latter took delight in teasing the romantic.

When Edith trod on his foot a second time in an effort to watch where Mr. Marke was leading her cousin, Elias winced. "Do you intend to call Marke out yourself? If you do as much damage with a pistol as you do with your feet, I wager you shall win."

The faintest bit of pink tinged her cheeks. "I assure you, nothing would give me greater pleasure than to meet all the Mr. Markes in England, one by one, at dawn."

"I don't doubt it! Though I imagine you might tire after a hundred such mornings."

"A hundred?" She raised her brows. "Have you such a high opinion of your sex? Or are you merely blind?"

"How many mornings do *you* think should suffice?"

She smiled, but the intensity in her eyes told him that she was very much in earnest. "Unless I engaged to meet more than one man each morning, I imagine death or disease should take me before my work was finished."

He blinked. So *this* was her opinion of men? "Surely there are not so many scoundrels as that."

She said nothing.

They pulled apart, coming to stand across the set from

one another. Elias glanced down the line of dancers, noting the fops and men far past their heyday. Not a scoundrel amongst them, he was certain. "I must count myself grateful not to be numbered amongst the rascals you refer to, I suppose."

A smile played on her lips. "What makes you think that you are *not*?"

He took her hand in his, and as they moved past one another, the same rush of vanilla surrounded him. "Do you frequently dance with men you wish to shoot?"

"Is there another type?" She was grinning—taking great pleasure in shocking him.

"And am I to understand that you hold your own sex to be innocent of offenses that merit a meeting at dawn?"

"Certainly not. But you cannot deny that the lion's share of the truly awful ones falls to men."

"I surely do deny it," he said.

Her brows shot up again.

They came together in the center of the set, Edith training her gaze on him, awaiting an explanation.

He frowned as he contemplated how to word his defense. "Men have the strength and the means to cause much physical harm, to be sure, and I shan't argue that they abuse it far too often. But I cannot allow your sex to be acquitted of their fair share of the suffering in this world. It is the harms that go unnoticed—the subtle, slow ones—which cause the most lasting damage. And it is my experience that women, much more so than men, excel at such harm."

"I think we shan't agree on this," she said.

"What a novel occurrence." He smiled, bowing to her as the last notes of the dance rang out.

She curtsied. He liked her hair back in its regular style—pieces coming loose here and there, escaped from the blue riband that made only the feeblest of attempts to contain the waves. It suited her. Neither she nor her hair could be contained.

Her eyes roved to the edge of the ballroom. "And now if you will excuse me, I have a man to speak with about a duel."

It was very much like her not to take his arm and allow him to escort her back to her father. He couldn't blame her for not wishing to return to him.

Elias followed just behind her, stopping at the refreshment table and taking a glass in hand as he watched her. She really was going to speak to Mr. Marke. It was none of Elias's business, of course, but he couldn't resist the role of spectator for such entertainment.

He edged closer to Marke, whose hand was clasping Viola's. Situated as they were between a plant and a curtain, they were hidden from view from the majority of the people in the room. The hue of Viola's cheeks betrayed precisely the nature of Mr. Marke's words, and the roundness of her eyes indicated quite clearly that she didn't know what to think of such conversation.

Edith strode up with a martial light in her eye that boded ill for either Mr. Marke or Viola—or perhaps both. Elias didn't envy them at all. And yet he was awed by Edith's confidence. He couldn't look away. Besides, he had been the object of her ire frequently enough that it was nice to observe it from a place of safety for a change.

"Yes, good evening and all that sort of thing," Edith said with the most brittle of smiles. "Viola, will you please get me a glass of ratafia? I am parched, and I wish to have a word with Mr. Marke."

Viola looked too overwhelmed to do anything but nod and walk the short distance past Elias to the refreshments.

"Good evening, Miss Donne," said Mr. Marke in his rich voice.

"Is it?" she said. "Yes, I happen to think it was. I was enjoying myself very well until I was obliged to watch you making up to my cousin in this corner, which seems to have become a favorite spot of yours, judging by the number of women you've managed to persuade here."

Elias's smile widened. So she had been enjoying herself with him, had she?

"Surely there is nothing untoward about a gentleman making conversation with a young woman at a ball."

"No, indeed." Her voice was cordial, and her mouth still pulled into a smile—a humorless one, but a smile all the same. "But I fail to see what that has to say to the situation at hand. My cousin is certainly a young woman, but you...." She trailed off, raising that thin brow that could send a man running for the hills.

Before Mr. Marke could respond, she was off again with that knifelike tongue. "There are plenty of women for you to swindle and flirt with here, Mr. Marke. So, if I see you speaking to my cousin again, I assure you I will have no compunction at all in telling her every last detail I know about you. And believe me, she is not so young or naive that she will then countenance your *conversation*, as you so delicately choose to describe it."

She executed a curtsy and swept away before Mr. Marke could say a word, brushing past Viola, who held a glass of the requested ratafia in her hand. Edith turned back to Viola, took the glass from her hand, raised it toward Mr. Marke with another smile, then threw it back, draining its contents in a few quick swallows.

Elias covered his mouth to stop a laugh. Perhaps Mr. Marke would have preferred a meeting at dawn.

In his mind's eye, Elias saw Edith, arm outstretched, hand grasping a pistol, sending man after man to meet his Maker, until she herself expired.

His mouth turned up in a crooked smile. A world without Edith Donne would be a dull place indeed.

Chapter Nine

Edith misliked what she was seeing in Elias's eyes. Whether she had been oblivious to the gleam of interest there before, or whether it had simply become more noticeable due to the time they'd spent in each other's company at Shipton House over the past few days, she couldn't be sure. She could swear there was the slightest hesitation in his rejoinders whenever she tried to engage him. And it made her uncomfortable.

And yet, somehow, she felt that, if she confronted him about it and made clear to him what her own feelings were, it was likely to change things between them forever.

She shut her eyes and let her head fall back. *Why* had the fool fallen in love with her? She had thought him above such silly nonsense.

At her father's insistence, Edith and her mother spent the late morning making a visit to one of the newer neighbors in the area.

"Wouldn't want to be remiss in welcoming them, would we?" he had said.

Surprisingly, Edith's mother had nothing to say against the

order—for there had been no mistaking the undercurrent of demand when her father had told them of his wishes.

Laden with a basket of Cook's warm muffins, Edith and her mother set out in the landau.

"Why did you agree to come?" Edith asked her mother as the carriage ambled toward the Cotters'. "You never let Father talk to you like that without putting up a fight." Somehow, after all these years, her mother still had enough spirit to resist the peremptory commands of her husband. She nearly always complied with them in the end, for there was certain retaliation if she didn't—Edith had a vivid memory of her father throwing every last one of her mother's political pamphlets into the fire after one of their more heated arguments—so Edith couldn't understand why her mother bothered at all. And today she hadn't.

"It is in both of our interests to befriend the Cotters. *He* wishes to secure Mr. Cotter's vote when the boroughs shift, and I wish to gauge Mrs. Cotter's interest in some of my own endeavors."

Edith settled back into the squabs. Her mother had taken it for granted that the vote would pass. Edith thought it very unlikely. "I thought perhaps you had simply tired of arguing with him."

"I never tire of a fight with your father."

"But you always surrender." Edith couldn't help herself. It was something she had never been able to understand about her mother. When Edith engaged in a battle, she didn't stop until she won. Her mother's efforts seemed like wasted energy.

Her mother raised a brow. "Do I?" She smiled slightly, eyes roving to the landscape. "Perhaps it appears that way."

Edith's forehead wrinkled. "I don't wish to offend, Mother, but there is no doubt at all, I'm afraid. You have surrendered every time."

"Every time? You are unaware of the majority of battles we engage in."

Edith turned her head to the side. "I am not. They have always been loud enough to alert the entire household. And, in the end, you give in."

Her mother's smile remained steady. "I have my way in secret often enough that I don't begrudge your father his perceived victories."

Edith looked at her mother through narrowed eyes. "Have your way in secret? You mean things that Father is unaware of?"

She nodded, a victorious light gleaming in her eyes. "I do plenty of things of which your father is unaware."

Edith couldn't blame her. She had the same stubborn streak herself. But she felt uneasy, all the same. "And if he *becomes* aware of them?"

"He won't. I am not so careless." Her pursed lips hid a knowing smile. "I have been holding meetings for my women's Whig society without his knowledge for years."

Edith blinked. She had long known her mother had a passionate interest in Whig politics. She had *not* known that it had amounted to anything besides expressing that opinion in a way that made Edith's muscles clench in expectation of reprisal from her father. She felt a flicker of dread at the thought of her father discovering the way in which his wife was undermining him. He was a Tory through and through, besides believing women had no place at all in politics.

Mr. Cotter was not at home when they arrived, but his wife received them gladly, and Edith was able to listen with uncomfortable admiration as her mother subtly ferreted out the family's political leanings. By the end of the visit, she had secured Mrs. Cotter's promise to drive out with her in two days' time.

"Father will be happy to learn of another Tory family in the vicinity," Edith said as they began the journey back to Shipton House. "A loss for you, though, I'm afraid."

Her mother tilted her head from side to side. "Their loyalties to the party seem tenuous—certainly not past changing. I think I may make quite a bit of headway with Mrs. Cotter, given a bit of time."

"Perhaps, but Mrs. Cotter is not the one voting."

Her mother looked at her. "You far underestimate the power of women in the political process. Certainly we are not allowed to vote formally as our husbands do. But I could tell you dozens of stories of husbands changing their votes thanks to the subtle influence of their wives."

"And yet your own husband remains the most loyal of Tories. You have not succeeded in changing *him*."

"Your father is very stubborn. But I have made much progress despite that. You see that he is lending his support to the bill to reform the borough boundaries. That is not a Tory cause." She smiled when Edith said nothing. "Your father need only be persuaded that a cause is in his own interest in order for him to support it. He may call himself a Tory and vote that way on any number of insignificant issues, but in time—and when it suits me—you will see his 'ayes' for Whig measures increasing, and those for Tory measures decreasing."

Edith was speechless. And frankly repulsed. The manipulation and subversion her mother was engaging in disgusted her. There was no choosing between her mother and father—neither seemed to care for anything but their own wishes. Perhaps they were perfectly suited after all.

"You are angry," her mother said. It was a statement of fact, said with a hint of curiosity.

Edith said nothing, merely gazing through the window at the passing hills.

"One day you will understand," her mother said, settling into her seat with a serene smile.

"Forgive me, but I don't think I shall."

Her mother watched her. "You persist in thinking yourself

above it all, don't you? Above your fellows. Above marriage. Above everything."

Edith's brows snapped together. "On the contrary. It is precisely because I know myself *not* to be above any of it that I choose not to marry."

That thin brow rose again. "I wonder if perhaps you might reconsider. There are a great number of benefits to marriage, my dear, and I believe you have a very good candidate."

Edith stilled. "What do you mean?"

"You and Elias Abram have known each other for more than half your life, my dear. He is very eligible—of good family and fortune." She locked her eyes on Edith's. "And he seems to be taking a greater interest in you than he has in the past."

Edith's heart pounded against her chest. Other people had been noting the shift in his demeanor?

"I have no interest in marrying, Mother. And certainly not in marrying Elias. I believed I had not only made that quite clear but also had the support of you and Father in that regard."

Her mother lifted a careless shoulder. "I certainly shan't force you to marry, and with your aunt's fortune at your disposal, you hardly need your father's or my blessing to do as you please. But I still think your decision a foolish one."

Edith crossed her arms, incredulous. "You truly believe I should marry Elias Abram?"

"I don't see why not."

Edith scoffed. "I should think the reason quite apparent to anyone who had ever spent more than two minutes in our company. We cannot agree on the most insignificant of matters."

Her mother raised her pointer finger. "You *choose* not to do so, and that is quite a different beast. Besides, there is something to be said, my dear, for marrying a man who at least believes you his equal, for I can assure you Eias would countenance none of your insolence if he truly believed himself above you. Given what I have observed over the past few days, I imagine he allows you to get the best of him in order to please you, and such a man would be tractable enough for you to mold him into what you will."

Edith's jaw fell open. She couldn't pinpoint what was more unwelcome: her mother's insinuation that Elias held back when engaging with her, or that she would wish to manipulate a husband into becoming some sort of pet, ready to obey her and submit to her whims.

"Oh, come, Edith," her mother said, the first hint of exasperation in her voice. "Don't look at me like that. These are important considerations, and you believe yourself above them at your own peril. A woman must fend for herself first and foremost, for if *she* doesn't, no one will."

"You mean like my sister has had to fend for herself? Did you know when you encouraged her to marry Richard that she would end as she is now?" Her mother showed the first signs of being ruffled. "You must admit, Mother, that between you and father and Lydia and Richard, you have not given me any reason at all to wish to marry."

The landau rolled to a stop in the courtyard of Shipton House, and, heart pounding and ears ringing, Edith thrust open the door of the carriage, flying past the figure of an astounded coachman, whose hand was extended in preparation to pull the door open for her.

She rushed along the drive, flinging gravel with every step, and into Shipton House with one destination in mind: she would set Elias to rights. The last thing she wished was for Elias to tread lightly around her in the name of whatever silly attachment he believed himself to have formed. She had taken pains to show him just how sharp her tongue could be, to put her faults on display, and yet somehow, he fancied himself in love with her—enough that others had noticed the change.

Well, he would soon realize his mistake—she would leave

him in no doubt whatsoever that he had chosen the wrong woman to place on a pedestal. She would blast the pedestal to smithereens in front of his very eyes. Much better that than for him to become disillusioned with her slowly and painfully.

If nothing else, he needed to know that there was no prospect at all of her returning his regard, no matter how many encounters he *allowed* her to best him in. She had no intention of returning anyone's supposed regard for her. She wouldn't become her mother and father or her sister and brother-in-law.

Elias was not indoors, and Edith's annoyance only built as she searched him out. He was found to be standing with Matthew at the edge of the small pond. As she stalked up to them, they both looked at her, exchanging uneasy glances.

"Leave us, Matthew." Edith indicated the way to the house with a peremptory hand.

Matthew's eyes flicked back and forth between Edith and Elias. The latter merely shrugged and nodded for Matthew to comply.

Edith waited until Matthew's footsteps died away completely.

"In your black books again, am I?" Elias said. He was smiling, but she saw the wary light in his eyes. So much the better. He *should* be wary of her.

"I assure you, Elias, that I will inform you if the day dawns when you are *not* in my black books."

He chuckled. "Let's have it, then. What have I done?"

She took in a large breath and let it out through her nose. Asking a man why he had fallen in love with her felt less simple than it had two minutes ago. But it had to be done. "Are you in love with me?"

He blinked three times in succession, and she knew a moment of misgiving. It was not the reaction of a guilty man.

It took a moment for him to recover, and his forehead wrinkled into a frown as he responded. "Let me ask you the same thing in return. Are you in love with *me*?"

It was her turn to blink in surprise. "Good heavens! What a question to ask. What utter folly!"

"Folly first committed by you!" The smile had disappeared from his face. He looked utterly dumbfounded.

She felt another moment of uncertainty, as though she had entered into waters deeper than she had first judged them to be and wasn't sure she could stay afloat. "It is folly to ask you what has already been communicated to me by my own brother?"

"What in heaven's name are you talking about? *What* was communicated to you by him?"

She hesitated. In truth, it had *not* been communicated to her by Matthew. It had been communicated by Matthew to Solomon, and from Solomon to Mercy, who had told Viola, not realizing that Edith was just beyond the garden hedge. "I...it...it was merely something I overheard."

He narrowed his eyes, and his shock was replaced by an intent curiosity. "Overheard? And what precisely did you overhear?"

She folded her arms, hoping it portrayed the confidence that was fleeing more and more with each moment that passed. "That you are in love with me but have been too afraid to confess as much for fear I would scorn your affections."

His mouth opened wordlessly, only to shut again, and his brow furrowed even more deeply.

She waited in a silence more supremely uncomfortable than any she had ever before experienced. Would he consider himself found out and confess his true feelings? Or would he refute it all?

He pulled at his lip with two fingers, staring at her thoughtfully. "When did you overhear this?"

She shrugged her annoyance. "What does it matter? A few days ago, I suppose."

He let out a scoff, dropping his hand. "Just as I thought. No, Edith. I am not in love with you. And you are not in love with me either, are you?"

She raised her brows at him. "How many times must a woman insult a man before he believes her not to be in love with him?"

His half-smile appeared. "And you are not merely denying it to save your pride?"

She glared at him. "Believe me, Elias. The revelation that you were somehow in love with me was not a welcome one. It altered my opinion of you for the worse, I'm afraid—something I thought impossible."

He acknowledged the hit with a smile. "Well, I am happy to report that I can now resume my prior place in your high esteem. We have been had, Edith. Tricked. Duped. Taken in." He tapped his fist against his mouth, shaking his head but smiling. "The clever fiends!"

"What in heaven's name are you talking about?" She was out of patience with Elias, annoyed that he seemed to be aware of something she was not—and perhaps even more annoyed that she had accused him of being in love with her when he quite obviously was not.

He seemed to remember her presence. "*You* overheard a supposedly candid conversation claiming that I was in love with you. *I* overheard another such supposedly candid conversation claiming that *you* were in love with me. You think this is some coincidence?"

"Someone said I was *in love* with you?"

He nodded his head. "Matthew said as much to Solomon. I had fallen asleep in the library—on the chaise behind the screen—I imagine you know the one?"

"Know it? I practically live on it. And you had no business being there. But go on."

His eyes grew slightly misty with memory. "I thought they

must have been unaware of my presence, for I was entirely hidden from view, but I rather think that they planned the conversation for my benefit."

Edith stared at him, images flashing through her mind of the day she had heard Mercy and Viola speaking in the garden. Had it all been a hoax—a plot and a conspiracy?

What alternative was there?

She shook her head. "I cannot believe it. Mercy would never agree to such a thing."

"Mercy?" he said, frowning. "I thought you heard it from Matthew."

She shifted her feet uncomfortably. "Not directly, no. But Mercy said she had it from her husband, who had it from Matthew, who had it from you."

He threw his head back and laughed. "All doubt is removed, then. A confirmed conspiracy! For Solomon claimed to have had it from Mercy, who'd had it from *you*."

"Nonsense! Fustian nonsense."

His jaw shifted from side to side. "They played it very well, did they not? I will give them that. They made veritable puppets of us, pulling our strings as they have." He let out a large breath and shook his head again, smiling widely. "And now I must go tell them that the game is up. I imagine they have been expecting us to discover their jest. They couldn't believe otherwise. I am only ashamed how long it took us."

Edith was hardly listening to him. She could hear her pulse beating in her ears and the heat emanating from her cheeks. How had she ever believed such absurdity? Had she not known that it was madness when she heard it?

And yet she had believed it! Like a simpleton. She had looked for evidence of their words and, as was wont to happen, she had found it where it did not exist.

And it had all been a game to her family—an opportunity

to make fools of Edith and Elias. What an easy victim she had made herself! Far too easily duped.

"No," she said suddenly, still staring at the lily pads in the long, narrow pool of water. Her breath came faster, and a smile tugged at the corner of her mouth. "We shan't tell them we know."

She looked up, energy coursing through her.

But Elias was gone.

Chapter Ten

Elias chuckled as he strode back toward the house through the gardens. He didn't want to stop smiling or laughing. He didn't want to explore what was beneath it. He had the uncomfortable suspicion that it was disappointment which lurked there. But he would never admit as much. Never.

Rapidly approaching footsteps sounded, and he turned toward them just as someone grabbed hold of him.

"Don't." Edith's breath was coming fast, her chest rising and falling, and her cheeks pink, but whether it was from coming after him or related to the energetic glint in her eyes, he wasn't certain.

"Don't what?"

"Don't tell them." She looked around them suspiciously and lowered her voice. "I have a much better idea."

He narrowed his eyes, aware of her hand still grasping his wrist, as though she didn't trust him to stay put. "What kind of idea?"

Her lips stretched into a full smile, her eyes full of vigor and purpose. She pulled him along with her, tugging him around the corner of a hedge with an insistent grip on his wrist. He thought about freeing himself from the clasp, of asserting himself somehow, but he found he didn't want to.

Edith's gaze raked over the empty hedgerow and, seeming satisfied, she turned back to him and let his hand drop. "What do you say to a bit of good old-fashioned revenge?"

He blinked.

She folded her arms, a self-satisfied smile on her lips. "Let us beat them at their own game."

His brows knit together. "And how do you propose we do that?"

A mischievous smile crept over her mouth, that delicate brow arching as it so often did when she was about to deliver the final blow—the thrust to end the sword fight. "We give them *more* than they bargained for. Much more."

He didn't even say anything. What was there to say? He hadn't the slightest idea what she meant, yet he hesitated to admit as much. He didn't particularly care for the prospect of looking slow or obtuse to Edith, and certainly not after the humiliating realization that she had never been in love with him. A man's pride inevitably suffered to discover such a thing.

She let out an impatient breath. "What do you imagine was the aim of this entire ruse they concocted?"

It was a home question, and he stared at her as he tried to come up with a satisfactory answer.

"Do you believe they wished for us to fall in love?"

Would they have wished such a thing? He couldn't believe they would. He shook his head. "Matthew is convinced I should marry someone docile—a woman who won't allow me to provoke her."

"Precisely. They would be horrified if we were to announce our intent to marry."

"So what do you suggest?"

She smiled, meeting his eyes with her intense gaze. He

didn't know whether to be dismayed or intrigued by what he saw there.

"We elope."

Silence.

"We *what?*"

Her smile grew. "It is what they least expect—and certainly not what they want. In fact, Mercy and Matthew would do their utmost to convince me against such a thing."

"I should think so! Revenge I can understand—beating someone at their own game and all that. But to elope? It is we who would suffer most and longest from such a course."

"I agree completely. There are no two people less suited to marry *at all* than you and I. And to marry each other?" She chuckled. "My will for revenge is not strong enough to subject myself to such a thing. No, what I mean is that we contrive to make them *believe* we have eloped."

He frowned, thrusting aside her uncomplimentary assessment of him. "Forgive me, Edith. I am no doubt an oaf—not all of us are as practiced as you apparently are in the art of false elopements—but how precisely does one give the impression of having eloped without *actually* eloping?"

She began pacing, her steps energetic, eyes glazing over. "We must first lay the foundation, or they shan't believe it. We shall have to appear to enjoy one another's company—to show a shift in how we engage together."

Elias said nothing, for the truth was he *already* enjoyed Edith's company. He enjoyed the back and forth, the need for an ever-prepared, sharp wit. He felt very much alive in her presence.

She stopped her pacing and looked at him. "Are you prepared to make such a sacrifice in the name of vengeance? It will be but a short commitment, for the longer we draw it out, the more likely they are to speak up before we have had the chance to perform our *magnum opus*. I think one or two strategic interactions will suffice—one of them observing us in a *tête-à-tête*, for instance, and then something small. After dinner perhaps."

He stared, trying to catch up with her ideas. "I hardly know whether to be fascinated or repulsed by your machinations—and the facility with which you have arrived at them."

She grinned and dipped her head, as if modestly accepting a compliment. There was fire and excitement in her dark eyes. "That foundation can quite easily be laid today and this evening, I think. And then tomorrow?" She wagged her brows once. "We elope!"

He opened his mouth to interject, but she didn't notice, taking to pacing again, her steps bringing her toward him, only to spin on the balls of her feet just shy of him and pace back the other direction. "The first stage of the journey is all that is needed, I think. Just enough to convince them—along with a note begging understanding and forgiveness, of course. I suspect they shall be on our heels immediately when they discover our intentions."

"This plan of yours," he said, tugging two of the small leaves off the boxwood hedge beside him. "Where does it leave your father?"

Mr. Donne detested anything that smelled of scandal. The vengeance they might take upon their friends could well be overshadowed by his wrath.

Edith showed the first sign of hesitation, but it lasted only a moment. "He shan't ever know. He leaves on business after dinner this evening, and we shall be back before his return tomorrow evening."

"You are certain?"

She looked at him with a knowing expression. "Afraid of my father, are you? I cannot say I blame you, for he would certainly ruin all the enjoyment if he caught wind of it. But yes, I am certain of his plans to leave. I could hardly be unaware of them, as he hasn't stopped talking about them for the past fortnight and more." She cocked an eyebrow at him. "What, then? Do you intend to forgo this opportunity out of fear of my father?"

Elias did stand in awe of Mr. Donne—wary awe. He had witnessed the man's temper on more than one occasion, and it was not so much fear-inducing as it was simply uncomfortable. But Edith seemed quite certain that he wouldn't know of their ruse, and Elias couldn't deny that the prospect of turning the tables on their friends was enticing. The expression on Matthew's face when he realized he had been duped was simply too much to pass up.

He smiled. "What must I do?"

The first step, Edith had insisted, was to arrange for a meeting—one that would be witnessed, supposedly unbeknownst to Edith and Elias, by one of the others. The meeting would serve two purposes—allowing them time to plan the details of the elopement, and giving their friends reason to believe it, for if they saw no evidence of newfound regard between Edith and Elias, their suspicions would immediately be aroused and the effect of all their work might be ruined.

With Elias's reservations regarding Edith's father overcome, he entered into the planning with vigor—and proved to be quite an asset, to her pleasant surprise. He had a long history of practical jokes that proved invaluable as he pointed out details Edith hadn't considered and ways to make their act more believable.

They parted ways with the plan to meet after dressing for dinner to execute part one of the ruse.

It had been some time since Edith had felt so much excitement and anticipation. It sharpened her senses and energized her in a way that was entirely novel.

Had the others truly assumed that there would be no attempt to repay the trick once it had been discovered? How little they knew her! And how quickly they would realize their error. Their dismay and sense of guilt would be overpowering—equaled only by their relief when they discovered what was truly afoot.

Time passed unevenly that day—the seconds barely ticking by some minutes, only for an hour to fly past without a trace. Lying beneath her anticipation, Edith recognized something new: nerves.

She and Elias had a part to play together. As careful and specific as they had been in their plans—going so far as to select the exact spot in the library where they would meet for their *tête-à-tête*—they had glazed over the details of what their interaction there would entail. To be convincing, it needed to be more than verbal, and it was *that* which caused an uncomfortable fluttering in her stomach.

Edith rarely ventured into unknown territory. She knew the limits of her wit, and she was glad to push those limits, for doing so increased her capabilities. But there was a difference between pushing a familiar boundary and sailing in uncharted waters, and physical proximity with a gentleman—even Elias Abram—was certainly uncharted waters.

How much practice *he* had was not something Edith knew or cared to ponder on for more than a moment. It bothered her that she would be the pupil and he the teacher.

She shut her jaw tightly and pulled on her gloves, clenching and unclenching her fists and noting how the fabric adhered to her fingers more than usual. At least the gloves would conceal the way her hands were sweating. She wouldn't give Elias the satisfaction of knowing she felt unsure of herself.

Trying to focus on the shock their interaction would cause

whoever witnessed it, she took a deep breath and forced herself to smile. A moment's discomfort and uncertainty would surely be made worthwhile when she and Elias were able to claim a laughing victory over their friends.

She picked up the pocket watch she kept on the small, mahogany table beside her bed. It was time.

She glided down the stairs, summoning as much confidence as she could muster.

It had become somewhat of a routine for Edith to slip into the library before dinner, catching a few moments in her favorite nook while waiting for everyone to gather. While her father told the staff and anyone staying at Shipton House that dinner was served promptly at six-thirty, he rarely put in an appearance until six-forty-five, at which point he would say something along the lines of, "Well, come on, then. Let's not dilly dally!" If anyone dared step into the drawing room after him, he had an unpleasant lecture on promptness at the ready.

Matthew had taken to popping his head in the library at six-forty to warn Edith. She was counting on him to follow habit this evening.

The library was empty when she arrived, and she felt somewhat calmed by the familiar scent there: old books, persistent dust, afternoons avoiding her governess, and refuge from the conflict that she could avoid nowhere else.

The door opened behind her, and Elias peeked his head in, then slipped inside, shutting the door.

"No," she said in a hushed voice. "Don't shut it. Leave it open—just enough that Matthew may see us. Or hear us, perhaps."

He nodded, pulling the door open a few inches. He turned to face her, sucking in a breath and looking around. His hair looked more precise than usual, though one stubborn lock stuck straight up, resisting the pomade that made the rest of his dark hair shine in the fading summer light penetrating the library windows in dusty, golden shafts.

The large standing clock pointed to six-thirty-two, ticking the seconds loudly in the silence. Why had they decided upon meeting so far in advance of the time Matthew would come? The dusty air suddenly felt thick and heavy.

Elias cleared his throat. "Shall we discuss tomorrow, then?"

Edith nodded quickly, grateful for the reminder of what else needed doing besides manufacturing romance out of nothing at all—worse, in fact. They needed to create it out of a history of heated debate and mutual antipathy.

She kept her voice low—she certainly didn't wish for *this* part of their interaction to be heard or witnessed. "I should think that a departure in the early afternoon—shortly after midday—will be the easiest. And though we shall need nothing for an overnight stay, I think we must pack some belongings to make it convincing, should anyone inquire with the servants."

"Very good." He stood three feet away from her, none of his careless confidence evident in the way he clasped his hands behind his back. And that patch of hair was ridiculous.

She glanced at the clock again. Six-thirty-four.

This was silly. And if Matthew decided to warn her a few minutes early—her father's temper was often at its most touchy on nights when he traveled to Bardon—he would walk in on a scene almost entirely unremarkable. He might be surprised at the lack of verbal daggers being thrown between Edith and Elias, but he was unlikely to spare it much thought beyond a furrowing of the brow.

She was being nonsensical. It was much better to take charge and ensure that their planning wasn't for naught.

"I think our parts are better played in closer proximity to one another, don't you think?" Perhaps there would be less awkwardness if they maintained their usual relationship. "Matthew will hardly be convinced we have persuaded ourselves we are in love if you insist on standing there like a starched-up vicar."

Elias's hands dropped to his sides, and he chuckled. "Forgive me" —he raised his brows at her— "but your posture isn't precisely the picture of romantic zeal either."

She looked down and noted the white-knuckled clasp of her hands. She forced a laugh, allowing them to break apart and fall to her sides.

He took two steps toward her, and Edith tried to imagine what Viola would instruct her to do in the situation. Elias was looking at her with a touch of amusement, as though realizing just how excruciating it was for her. He was close enough that the lock of rebellious hair was barely visible in the periphery of her vision.

He took another step toward her. She felt her muscles stiffen, and she *knew* he had noticed.

His eyes twinkled. He was thoroughly enjoying himself now. He took yet another step toward her, and she had to tip her chin up to meet his gaze.

"Regretting your plan now, are you?" There was so much satisfaction and confidence in the way he looked at her, she wanted to slap him. But that would hardly be conducive to their goal.

"Not in the least," she said through clenched teeth.

"Then why are you retreating every time I draw nearer?" He moved his feet so that the tips of his boots were hidden by the hem of her dress, the top of his thigh brushing against her hip.

She forced herself to stand her ground. "You see what you wish to see, Mr. Abram. I am perfectly comfortable."

"Is that so?" He spoke more softly, as if to emphasize how near they were, and his breath brushed her face.

Edith hardly needed a reminder of their proximity. She was well aware that the force of her heart beating against her ribs could likely be felt by Elias through the nonexistent gap between their chests.

His gaze flitted to her hair and then back to her eyes as he reached a finger to one of her waves and brushed it back. It was the merest hint of a touch, but she felt it in every inch of her body. He was near enough now that she could see the small spot his valet must have missed while shaving him—for there was no doubt at all that he was just shaven. He smelled of soap, and she tried to focus on what its ingredients were. She thought she detected rose water.

"If you are so comfortable, why did you refer to me just now as Mr. Abram?" he said.

How did his eyes manage to smile and challenge her at the same time? He was right, though. She had slipped and called him Mr. Abram—perhaps as a way to increase the distance between them the only way she knew how. But she wouldn't let him come off conqueror in this battle.

Footsteps sounded in the corridor, growing steadily louder and nearer. She met the challenge in Elias's eyes and in the small quirk of his brow, knowing that her brother's head would appear in the doorway any second.

"This was *your* idea, Edith," Elias said softly, his smirk lighting a fire inside her.

She had to act—to prove to Elias that she was perfectly mistress of the situation.

Reaching her hand around his neck, she pulled his mouth down the final inches to hers, locking their lips together and forcing her heart back down into her chest as their mouths met.

He froze, his muscles as rigid and tight as hers, but the next second, one arm was around her waist, the other cradling the back of her head. Her senses filled with the scent of rose water, the touch of soft lips, and the sound of his breathing. A heat burned through the thin fabric of her dress where his hand rested on the small of her back, pressing her toward him.

And she forgot. She forgot that the kiss was for Matthew's benefit. She forgot that it was to prove her mettle to Elias. She forgot that it was all part of revenge.

Responding to the insistent tug of Elias's arm around her waist, she let him pull her toward him, and even though her body rested against his, it somehow didn't feel close enough. Their mouths moved in concert, and Edith's head swam.

She had always strived for strength around Elias, but just now, she felt malleable, like dough in his hands. And she could feel herself baking from the heat between them.

The door creaked, and they broke apart.

Matthew's wide eyes and open-mouthed surprise met Edith's stunned gaze. There was no acting involved in the shock she felt, and her chest heaved, as though she was trying to catch up with what had just occurred.

"I...I..." Matthew stuttered.

If Edith herself hadn't been so entirely bemused, she would have laughed at her brother's confusion. It was so perfectly what they had been hoping for. But all she could manage was wonder at the impossible speed at which her heart was beating and the way her lips tingled so that she had to resist pressing a hand to them.

She needed to pull herself together. It mattered what happened now.

"Elias was just helping extract a stubborn eyelash from my eye." She blinked quickly, brushing a finger at her eye and looking to Elias to confirm her words.

He wasn't even looking at Matthew, though. He was staring at her, his chest rising and falling just as hers was. He shut his mouth, pulling up a finger and squinting at it. "I believe I managed to get it. Yes, there it is." He blew a quick breath at the finger and watched an imaginary eyelash float away.

Matthew said nothing, still staring at them for another pregnant moment. He swallowed. "Father should be down any moment."

Edith stifled a victorious smile. Matthew didn't believe their story for a second. And that was just as she wanted it to be.

"Perfect," Elias said. "I have been starving this last hour and more."

Matthew cleared his throat and nodded, disappearing from the room with a few mumbled, unintelligible words.

Edith's skin tingled. They were alone again, and the kiss hung in the air, unavoidable, demanding to be acknowledged. But she couldn't—she wouldn't—look at Elias and acknowledge what had happened. Instead, she followed Matthew from the room without even a backward glance.

Chapter Eleven

Elias waited to leave the library until his breathing slowed. The clock read six-forty-two, and he let out a long exhale, paying attention to the slow falling of his chest in order to occupy his mind, then followed behind Edith.

Perhaps it was for the best that he hadn't more time to reflect on what had just happened.

What *had* just happened?

Edith Donne had kissed him. Of course he had taunted her past her ability to bear it—he knew that. But he had expected her to slap him, honestly, not kiss him. And certainly not kiss him like *that*.

He blinked, trying to right his vision, which swam every time he revisited the past few minutes.

It had been part of the act, nothing more. An impulsive, spur-of-the-moment decision prompted by the approach of Matthew.

Well, if that was the result of Matthew approaching, Elias couldn't help wishing he'd approach more often.

He clenched his eyes shut, stopping at the drawing room door. He was being a fool, and he needed to rein it in before entering—before seeing her again. Their conduct would be under scrutiny by Matthew at the very least. And they still had to execute the second part of their plan for the evening. Providing Edith hadn't changed her mind....

Had it really been so long since he'd kissed a woman for it to affect him so? It *had* been long. But surely, he wouldn't have forgotten the feeling he'd just had in the library, hand tangled in Edith's hair, body pressed against—

He shoved the door open. That was quite enough.

All eyes were on him, including those of Mr. Donne, who looked none too pleased to forfeit his place as last-into-the-drawing-room to Elias. Matthew was staring at him with a strange, stricken look, and Edith met his gaze with her color only slightly heightened. Had she thought better of their plan? Decided it wasn't worth it?

But a few minutes later, when the company sat down for dinner, she took the chair beside him at the table. Elias hadn't realized the tension he had been holding in his body until it relaxed at her approach.

She was at least not so angry that she had given up the ruse. Nor did it seem she was angry with him.

Or else she was a *very* good actress. Perhaps as good an actress as she was a kisser.

The execution of part two was expertly accomplished by Edith. It took every ounce of self-mastery for Elias to stifle the appreciative grin that rose to his lips when Edith slipped a folded note into his hand in the drawing room after dinner. It had all the appearance of subtlety, yet there was no doubt in Elias's mind that Matthew had observed it.

For Matthew's benefit, Elias let his eyes linger on Edith's receding figure for a moment—her soft curves swaying slightly with each step—before tucking the note between his shirt and waistcoat.

She was a marvelous creature to behold. A feisty one, but certainly marvelous.

He put a hand to his waistcoat, reassuring himself that the note was still there. He was curious to know what, if anything, was written on it. No doubt it would be some pithy insult.

Edith reached the other side of the room, where Viola and Mercy were going through the collection of music available at the piano. She turned her head back toward Elias for the briefest of moments, her mouth pulling into the veriest hint of a smile, and her lashes quickly veiling the bewitching glint in her eyes.

The effect was to set Elias's heart galloping. What was *that* about?

He shot a quick glance at Matthew. Ah, of course. Matthew's gaze was fixed on Edith, and Elias averted his own gaze an instant before Matthew's came to rest on him.

Edith was far too good at this.

While Elias had told himself he wouldn't open the note until he retired to his room for the night, he found himself itching to pull it from his waistcoat during the time in the drawing room. Positioning himself in the back of the group as Mercy and Edith performed a number at the pianoforte, he slipped the note out and cringed as the crinkling seemed to reverberate through the room. He surveyed the others, but no one had noticed.

His gaze hovered on Edith, sitting at the piano, her eyes alternating between the sheet music and Mercy's face, her mouth drawn into a joyful smile. They seemed to be performing a piece they had sung together many times before, and Elias stood transfixed, forgetting the note for a moment.

He had seen Edith in a rage. He had seen her indignant. He had seen her energized and victorious. But *this* was Edith at her most beautiful—spilling over with badly controlled laughter whenever she or Mercy made a mistake, the skin around her sparkling eyes wrinkled with joy.

The song ended, and Elias realized he was still holding the folded note, his mouth pulled into an unconscious smile. He swallowed and hurried to open it.

It was blank.

He would have almost rather it contained some insulting jibe—any acknowledgment of what had happened in the drawing room. But either the kiss had been so unexceptional as to merit no remark, or Edith had chosen to pretend it never happened. She had certainly acted as though nothing out of the ordinary had occurred, walking out of the library without a word or a glance.

The thought crept into Elias's thoughts unsolicited: had Edith kissed other men that way?

His stomach clenched, and he tucked the note away again.

He had to admit that Matthew's reactions to their plan were every bit as humorous as he had hoped they would be. True to what Edith said, Matthew looked dismayed, troubled even, by the interactions he witnessed between the pretended lovers. Elias was convinced that Matthew had managed to communicate at least some of what he had seen to the others, for their eyes seemed to follow him and Edith more frequently than usual.

When Elias noted it, he took pains to concoct a few of his own little confirmatory gestures—a hand held a moment too long, a gaze too pointed, anything to make them wonder what beast they had unwittingly created.

Edith had of course noticed the scrutiny as well, and she sent him more than a few lashed glances over the course of the evening, the perfect combination of subtle but speaking. Elias found himself thoroughly enjoying the dance they were leading —even if it did set his heart pattering in earnest—and by the end of the night, he was halfway to convincing himself that the kiss he had shared with Edith didn't matter. It meant nothing. It was merely a means to an end that promised to be deliciously triumphant. They had made it convincing because it needed to be.

The next day dawned gray, with large, rolling clouds making their way across a sunless sky. It was a bit of a dreary backdrop for a day promising to be full of excitement, but Elias didn't let it bother him. He hoped to avoid Matthew as long as he possibly could, for he suspected that it wouldn't be long before Matthew confronted him about what had happened the night before, and he wasn't entirely sure how to handle such a confrontation.

He asked for breakfast to be brought to his room, but he couldn't avoid going downstairs altogether when he and Edith weren't set to leave until midday. He would venture outside for a stroll in hopes of avoiding Matthew a bit longer.

It was with tight-jawed consternation that he saw Matthew at the base of the stairs—almost as if he had been waiting for Elias.

He greeted his friend with as regular a manner as he could, but it wouldn't do. There was obvious purpose in Matthew's eyes.

"Eli." Matthew took him by the arm, pulling him into the library. That hint of vanilla, mingled as it was with the smell of books, wafted around them, taking Elias back to the night before.

He had to concentrate.

"What the devil is going on between you and Edith?"

Right to it, then.

"I don't know what you mean."

"Dash it, Eli! Don't play the fool with me. I caught you kissing her. Kissing my sister. Right here!" He pointed an impassioned finger at the floor. "Not to mention looking like a lovelorn buffoon in the drawing room last night while she played the piano."

"I did not!" The words escaped him involuntarily. Out of all the play-acting he and Edith had done last night, Matthew chose to point out the one part of the evening when Elias *hadn't* been acting.

"Yes, I know," Matthew said dismissively. "Helping her with an eyelash! Is that what people are calling it nowadays?" He shoved his finger into Elias's chest. "Stay away from my sister, Eli! I happen to care about her, and I know your views on women too well to sit by while you lead her on some silly dance for your own enjoyment."

Elias was momentarily bereft of speech. He had taken pains over the years to keep up appearances—flirting with women and even concocting stories of short *liaisons* to appease his friends—anything to stop questions about his plans to marry. Well, clearly, he had been successful in his aims. Matthew thought him incapable of anything but dalliance and cynicism when it came to women.

Perhaps that was for the best—whatever could inspire Matthew with a determination not to allow Elias and Edith to form an alliance.

"Your sister has proven herself more than capable of fending off unwanted suitors."

Matthew shook his head, his nostrils flaring. "She takes pains to appear that way, but I know better." He jabbed Elias in the chest again, punctuating each word. "Leave her alone." And with a slamming of the door, he was gone.

It was exactly what Elias should have wanted, and yet the encounter had jarred him.

Edith was nowhere to be seen during the morning hours, and it was with the assumption that she would have sought him out if anything had changed that Elias began packing a few things—a change of clothes, fresh cravats, and a few other items he imagined a man eloping would take with him. It needed to look convincing if Matthew came charging into his room, looking for evidence of the elopement.

Just before noon, a note was brought to Elias's room by one of the maids.

Meet me at the stables at half-past.

His lip tugged up at the corner. The day promised to be very much out of the ordinary. He felt jumpier than usual—the prospect of spending the afternoon with Edith was equal parts enticing and unnerving. Would she bring a maid with her? They would only be gone a few hours, but he trusted she had taken all the necessary precautions to avoid any hint of scandal that might be attached to their spending time in a closed carriage. Though, to be fair, anyone who had witnessed their kiss in the library the day before couldn't be blamed for making assumptions.

No, having a maid in the carriage would be for the best. It would keep Elias from his persistent curiosity. He had been wondering what it might have been like if Matthew had given Edith and him another minute—or five—to...search for the eyelash.

A little rumble of thunder filled the darker skies in the distance—the area not far from Wooldon, Elias's own estate—as Edith arrived at the stables, followed at a discreet distance by her shy maid, who carried a trunk. Edith wore a pleasant expression, carrying herself with an energy that told Elias she was looking forward to the prospect before her.

"So, you didn't lose your nerve," she said as she approached.

"Nor you your imagination."

Another rumble of thunder sounded, a bit louder than the last. He looked up at the sky. "Though perhaps it *would* be wise to postpone this adventure until tomorrow—to ensure its success."

She raised a brow at him, as though he had just proven her

point about losing his nerve. "Don't be ridiculous." The trunk was taken from the maid and hefted by the driver into the box behind the chaise. "It is today or never. My father will return this evening, and then the window of opportunity will be firmly shut. Besides, the gloom will not only add to the impending doom my brother and cousins feel upon reading my note, but it will lay to rest any questions they have about how earnest we are."

Elias pursed his lips, hesitant to make himself sound worried about a bit of rain.

Edith glanced at him, tilting her head to the side. "You mustn't mind the clouds in the south. The worst weather always follows the coastline."

"Very true." He assisted her into the chaise, following behind her maid with a slight fluttering of nerves.

It was time to elope.

Chapter Twelve

Edith smiled as the chaise left the courtyard of Shipton House. In twenty short minutes, her note would be delivered to Matthew, and chaos would ensue. She was only sad she wouldn't be there to witness it.

"Your brother took it upon himself to warn me, you know."

She looked to Elias curiously. "Did he?"

He nodded, and a smile grew on his face. "He seems to think you far more vulnerable than you appear, and he sternly warned me to leave you be."

She scoffed, but there was affection in her amused smile. "Matthew has always feared himself the weaker sibling. If it makes him feel better to believe that I am secretly a helpless kitten, then" —she shrugged— "so much the better. It will be all the more amusing when he arrives at the inn and realizes his role of protector was entirely unnecessary. Speaking of which, we have a few details to discuss."

She glanced at Susan beside her, but the maid's head was slumped over against the side of the chaise. Whether her fast-achieved sleep was pretended or authentic, Edith didn't know, but she was grateful for it, either way. Of necessity, Susan would be aware of the general plan, but Edith had no desire to add fuel to the fire of the servant gossip that would no doubt rage upon their return later that day. Better Susan than any of the other servants, though. She was a timid creature—and never more so than when she was with Edith. She would likely fear Edith's sharp tongue if it became known that she had spread information.

Edith shifted in her seat so that she was sitting forward, her gaze as close to level with Elias's as possible. He leaned in, ready to listen, and the image of his face inches from her own flashed across her mind. She thrust it away.

"We will need to wait at the inn in Ilmarsh for a time while whoever comes after us catches up. In that twenty or thirty minutes, we will need some explanation for our situation—or names at least that convey that we are related. We are unlikely to encounter anyone of note there, truthfully. I have instructed us to be driven to The Old Dog and Pheasant. It is generally passed over in favor of The George in the village just before it."

"Hardly any wonder, I think, with a name like that," Elias said with a chuckle.

Edith ignored his comment. "I have no desire to test how discreet the servants at The Old Dog are, though. I think we should use false names."

Elias nodded thoughtfully. "What will it be, then? Ned and Wilhelmina Myerscough, brother and sister?" He grinned.

She gave him an unamused tip of the eyebrow. "I shall keep my first name, thank you. But I think it might occasion less comment if we go under the guise of a married couple." Why in heaven's name were her ears and cheeks beginning to burn? "Whoever comes after us—I expect Matthew at least—will likely storm into the inn, inquiring after an eloping couple, and if we have given the story that we are brother and sister, it is likely to draw even more unwanted attention."

Elias held her gaze, but she thought she saw a tremor at the side of his mouth, as though he wanted to say something but decided against it. "I concur. What will our names be, then, madam wife?"

Her lips compressed into a thin line at the epithet.

He raised his brows. "I sincerely hope you will manage to respond to your husband in a more seemly manner by the time we arrive. Or are we assuming the role of dashing husband and shrewish wife?"

She suppressed a smile, but he knew her too well to miss it, and a satisfied glint appeared in his eyes.

"Mr. and Mrs. Cherriman," she said. "On our way to visit family in Somerset."

He gave an exaggerated nod. "So be it."

The muted sound of hoofbeats on dirt shifted to a loud clopping as the chaise rumbled over a stone bridge. They were only a few minutes from The Old Dog. The journey had passed much more quickly than Edith had anticipated, but as the carriage moved back to the dirt road, a new sound assailed their ears: the pattering of rain on the roof of the chaise.

Her gaze met Elias's. She pulled up the shade to peer outside and knew a moment's misgiving at the view before her. Dark, roiling thunderheads seemed to be coming nearer, flying in the face of her confident comment about the worst weather keeping to the coast.

Elias's eyes were on her, and he seemed to sense her misgiving, as he scooted over toward the window. "May I?" His leg came up against hers, much like it had in the library.

She hesitated, then shrugged, moving to allow him space.

"Gad!" he said, pulling back and looking at Edith with alarm. "We are in for no small storm. So much for your forecast, Mrs. Cherriman."

The thought of turning back crossed Edith's mind. It was undoubtedly the safer option. But to turn back would be to forgo the best part of their charade—the finale. It would sap their victory of its potency, and Edith intended to have her full revenge upon Matthew and the others—now more than ever. For it was their ruse that had landed her in the humiliating situation in which she found herself—having forcibly kissed Elias Abram. And having enjoyed it immensely.

She had never kissed anyone before, and she now found herself in the mortifying position of wondering whether she had entirely botched it. Had it been enjoyable for Elias too? Did all kisses feel as that one in the library had?

Shaking herself mentally, she refocused on the matter at hand. The rain was still pattering, perhaps a bit stronger than it had been even a minute ago, but certainly nothing to alarm anyone. Besides, she had known plenty of ominously dark clouds to taunt and threaten, only to pass over after scattering a handful of raindrops on the area.

"I wish to go on," she said decidedly. "But if your courage is failing you...."

He shook his head. "I quite enjoy a good downpour myself."

The chaise rumbled into the wet yard of The Old Dog, and Elias began taking off his coat as the chaise stopped.

"What are you doing?" she asked, frowning.

The door opened, the stairs were let down, and Elias hopped to the ground, coat draped over his arm. His eyes squinted as rain and wind pelted him, flattening his hair in a matter of seconds. He put out a hand to Edith, and she took it hesitantly, still bemused by his decision to remove his coat at the time when it was most useful.

She gave a sharp intake of breath as she stepped out, drops of cold rain slapping against her cheeks. And then stopping unaccountably.

Elias was holding his coat over her head, his eyes still squinting to keep out the pelting rain. "Come, Mrs. Cherriman!"

Secretly touched by his thoughtfulness, Edith rushed

alongside him to the inn door, which stood open, the innkeeper beckoning them in. Edith's maid followed them, assisted by the driver of the chaise, who held his tricorn hat over her head.

The innkeeper—a Mr. Drew by name—accepted their explanation without batting an eye. And indeed, why shouldn't he? He was more concerned with instructing a servant to add a log to the fire in the coffee room, and for a cup of coffee and a bowl of warm stew to be served to the Cherrimans without delay. Based on the intensity of Mr. Drew, Edith doubted it was very often that he had guests at The Old Dog who were as obviously genteel as the Cherrimans.

The stew was surprisingly palatable, and it warmed Edith's throat and stomach with each bite, a welcome little mercy in contrast with the bleak prospect the windows afforded.

The storm was already unleashing its full fury on the area, smacking the window panes with such a din that it wasn't until Edith heard the sound of voices that she realized they were no longer the newest guests. They had been there but a matter of ten minutes, but a quick trip to the rain-blurred window led Elias to raise his brows.

"What is it?" Edith asked, setting down her cup of coffee.

"Two carriages."

"What?" She stood, crossing over to join Elias at the window. He shifted his shoulder to allow her space, putting a hand on her back to guide her forward in a way that caused Edith to glance up at him.

But he was still staring outside. Sure enough, the bleary outline of two equipages met her gaze. "Matthew already?" She squinted as if that might help bring the details into focus, but it was no use. The sheet of rain covering the window was too thick.

"I don't think so. It's too soon, isn't it?"

She twisted her mouth to the side. "Yes. The rain must be forcing people on the road to stop shy of The George." She looked at him with a hint of worry. "Perhaps we should request a private parlor?"

He nodded. "I shall do so right now. Mrs. Cherriman." He glanced down at his hand on her back, and it dropped before he left her side.

Chapter Thirteen

It was two or three minutes before Elias had the attention of Mr. Drew, taken up as the man was by assisting the new arrivals to the inn.

One of those new arrivals was vaguely familiar to Elias and certainly a member of the gentry. He was middle-aged, with traces of sandy hair visible under his sleek top hat, and a strong but straight nose.

"The Cedar Room will do." The man's voice was low and strong, his words quick and dismissive, as though he took for granted that his orders would be obeyed. He brushed at the shoulders of his coat, and a few droplets of water flicked onto Elias's face.

Mr. Drew, whose face was beet red, with beads of sweat gathering on his brow, turned to Elias.

"Mrs. Cherriman has requested a private parlor, if you please. Straightaway."

Mr. Drew clenched his teeth together. "Very good, sir, except that I'm afraid The Old Dog and Pheasant is only equipped with two private parlors—we are but a small establishment, you see—and the second has just been claimed." He grimaced apologetically and glanced at the man in the top hat, who seemed to have overheard.

He turned to Elias, surveying him with a critical eye, and seemed to be satisfied with what he saw.

The door of the inn opened again, and a young woman, attired entirely in black, stepped in, followed by a maid. Mr. Drew sucked in nervous breath and excused himself to attend to her.

"Did I hear correctly that you are in need of a private parlor?" The older gentleman addressed himself to Elias.

Elias dipped his head. "My wife" —he cleared his throat, trying to accustom himself to the word and hoping he sounded natural— "desires more privacy than is offered by the coffee room, sir. We hadn't expected to stay longer than would allow for a quick cup of coffee but"—he nodded toward the window with a smile—"it looks as though we will be here for a while at least."

The man didn't smile, but he looked to be thinking. "You may take refuge in the Cedar Room for a time if you and your wife aren't opposed to sharing it with me."

"It is very kind of you, sir. And who shall we thank for the kind gesture?"

"Stratton. John Stratton."

Another carriage rumbled into the courtyard.

"Pleased to make your acquaintance, sir." Elias hesitated a moment. "The name is Cherriman." He didn't wish to provide a false given name in the event that Edith accidentally addressed him by the real one.

"Charmed." The man bowed, looking anything *but* charmed, then strode toward a door that had a small sign above, with the words *Cedar Room* carved into the wood.

Mr. Stratton likely wouldn't be the most amiable man to share a parlor with, but Elias wasn't going to look this gift horse in the mouth. The man had no obligation whatsoever to share the space with them—he had requested it first, fair and square—and yet he had offered it all the same.

The door to the inn opened, and Elias's eyes widened. A man, tall and muscular, with a many-caped greatcoat draped over his shoulders, entered the inn.

"Oxley?" Elias croaked out.

The man glanced at Elias as he removed his hat, a smile growing on his face. "Abram." He strode over and wrapped Elias in a crushing embrace. "Fancy meeting you here!"

This was a fix indeed. Elias trusted Oxley—they were friends of old, after all—but it was the deuce of a situation to explain.

"Indeed. Are you on your way to Oxley Court, then?"

Lord Oxley shook his head, tipping his hat from side to side and watching a few rivulets stream down and onto the floor. "No, in fact. Taking a short journey to Weymouth on a matter of business. I didn't think I should nearly die on the way, of course."

Elias chuckled. "This storm isn't as bad as that."

Oxley raised his brows. "My carriage barely made it over the bridge before a gush of water flooded it. Seconds later, and I might not have been here to tell the tale."

"Gad," Elias said in hushed surprise.

"Flooded?" a distraught voice asked.

Elias's head whipped around. The young woman in black was wringing her hands, staring at Oxley, who nodded. "I'm afraid so."

Alarm grew in her eyes. She couldn't be more than seventeen, and aside from a maid, she seemed to have no company. Perhaps she was journeying back to a seminary or some such thing.

She looked to Mr. Drew. "Does this happen often? How long do you expect it will take for the waters to recede?"

"I couldn't say, miss. It happens once a year, perhaps, but it all depends on the weather, of course. It could be a matter of an hour, or it could be a matter of days."

Elias tried to hide his own dismay as the young woman sucked in a breath, clearly destabilized by the answer. "Days?" she said in a weak voice.

"Come," Mr. Drew coaxed. "Have a cup of coffee, miss. At the inn's expense." He shot a look at Elias and Lord Oxley that quite clearly spoke his opinion of the fragility of women.

Elias couldn't stifle a smile. Mr. Drew's opinion might well change if he became better acquainted with Edith. She was as fragile as a block of marble.

The young woman's maid put an arm around her, and she allowed herself to be led into the coffee room.

The door to the Cedar Room opened, and Mr. Stratton reappeared, glancing quickly at Elias and Lord Oxley. He looked a second time at Oxley, and he seemed to straighten, his mouth pulling into the first smile Elias had seen. It had a forced quality to it.

"Lord Oxley," Mr. Stratton said, coming over to them and stretching out a hand.

Oxley took it, inclining his head briefly. "Stratton."

Stratton's eyes moved to Elias again, then back to Oxley. "I see you have met Mr. Cherriman."

Oxley's brows came together, and Elias rushed in, putting a friendly arm around Oxley's shoulders. "Oh, yes. Ox and I go back years. Ask anyone at Oxford, and they'll have heard of that deadly duet: Oxley and Cherriman."

Oxley let out a forced laugh. "Indeed."

"Well," Stratton said, "if you are in need of a private parlor, you are welcome to join Mr. and Mrs. Cherriman and me in the Cedar Room." He turned to indicate it, and Oxley shot Elias a glance of puzzlement and suspicion.

"Thank you," Oxley said, "but I intend to stay the course after giving the rain a few minutes to subside. The skies are much clearer in the direction I am headed than they are where I've come from."

Mr. Stratton bowed and excused himself to go upstairs.

They watched him disappear around the corner before Oxley turned toward Elias, who looked up at him with a smile full of clenched teeth.

"Mr. and Mrs. Cherriman?" Oxley said, with the hint of a baffled smile.

Elias nodded. "For the day, yes."

Oxley raised a single brow. "Do I even want to know?"

Elias shook his head, and Oxley nodded with an amused grimace that said he washed his hands of his friend. He strode over to the window and peered out. "It's not letting up, but the longer I wait, the muddier the roads shall become. I am tempted to ride and have the carriage follow behind once the roads are more passable."

Elias was looking thoughtfully at the stairway Mr. Stratton had gone up. He strode over to join Oxley at the window. "What do you make of that man—Stratton? He seemed a surly fellow when I first met him, but he was quite smiling to you. Shall I forever regret accepting his invitation to share a private parlor?"

Oxley chuckled. "He fears me. But no. He isn't someone I should choose as part of my inner circle—or my outer circle, truthfully—but he's harmless enough for an afternoon." He let out a large sigh. "Well, Abra" —he caught himself— "Cherriman. It was a nice surprise running into you, but I must be off. This business won't wait. Stop by Oxley Court if you're still in the area in two days."

Elias nodded, giving Oxley a friendly slap on the back. Oxley set his hat squarely onto his head and strode purposefully out into the storm. Elias's jaw shifted thoughtfully from side to side. He hadn't any idea what to do with the information about the bridge.

He made his way into the coffee room. Edith was still

sipping her coffee, her gaze trained on the young woman in black. She directed a raised brow at Elias upon his entrance. He took the chair beside Edith, and her eyes remained fixed on the young woman.

Elias shook his head. "I think we shan't be seeing Matthew —or anyone from Shipton—for some time. Apparently, the bridge we crossed over shortly before arriving is flooded."

Edith's eyes shot to his, widening and then shutting in exasperation. "A flood?" she asked in dismay.

He nodded. "Just heard as much from my friend. He stopped here for a few minutes on his way to Weymouth. Seems his was the last carriage to manage a crossing—and that only just barely—before the flooding."

Edith rubbed her forehead with her bare hand; her gloves laying neatly in her lap. "And what did you tell this friend of yours?"

"Oxley? He didn't ask any questions. He knows me well enough."

She raised a brow. "Naturally he is accustomed to meeting you in such a way." She looked to the windows with a sigh. "The rain gives no sign of abating."

Elias's mouth twitched slightly. "One can only wonder what kind of storm the coast is being assaulted with."

She glowered at him, unamused. "Have you acquired a private parlor?"

He tilted his head from side to side. "Yes and no. There are evidently only two, and both have been spoken for. But a gentleman was kind enough to invite us to share one with him. I suspect he frequents the inn, based on the deferential treatment Mr. Drew afforded him. He seems a surly fellow, but it will have to do, I'm afraid, unless we wish to inquire about two rooms where we could both retire for the time being. Besides, he seems not to be using the parlor for now."

"It is quite all right. Where is it?"

"The Cedar Room—second door in the corridor next to the stairs."

He glanced at the young woman in black. She was sipping at her cup of coffee with a worried brow, her uneven color betraying the fact that she had been crying recently, her eyes unfocused as they stared into the fire. "I think I shall see if I might be of any assistance to the young woman before we go in. She looks to be alone, save for her maid, and too young to be without better escort."

Edith assented to this, and he took a swift gulp of coffee before rising from the table.

Mr. Drew might be right—the young woman might simply be easily overset—but somehow Elias doubted it. Given her mourning attire, he thought it more likely that she was leaving from a funeral, her grief still fresh as she made her way back to the seminary. Elias remembered how even the smallest bout of ill luck made him feel as though the world had turned against him after his father's death. Certainly a flooded bridge would be enough to upset even someone *not* laboring under heavy emotion already. In any case, she wasn't likely to receive much sympathy from Mr. Drew beyond the steaming cup she held in her fidgeting fingers.

He hoped he wasn't overstepping his bounds, but he had to do something. He knew well what it meant to be alone with grief.

Chapter Fourteen

Edith wrapped a hand around her mug of coffee. It was barely warm now, and she had drunk all but a few sips as she observed Elias speaking to the young woman. His desire to see to the girl had come as a surprise. She had assumed he would have little patience for weeping women.

Well, obviously she had been wrong. He was showing a great deal of sympathy—his brow furrowed as, by turns, he listened and then spoke softly. The girl's maid—if that's what she was—seemed to approve of him, as she had relaxed her protective posture and was looking on the two of them with a sort of maternal permissiveness.

Perhaps Elias *did* need a soft-spoken woman like the one before him. An image flashed across her mind of him closing the distance between him and the girl, taking her in his arms, and kissing her the way he had kissed Edith.

Her cheeks warmed even as her stomach tied in knots, and she looked away, letting her eyes rove toward the window. The rain hadn't let up in the slightest from what she could tell. Anxious for something to do besides scrutinizing the interaction between Elias and the girl, she rose and walked to the window, leaving her own maid Susan at the table.

Susan sat on the edge of her chair, hands folded in her lap, eyes cast down.

Edith's lips drew into a thin line. The girl looked like she could use a kind word. Edith only wished her own skill wasn't so undeniably for *unkind* words.

She turned her eyes to the window. The vista outside presented a very gloomy picture indeed. It was little wonder that the bridge had flooded. Outside, little rivulets of water on the ground fed into larger ones, snaking through the yard of the inn and pooling in large, murky puddles. It couldn't persist like this for too long, though. Surely there was only so much rain in the skies?

Yet another carriage pulled into the yard, and Edith straightened. Matthew?

No. Even through the blurry window, Edith could tell that this was a stage coach—and coming from the opposite direction as Shipton House. She brushed off the panic that began to bubble inside. It was but three o'clock. There was still time before her father's return.

Soon, more people would be in the coffee room, despite there being just two empty seats left.

Edith motioned to Susan, who rose and followed her out. Elias could come at his leisure. His presence at the inn occasioned far less curiosity than Edith's did. She glanced at the doors in the nearest corridor and passed by the one with the words *Oak Room* engraved over the top in favor of the second door, labeled *The Cedar Room*.

She pushed the door open and stepped in, glancing quickly around the room. There was no one. Susan closed the door behind them, and Edith took a seat near the fire. She wasn't feeling terribly cold, but the dreary prospect outdoors made the light of the fire appealing.

She surveyed the room again, looking for any indication that someone had been there, but found none. Perhaps he had decided to give up use of the private parlor altogether.

The door opened, and she rotated in her chair, freezing at the sight before her.

John Stratton stopped abruptly in the doorway, frowning. "Miss Donne!"

Her heart beat wildly in her chest. *No, no, no.* It was too unkind—too much like a bad dream, where the most unlikely misfortunes were forever plaguing one.

But this was no dream. The rain slapped against the roof of the inn, and the room brightened momentarily with a flash of lightning outside.

"Mr. Stratton." She cleared her throat and rose from the chair.

He didn't move, and the look of confusion on his face intensified.

Her mind scrambled. The story she and Elias had contrived wouldn't do. Mr. Stratton was well aware that she was unmarried—only recently, they had spoken in passing. But how much did he know of her family? Would he bat an eye if she claimed that Elias was her brother? She feared he would. Her father made it his business to know everything he could discover about Stratton, and she imagined the reverse was true as well.

"I requested use of this parlor," he said, leaning back and glancing at the engraving above it as if to ensure he hadn't entered the wrong room. Seemingly satisfied that it was indeed the correct room, he took a step in.

She forced a smile and rose, directing a speaking glance at her maid, who followed suit. "Of course. I apologize—the fire was so inviting, and the quiet, too, that I couldn't resist stepping inside when I saw it was vacant. But I am quite warm now, and I shall leave you in peace." She snatched her bonnet from the sofa and moved to leave.

A CONSPIRATORIAL COURTING

Footsteps sounded, and Mr. Stratton moved out of the way.

"Ah, there you are, darling." Elias's mouth was stretched into a full smile, while every muscle in Edith's body tensed. "I didn't see you leave the coffee room." Eyes wide, Edith gave an infinitesimal shake of her head.

Mr. Stratton's eyes darted between her and Elias. "Mr. Cherriman?"

Edith tried valiantly to issue a stronger wordless warning to Elias, but he wasn't looking at her.

"Yes," he said, dipping his head in acknowledgment. "And I see you have met my wife."

Edith shut her eyes in consternation. Devil fly away with Elias!

"Your wife?" Mr. Stratton's eyes were fixed on Edith. "Am I to felicitate you, Miss Donne?"

Elias seemed to finally realize that there was more to the situation than he had anticipated, and his smile faded slightly. "You are already acquainted?"

"Yes," Edith said, her jaw tight. "Mr. Stratton represents Kingsbridge in the House of Commons alongside my father."

Mr. Stratton bowed. A curious glint had come into his eyes, and his mouth drew into a smile. Edith recognized it instantly—the hint of victory in it.

"Excuse me," Edith said. "I think I heard the arrival of another coach, and I should like to see whether my brother Matthew has arrived." Without waiting for any acknowledgment from either man, she brushed past them—allowing her elbow to jostle Elias roughly as she swept by.

She indicated with a nod to Susan to close the door behind them, and as soon as it was shut, she rushed toward the coffee room. It didn't matter who saw her now. Anyone—*anyone*—would be preferable to Mr. Stratton. It couldn't possibly be any worse than it already was. She hurried to the window, clenching her eyes shut at the unchanged view of the raging storm outside.

Why had she been such a fool?

Footsteps sounded behind her, and she felt a hand on her arm.

"What in heaven's name, Edith?"

She turned toward Elias, her nostrils flared, and her teeth clenched so tightly that her jaw ached.

"Who is Stratton?"

She blew a frustrated puff of air through her nose, pulling her arm from his grasp. "I thought you knew him—he was at the Haynes' ball."

"Yes, he and a hundred other people!"

She clenched her teeth harder, hardly believing her bad fortune. "He is my father's political rival."

Elias stared at her, dismay gathering on his face. His eyes searched hers, and he muttered an oath.

"Just so," she said, turning her head to look through the window.

"Forgive me," he said. "I shouldn't speak so."

"That is hardly in the realm of our current concerns." She closed her eyes and let her head fall back. "*Why* must you needs barge into an unfamiliar room speaking of your wife?"

He rubbed his forehead harshly. "I *thought* you would be pleased with my convincing act."

She said nothing, the feeling of dread closing in around her. She knew it wasn't Elias's fault, but it felt good to direct her anger somewhere when she felt the walls closing in on her— and no one to blame but herself.

"Besides, this" —he motioned to the room around them with a hand— "was hardly *my* idea in the first place. I believe I expressed my hesitations on more than one occasion."

He was right, of course. And she hated him for it. And even more, she hated how she couldn't look at him without smelling the soap on his face and feeling the traces of his hands around her waist.

Soft sniffling sounded behind them, and Edith turned toward it and then back to Elias.

His mouth twisted to the side, and his brown eyes grew somber. "Miss Susanna Perry. She is traveling to her brother's funeral at Ivybridge and very concerned at the thought she might miss it."

Edith let out a *hmph*.

"What?" Elias asked.

"It is not as if she can attend the service or the committal."

"No, but surely she wishes to participate in the other rituals."

Edith shrugged lightly. "I should think it might be a relief to miss it."

Elias's eyebrows snapped together, and she felt the need to explain herself. Her eyes roved to Miss Perry. "Do you not find funerals to be a bit...hollow?"

He gave a chuckle that held incredulity. "What, honoring someone's life?"

"What good is honoring someone when they are not there to hear any of the praise? If we really cared about the person, I imagine we would express those things while they were still alive."

His brows pulled together. "That is certainly a noble idea. But it doesn't follow that there is no value at all in commemorating a person—particularly if you believe that we continue to exist even after death."

"Do *you* believe that?" It was strange, but even after knowing Elias so many years, there was so much she didn't know about him.

He shifted in his seat. "I think so. I hope it."

She gave a little shrug. The idea of life continuing after death was one she had always struggled with, but she didn't particularly wish to delve into the topic. "It just seems like more pretense at times than anything—more for the benefit of those still living than for the person who has died."

"Can it not be both?" There was a touch of impatience in his tone. Or perhaps it was annoyance. "Do you expect life to go on as if nothing had happened after a person dies? There is a purpose to mourning and remembering someone. Death leaves wounds that need healing and a void that deserves to be understood."

Edith swallowed, suddenly feeling self-conscious, as though her words had lowered Elias's opinion of her.

What did she care, though? She wasn't obliged to explain herself to anyone.

Elias was still regarding her through puzzled eyes, as though he didn't know what to make of her. "I assure you there will be a great deal of mourning when *your* time comes."

Her cheeks flamed, betraying her. She forced a laugh to diffuse the discomfort she felt at his serious tone and intent gaze. "Well, I shall never know, shall I? Unless, of course, you are right about it all, in which case, I shall be watching very carefully from above to see just who appears at my funeral and what false praise people manage to give in my honor." She tilted her head. "Or perhaps I shall be watching it all from below."

Her words achieved only the vestige of a smile from Elias, but it was forced—more disturbed than anything—and she hurried to change the conversation.

She indicated Miss Perry with a nod of the head. "When is the funeral?"

"The day after tomorrow, I believe."

Edith looked at him aghast. "And she despairs of making it in time? Surely we will not still be here the day after tomorrow —or tomorrow even! The rain cannot continue like this. And we cannot stay the night here."

Elias bared a mouth full of clenched teeth, lifting a shoulder. "Whether it can or not, we must certainly hope that it doesn't."

The young woman glanced up at them, and her ears, covered partially by a bonnet with black ribbon, grew red.

Elias beckoned to her. "Come, Miss Perry. I would like to introduce you to"—he hesitated, glancing at Edith.

"His wife," Edith said, pulling out the chair beside her to make room for Miss Perry. "Edith Cherriman."

The girl summoned a pathetic smile, framed as it was with red eyes and her sorrowful brow. "Susanna Perry, ma'am."

Ma'am. That was certainly something Edith was unaccustomed to. "My husband" —she avoided Elias's eye— "has been kind enough to inform me of your situation. I am very sorry to meet you under such sad circumstances."

"Thank you," Miss Perry replied. "It is very kind of you to invite me to sit with you, but I am afraid I am very poor company, and I have no wish to cast my gloom upon you."

Elias shook his head. "I quite understand, but you needn't worry about such a thing. My wife is of a somber temperament by nature, so your mood will suit her quite well." His mouth twitched ever so slightly at the corner. "And I am the last person to reproach you in such circumstances," he said. "A loss like the one you've sustained cannot merely be brushed aside for the sake of civility. And we certainly don't expect such a thing."

She raised her eyes to him, and her hand fiddled with the silver pendant on the necklace she wore. "Have you ever lost someone near to you?"

Elias seemed to hesitate a moment, his eyes flicking to Edith as though he didn't wish to answer in her presence. All traces of humor had disappeared from his face. "My father. And a younger sister." The words were tight.

Edith averted her eyes, feeling as though she was eavesdropping.

Miss Perry's brow furrowed even more deeply. "I am terribly sorry."

Elias cleared his throat, and offered a quick, polite smile. "Thank you."

She lowered her head, and her eyes squeezed shut tightly, forcing out a tear. "How did you bear it?"

Elias's throat bobbed, and Edith knew an impulse to take his hand. Miss Perry wouldn't think anything of it, surely—a wife comforting her husband.

But she felt suddenly stiff—immobilized. Whether by fear or pride, she didn't know.

Elias cleared his throat. "Though it sounds impossible right now—the weight of grief can be crushing—time does provide healing."

"But...but..." Miss Perry's chin trembled, and her eyes traveled to the window as she brought her sagging handkerchief to her nose. "It is too cruel that I should be deprived of saying goodbye in both life and death."

Edith looked to Elias, waiting for him to comfort the young woman with his experience, for she had none to offer.

But he was staring into the fire, his brows drawn together, and an unfocused look in his eyes that told Edith his thoughts were far away—far away and unhappy. She knew one desire to stare and another to look away, for the sight was in such contrast to the man she knew—the jester who never came into a room without a ready laugh and a stinging retort on his tongue. *That* man she could tease and provoke, prodding him with the assurance that his armor of wit was nearly impenetrable.

But the man before her now? He seemed fragile and out of her reach. And of no help with Miss Perry.

She cleared her throat lightly. "You were very close, then, with your brother?"

Miss Perry gave a jerking nod, her fingers moving again to

the simple pendant that lay just below her neck. "He is but eleven months older than I and the very dearest of brothers. Or he *was*."

Edith put her hand over Miss Perry's. "Whether you attend the funeral in person or are cooped up in this inn with us, your efforts to be there are not in vain, my dear. I imagine that your brother—what is his name?"

"Robert."

Edith squeezed her hand. "I imagine Robert is aware of your desires where he is now" — her conscience pricked her for saying something she wasn't sure she believed— "and that he would not wish for you to berate yourself for circumstances so far outside your control."

Miss Perry's shoulders shook, and Edith scooted closer to her, wrapping an arm around the girl's slight frame in a gesture that felt as right as it felt uncomfortable.

Miss Perry sniffed softly. "If the flooding does not clear, I shall be the only one absent in my family—I who loved Robert best of all." She lifted her shoulders in a helpless gesture. "Perhaps I should just return to school. It is too painful to be so close and yet so helpless."

Edith sighed. She couldn't help feeling that Miss Perry's despair was premature—there was still plenty of time for the weather to clear up, and Ivybridge was only ten miles distant. More likely than not, she could be on her way within a matter of hours—muddy though the roads would certainly be. "It is very unjust, to be sure. But surely your family will wish to see you, whether the flooding has receded in time for the service or not. I cannot lay claim to any personal experience with a loss so near as yours, but I imagine that you would be missed terribly if you chose not to return home at all. I doubt Robert would wish you to mourn on your own."

Elias turned his head away, a hand gripping at his mouth—

the first sign that he was conscious of the conversation happening around him.

Edith hadn't any idea whether what she was saying was true or utter fiction, but she was encouraged to see Miss Perry's sorrowful expression lighten slightly.

Ominous thunder clapped outside, drawing their gazes to the windows. The dreary, colorless vista made it difficult to say for certain, but the skies seemed to be darkening further, and with no sign of the rain stopping—or even slowing. Even if it did stop within a few hours, driving on dark, muddy roads would be dangerous.

It was looking less and less likely that anyone was coming from Shipton House or that Edith and Elias would be able to journey back until the morrow. A wave of nausea washed through her at the thought of what her father would say.

Mr. Drew stepped into the coffee room and, seeing the three of them together, strode over.

"Excuse my intrusion," he said, bowing deeply. He looked deeply frazzled, with cheeks as red as autumn apples and an erratic quality to his movements. "I merely wished to discover whether you intended to pass the night here or not? I fear we may have more guests than we can house."

Edith's brows went up. This was all they needed—to be stuck at an inn, pretending to be married, with nowhere to sleep.

Mr. Drew seemed to notice her reaction and rushed on. "Naturally, I wished to give preference to you and Mr. Cherriman, for you were the first to arrive today, and so I took the liberty of setting aside the large room upstairs."

Edith swallowed, panic rising from her stomach and into her throat. No doubt Elias would think it a fine joke indeed— much as he had taken joy in her discomfiture in the library.

But when she looked at him, there was no amusement in

his face, only dismay—it would have been comical had the stakes not been so high.

"I am afraid that Mr. Cherriman and I require separate rooms," Edith said, summoning a pained look. "He snores as loudly as thunder, the dear thing."

Elias held her eyes for a moment with a promise of vengeance before saying, "Inherited the tendency from my mother, I fear." He shook his head regretfully.

Mr. Drew nodded. "I quite understand. Mrs. Drew suffers from the same malady. Might I suggest adding an extra pillow to prop up your head at night, Mr. Cherriman?"

Elias accepted the suggestion with a humble nodding of the head and a stilted "thank you."

Mr. Drew frowned. "Mr. Stratton must of course have his regular room, and then the two others have since been reserved." He counted the rooms on his fingers, then brought his head up so that his gaze rested on Miss Perry. He hesitated. "I am afraid, miss, that it leaves no place for you."

Chapter Fifteen

Elias could hardly bear the look of alarm on Miss Perry's face.

Mr. Drew fiddled his thumbs, glancing at Edith and then Elias, as if it was their ill opinion he feared. "We are just a small establishment, you see."

Silence hung heavy in the air.

"Miss Perry cannot possibly leave the inn," Elias said, tossing a hand in the general direction of the window, where lightning lit up the sky, as if on cue.

"No," said Mr. Drew. "I quite see that. I am afraid that the only other beds we have are in the servant quarters." He flinched, as though someone might strike him for the suggestion.

"Good heavens!" Edith said. "No, that will not do at all." She took in a breath in the manner of someone determined. "If you are agreeable, Miss Perry, I would be happy to share my own chamber with you." The corner of her mouth trembled. "Provided you don't snore, that is."

Miss Perry gave a little laugh, her mouth spreading into the first smile of the day. "I do not—that is, I do not *think* I do. Do

I?" She turned to her maid, still sitting at the nearest table, who shook her head. Shoulders dropping with relief, Miss Perry turned back to Edith.

"Very good, miss," said Mr. Drew. "There is just one thing. The rooms have only one bed—large enough for two, of course"—he glanced at Elias, then hurriedly looked away. "We might lay a few extra blankets on the floor for Miss Perry, I suppose."

Edith's hesitation was so brief it likely went unnoticed by Mr. Drew and Miss Perry. But not by Elias.

"Nonsense," she said with a great attempt at nonchalance. "If anyone shall sleep on the floor, it shall be me."

"Oh dear," Miss Perry said. "I could never allow such a thing. I assure you, Mrs. Cherriman, that I have been used to sharing a bed from time to time with my sisters. That is, I wouldn't presume to—I only wished to say that—oh, it is a great inconvenience, I fear!"

Elias was nearly sure of it. Edith did not seem the type of person who wished to be touched while she slept—or perhaps ever. Though she had seemed very willing indeed in the library.

He forced his thoughts back to the present. Miss Perry's agitation and desire not to trouble anyone—to say nothing of her pitiable circumstances—was affecting, and Elias could see Edith's impulses warring.

"It is no inconvenience at all," she said. "It *is* rather cold today, so I imagine we will be glad for the extra warmth in the bed."

It cost her. Elias could see it in the tightly-balled fists that rested in her lap. But her words had been convincing enough to draw another breath of relief from Miss Perry and to fill her eyes with tears anew—this time tears of gratitude, which Edith brushed off uncomfortably.

Elias could have kissed Edith. For all she tried to seem cold and unconcerned, she had a kind heart inside her—embarrassed of it though she might be.

They shared a table for dinner with Miss Perry. Elias had thought to offer it, but Edith beat him to it, engaging the young woman by asking her questions about her brother and then listening politely as memory after memory was recounted. Miss Perry was at her most animated when speaking of her brother, and Elias sent Edith a grateful glance on more than one occasion. He wouldn't have guessed that speaking of her deceased brother would *improve* Miss Perry's mood, but it certainly had.

No one had ever comforted Elias after his father's death like Edith was doing for Miss Perry. Indeed, he had hardly spoken of his father since, except in passing. There was something very intuitive and maternal in what Edith was doing, though Elias thought she might throw her plate of food in his face if he told her as much.

Miss Perry rose from the table before them, insisting they should enjoy at least a portion of their meal without her intrusion, and when Edith dismissed such concerns, Miss Perry confessed herself very tired indeed. She curtsied, then wished Elias a good night, reassuring Edith that she needn't worry about waking her when she came upstairs to retire.

Elias watched Miss Perry leave the room. "You needn't share a room with her, you know. And certainly not a bed."

Edith's brows went up skeptically. "Needn't I? What alternative do you propose?"

Elias shrugged. "I suppose I might sleep on that sofa over there, then both of you could have a room and bed of your own."

Edith laughed. "What? And endure your complaints all day

tomorrow, laid at my door? No, I thank you. It is only one night, and besides, I think Miss Perry should perhaps not be left alone. In fact" —she dabbed at the edge of her mouth with a napkin, then set it on the table— "perhaps I should go to her now." She gave a nod to her maid to send her ahead to the bedchamber.

"You are certainly the right person for the task," Elias said. He knew a pang of envy. How might it have been to have someone as concerned with his well-being after his father's death? To ensure that he didn't drown alone in grief?

"Hardly. I haven't the first idea what is helpful or not to someone in mourning."

"And yet you have managed to soothe her—and even make her laugh. I confess I was nervous when you began asking her questions about her brother, but you were right to do so. It seems to be precisely what she needs."

Edith hesitated a moment, putting on her gloves, then looked at him. "Did that sort of thing help *you*?"

He stiffened slightly and made an effort to relax. "I wouldn't know." He rose to help Edith from her chair, not wanting to say more. He didn't need Edith to think him any weaker than she already did. It was easier to focus the conversation on Miss Perry—or to engage in the usual banter. He would have plenty of time to ponder on the subject in the coming week—two years since his father's death, and twelve years since his sister Caroline's.

He cleared the thoughts away. "Allow me to escort you upstairs, Mrs. Cherriman." He glanced at the couple dining at the table near them and raised his voice a bit. "I know how your knees bother you on the stairs these days."

Edith pursed her lips, and Elias grinned, offering her his arm. She took it, squeezing it so tightly that he was obliged to stifle a protest. "You are too kind, my dear," she said.

They smiled and inclined their heads at the nearby couple, then made their way out of the coffee room.

A servant showed them to the room prepared for Mrs. Cherriman and Miss Perry and pointed Elias in the direction of his room. "Just past Mr. Stratton's, sir, but if you reach the door at the end of the corridor, you've gone too far, for that's naught but a closet for linens."

Edith and Elias broke arms in front of Edith's door, waiting until the servant's footsteps faded. She was gazing down the corridor with a worried brow.

"What is it?" Elias asked.

She shook her head. "Nothing. There is nothing to be done."

Elias glanced at the door that led to Stratton's room. "You are concerned about Stratton?"

She met his gaze and nodded, a wry smile touching her lips. "You will say that it is all my fault. And you will be right."

Her feeble attempt at humor wrung his heartstrings. "Ah, but why state the obvious?"

She chuckled lightly, but the wrinkle in her brow remained.

He reached for her hand, surprising himself. He wondered if she might refuse the gesture, but she didn't. "We will come about, Edith." He smiled. "Mr. Stratton is no match for the two of us. Besides, we have observed propriety quite rigorously, I think."

She nodded, but there was no alleviation of the worry on her face as she took her hand from his to open the door to the bedchamber.

He didn't want her to leave. He wanted to ease her worry. He wanted to follow her into the room and reassure her until she believed that he wouldn't allow any harm to come to her reputation.

A bit counterproductive, that idea.

Her gaze met his as she bid him good night. Was he only

imagining the reluctance there? He was no longer certain how to interpret Edith's actions and expressions, all because of a stupid prank.

The door closed softly behind her, and Elias stood in the same spot for another moment, hearing the muffled sound of Miss Perry saying, "Oh, Mrs. Cherriman," in a surprised voice.

Mrs. Cherriman. His pretended *wife*. It was a word he had disdained for as long as he could remember. And yet tonight...

He sighed and turned down the corridor to his own room.

Chapter Sixteen

Edith awoke in the morning to the light pattering of raindrops on the window pane and the roof above. She kept her eyes shut, holding on to the last bits of sleep and trying to discern how heavy the rain was. She dreaded the moment she would have to pull back the bedcovers.

It was so very warm in the bed, a warmth accentuated by the way the cool air in the room nipped at the exposed skin on her face. She didn't have to look to know that there was no fire in the grate, for she could hear raindrops pattering on the old ashes.

Perhaps she would stay in bed all day—the prospect of interminably looking through the drizzle on the windows in hopes that it would stop was hardly appealing, and pondering on the conundrum she was now in even less so.

She took in a deep, drowsy breath. If only her entire body could be as warm as her arm felt.

She stilled, her muscles going rigid.

As slowly as she could manage, she turned her head on her pillow, letting out an enormous sigh of relief as her gaze landed upon Miss Perry.

A CONSPIRATORIAL COURTING

Not Elias. Of course not Elias. She had *not* invited him into her room. And she had certainly not kissed him again. Wisps of a dream—that's all it was.

Of course, it was strange to lie beside Miss Perry, too. Edith had never shared a bed in her life. But Miss Perry looked so serene in her slumber, none of the grief that had been so apparent in the lines of her face yesterday visible now.

Edith slipped quietly from the bed, shivering as her feet met the cold planks, and hurriedly reached for her wrapper. She pulled her loosely plaited hair over her shoulder, tugging on the loops of the ribbon that tied the bottom to tighten the bow.

She hesitated with her hand by the bell. She didn't wish to wake Miss Perry, but she needed to dress. The rain had certainly lightened, and she was anxious for news of the bridge. She could only hope that Mercy and Matthew had come up with some credible excuse for her and Elias's absence.

She clenched her eyes shut. More than likely, they had told Edith's father of the elopement, for Edith and Elias had taken pains to make them believe their act.

She pulled the door open a crack, wincing as it creaked slightly. But Miss Perry didn't move a muscle.

Edith only had to wait a matter of thirty seconds before a servant passed by, whom she instructed to have her maid sent up. Edith and Susan managed to prepare her for the day in near-silence. But even the noise they had made didn't seem to rouse Miss Perry. Perhaps the weight of her grief made her sleep heavy.

Had Elias been like Miss Perry after the death of his father or his sister? It seemed impossible, and yet yesterday Edith had seen a glimpse of just how little she knew Elias Abram. He was not all confidence and wit and arrogance. Miss Perry's grief seemed to affect him strangely—as if inspiring his sympathy but also a sliver of resentment or disagreeable memories or... what was it? She hardly knew.

Edith and Susan tiptoed from the room, the former making her way to the coffee room, hoping Mr. Drew might have some news regarding the state of the roads.

She stopped in the middle of the staircase, noting Mr. Stratton speaking with the innkeeper at the base of the stairs. He glanced up at her, and her stomach dropped at the knowing glint in his eye.

"Miss Donne." He addressed her by her real name, making it clear that he didn't believe the story she and Elias had concocted.

Mr. Drew's brow furrowed at the appellation, but he said nothing. Edith could hardly blame him. Mr. Stratton would not welcome his behavior being questioned by the innkeeper, however strange the behavior might appear.

"Good morning, Mr. Stratton." She continued down the stairs, determined to stay poised. The more she showed the fear she felt, the more suspicious the situation would seem.

"Go," he said to Mr. Drew, and the innkeeper scurried away with a bowed head. Edith had half a mind to go after him, not only to inquire about the roads but to escape Mr. Stratton. But she resisted the impulse. Dealing with Mr. Stratton was every bit as urgent—indeed more so—than discovering how soon she and Elias would be able to return to Shipton House. The thought of the necessary interaction was not a pleasant one.

Surely an innocent trick had never gone so awry as this one.

Mr. Stratton turned toward Edith, smiling in a way that made her feel uneasy. "I said Miss Donne, but perhaps you prefer Mrs. Cherriman?"

She laughed. "Mr. Abram would be delighted to hear you call me Mrs. Cherriman, for it amuses him to vex me."

"To vex you." The words were skeptical.

"Yes, indeed. I assured him that no one would bat an eye at

someone who is so much like a brother to me escorting me here, for I came to intercept a friend returning home for a funeral, you see." She waved an impatient hand, secretly determined to seek out Miss Perry as soon as she possibly could to beg her understanding and collusion. "In any case, when it became clear that the weather would not permit our departure, Mr. Abram was convinced that he needed to protect my reputation—brothers *will* insist on such dramatics, I have found—and so, very much against my wishes, he has maintained that we are Mr. and Mrs. Cherriman. You must forgive his irrationality, though, Mr. Stratton, for it is all very well intended, even if somewhat ill conceived."

"As you say, miss," Mr. Stratton said with a slight bow of the head.

Oh, how uncomfortable he made her!

"And what of this friend of yours?" Mr. Stratton asked. "I take it she is the young woman in mourning I noted yesterday? Was Mr. Abram not so concerned with her reputation? I confess I am not acquainted with him, but it seems, from what you have told me, as though he would be troubled on her account, as well."

For a moment, it seemed as though her story was unraveling, but she had too much determination to accept defeat. "You should have seen him worrying over the matter, but he felt that Miss Perry's reputation could not be in question if it were known that she was traveling with Mr. and Mrs. Cherriman."

"No one would dare, I'm sure," he said ironically.

She ignored the barbed comment, glancing at one of the maids coming out of the coffee room. "Would you excuse me, Mr. Stratton? Miss Perry and I were obliged to share a room last night, and I assured her when I left a few minutes since that I would see to it that fresh kindling was brought and a fire lit, for we were obliged to huddle together the entirety of the night to stay warm."

Had it been too obvious? She wanted to leave no room at all for Mr. Stratton to make any assumptions about the relationship between her and Elias—or what might have occurred under cover of nightfall. "I apologize for taking far too much of your time with information which has no doubt been most tedious to you."

"Tedious?" He smiled politely. "On the contrary. I found it fascinating."

She stifled the impulse to swallow uncomfortably, then curtsied and strode to the maid who was scaling the stairs. Edith gave her a few quick instructions then continued to the top.

Edith didn't dare look back to see whether Mr. Stratton was still standing at the base of the staircase, so it was not until she was obscured by the corridor wall upstairs that she stopped and let out a long, slow exhale.

Never had her powers of mind been taxed so heavily. Nor had she ever spoken such longwinded poppycock. She was known for being quick. Abrupt. Pithy. She could only hope that Mr. Stratton didn't refine too much upon the change in demeanor.

And that Miss Perry wouldn't mind perjuring herself.

And that Elias would take it in stride that she had made him out to be a ridiculous but well-meaning fool.

She smiled slightly. He was accustomed to Edith's ways by now, surely. And even if he wasn't, there was too much at stake to worry about such things.

Chapter Seventeen

Elias was relieved to find that the pounding rain had lightened to a rhythmic pitter-patter when he woke. His next thought was how Edith had fared sharing a bed with Miss Perry for the night. He felt a large measure of guilt, having all the space of his own bed to himself, but there hadn't been a good alternative—at least not a suitable one. His heart quickened as he thought what it might be like to share a bed with Edith.

When he stepped into the coffee room after dressing for the day, Edith and Miss Perry were already there, partaking of tea and toast. He surveyed Edith for a moment, noting the faint crease between her brows. Was it a result of having passed a bad night? Or was she still plagued with worry over the situation?

He strode over, pulling out a chair and greeting them.

"There you are!" Edith said. "You've been snoring your life away, no doubt."

He grinned. "I slept very comfortably, thank you. How did you fare? Were you forced out of bed by your bedmate, Miss Perry?"

Miss Perry glanced at Edith, who glared at Elias.

"Not at all," Miss Perry said, setting down her cup. "In fact, I don't think I woke at all, save for very quickly when I found my arm to have fallen asleep." She laughed with timidity and glanced at Edith. "I discovered that you had wrapped your arms around mine, as though you thought me a pillow or some such thing. Robert always used to clutch at his blankets in much the same way while he slept." She smiled fondly at the memory of her brother. "I was glad that I didn't rouse you when I extricated my arm."

Edith's color was considerably heightened.

"How fascinating," Elias said. "Mrs. Cherriman must like you better than me, for I am more likely to receive a flung arm to the face than—"

"She knows, Elias." Edith cut him off. "I told her."

He looked back and forth between the two of them, Miss Perry attempting to suppress her amusement, and Edith's face still pink and annoyed.

"I was obliged to concoct a story for the edification of Mr. Stratton—thanks to your need to publish about our pretended relationship—and Miss Perry has kindly offered to corroborate the story I told." She sent a smile at Miss Perry.

"It is no trouble at all," Miss Perry said. "I assure you. The weather took us all by surprise. You couldn't have known that you would be obliged to spend the night here."

Edith rose. "The flooding has receded now, so I think we should be getting on our way as soon as possible."

Miss Perry set down her cup of coffee. "Yes, I should be on my way as well."

They left Elias to swallow a quick breakfast before gathering his things to leave.

The few items Elias had used during their time at the inn were packed away again, and he instructed one of the inn servants to convey the portmanteau to the coach. The ride would be unpleasant and muddy, but he looked forward even less to arrival at Shipton House. In their efforts to turn the tables on their friends, they had only managed to make fools of themselves—and likely worse. Elias cringed to think of the inevitable encounter with Mr. Donne. He and Edith would have to come up with a way to placate the man. He would be mad as fire when he discovered everything. And the thought that Edith's reputation might be in danger made him feel sick to his stomach.

Elias strode down the corridor, his boots thudding loudly as he approached the room Edith and Miss Perry had been occupying. He hoped to borrow a horse from Mr. Drew and ride beside the chaise—whatever he could do to lessen the wrath of Mr. Donne and convince him that they had been meticulous in safeguarding Edith's reputation.

He would arrive at Shipton House with clothing caked in mud, no doubt, and he acknowledged a feeling of disappointment at the prospect of sacrificing time in the carriage with Edith, but it was a small price to pay if it meant sparing her some of her father's unpleasantness.

"I cannot think what might have happened to it." Miss Perry's distressed voice sounded through the bedroom door, left ajar.

"Might your maid have it?" Edith asked.

"No, for she knows that I care for it myself—I am quite particular about it. Oh, dear!"

"No need to distress yourself just yet. I shall go look in the coffee room. Perhaps the clasp came undone while we ate." Edith emerged from the room, stopping short when she saw Elias. She pulled the door shut and sighed. "Miss Perry has lost her necklace."

Elias frowned. "A shame, I'm sure, but I would think such a consideration would be superseded by her desire to be to the funeral in time."

"Yes, I thought so too, but it is not just any necklace. It was a gift from her brother."

Elias sighed. "If it is the piece of jewelry I am remembering, it could be anywhere—slipped between a crack in the floorboards, swept up by a servant, *stolen* by a servant...." He shrugged. "It was a small little thing. We could spend the rest of the day in search of it, I should think. And who knows how long the rain will hold?"

Edith brushed past him, with a saucy look over her shoulder. "Then stop jabbering, and help me find it."

Mr. Stratton was found to be on his way out, a many-caped greatcoat enveloping him and a cane in hand.

After a quick greeting, Edith brushed past him toward the coffee room, and Elias followed. He couldn't like the way Mr. Stratton's eyes pursued them.

Elias inquired with one of the servants about the necklace, explaining that it held great sentimental value for Miss Perry, whom he noticed through the coffee room door, her eyes frantically searching the floor.

He went to her, explaining apologetically that nothing had yet been found.

"Is there something I can be of assistance with, Miss…?" Mr. Stratton stood behind Elias, looking a question at Miss Perry.

"Perry, sir." She wiped at her eye quickly. "I don't wish to trouble you, sir. It is only that I seem to have lost the necklace I was wearing yesterday. It is very important to me."

At Mr. Stratton's request, she described the appearance of the necklace.

"I'm afraid I haven't seen it," he said. "I wish you luck, though, in your search, Miss Perry. Mr. Cherriman." As he met Elias's gaze, his brow lifted slightly along with the corner of his mouth, then he tipped his hat and returned to the entryway.

Twenty minutes of searching passed, with two servants joining the quest, but the necklace and pendant were nowhere to be found. Elias's mount and Edith's chaise stood in the courtyard, impatient horses pawing at the stones below, their coats glistening with the slow-falling rain.

Elias exchanged an anxious glance with Edith, who nodded.

Gingerly, he approached Miss Perry, who was on hands and knees searching, dashing every now and then at a tear.

"Miss Perry," he said gently. "I'm afraid none of us has had any success in locating your necklace. I think it would be wisest to set out despite that, for we cannot tell how long the rain will continue so light. We can instruct Mr. Drew and his staff to continue looking for it—I would be happy to pay for the cost of sending it to you should it be found, or even to come retrieve it myself."

Miss Perry stood, shaking her head, her hold on her emotions quite obviously tenuous. She brushed her hands down her dress. "You are right. I should be on my way, and I am sure that you are both anxious to leave. Thank you for your assistance. You have been so very kind to me."

Coming up beside Elias, Edith reached a comforting hand to Miss Perry's arm.

The door to the inn opened, and Mr. Drew appeared, his hair damp from the rain. He looked at the three of them, and an apologetic grimace pulled down at the corners of his mouth.

He lifted his shoulders. "I am sorry to report this, but passage over the bridge is quite impossible. It held up for a number of equipages this morning, but it seems it was weakened by the storm, and it is no longer safe. Part of it gave way."

Edith shut her eyes and bowed her head, while Miss Perry's black glove flew to her mouth. Elias put a hand on Edith's shoulder, hoping to reassure her, though it was becoming less and less clear how everything was to be settled, given the debacle they were in.

"You are very welcome to continue your stay here, of

course," Mr. Drew continued. "I imagine the bridge will be repaired as quickly as possible, if only the weather will cooperate."

The rain continued to fall outside, though it seemed to be lighter than it had been even an hour ago. The skies were gray, but they lacked the threatening purple and charcoal hues from the day before.

"Is there no other way to Ivybridge than the main road?" Elias asked the innkeeper.

He shook his head. "Beyond slipping through one of the hedges and riding across the countryside, I'm afraid not. I suppose one might take the road all the way back to Hebury Heath, and then take the village roads that wrap around north, but that would be a *very* long route." One of the servants was heard calling for the innkeeper, and he excused himself.

"Repairing a bridge in the rain?" Miss Perry said, staring at nothing in particular. "That could take days! I shall surely miss the funeral."

Elias took her gloved hand, hoping to keep her grounded. "Miss Perry, I promise that you shall attend your brother's funeral, even if it means I must escort you on horseback myself—just like Mr. Drew mentioned."

"Would you really?" Hope bloomed in Miss Perry's face, and he could see Edith's blinking surprise from the corner of his eye.

He nodded.

Miss Perry glanced at Edith and then back to him. "It is so very kind, particularly when I have ruined everything for you. You might have been on the road an hour ago if it wasn't for me and my necklace. And now you are forced to wait here indefinitely."

She was right, and Elias stole a glance at Edith, wondering how she was feeling with the knowledge that they would be stuck at The Old Dog and Pheasant for even longer.

Edith met his gaze, then applied herself to Miss Perry. "Better safe here than drowned in the river, for who knows but what it might have given way underneath us?"

The thought made Elias's stomach clench, and his hand gripped Edith's shoulder harder. When had he even placed it there? He removed it gently, hoping Edith hadn't noticed. He was quickly losing control of himself, and he foresaw nothing but hurt ahead if he didn't manage to regain it.

After instructing her maid that her belongings be returned there, Miss Perry made her way back up to her room, and Elias turned to Edith.

"I know, I know," she said, not meeting his gaze. "It is my fault again. I should never have agreed to help look for that cursed necklace, and all our efforts were for naught, as it is still lost." She finally looked at him.

He smiled. "I wasn't going to say anything of the sort. In fact, I am getting quite comfortable here. I have a mind to stay indefinitely."

"It isn't a bad idea," Edith said significantly. "Not if it means we never have to face Matthew or Mercy or my father again." She held his gaze, unspoken apology written in her eyes. "We shall pay dearly for our trick."

"You shan't," he said, taking her hand. "I won't let you."

"It is very valiant of you," she said, pressing his hand gratefully, "but my father's wrath will be growing with every hour we are absent—and that is *without* knowing of Mr. Stratton's presence. If he feels I have jeopardized any of his political plans, he will yell me into my grave."

"Let him direct his wrath at me, then." He winked at her. "I can be quite deaf when I choose to be."

"Deafness is only half the equation, I'm afraid. You shall feel the very ground rumble beneath your feet."

"Much like when I snore?"

Her mouth trembled, and he knew a sense of victory at

having pierced through her gravity. He was growing very attached to her reluctant smile.

"Oh, no. Nothing can rival *that*." She turned on her heel and tossed a saucy look over her shoulder.

He watched her with a smile tugging at his lips. She always loved to have the last word—and the truth was, she generally earned it. She surpassed him in wit, little though he liked to admit it. And even had she not, he thought he might let her have the last word if only to see that look she gave him.

It was victory, yes. But even more, it was connection. It was an invitation to try her again, to come back for more. And Elias was more and more certain with each passing hour in Edith Donne's company that he would keep coming back as long as she let him.

Chapter Eighteen

❧❀❧

When Edith realized that Miss Perry had every intention of passing the majority of the day in the bedchamber, she pursed her lips.

"I think not, my dear," she said, taking the girl's hand and pulling her up from the bed. In such a place, there was little else for Miss Perry to do but dwell on her misfortunes, and the gray view onto a muddy stable yard from the window could hardly do anything but enhance the gloom.

For Edith's part, the prospect of her arrival home held more than enough anxiety and unpleasantness. What they all needed was distraction. Something to lighten the mood.

"*I* think we should get up a game of bullet pudding." Edith wagged her eyebrows, and Miss Perry looked intrigued but skeptical.

"Would it be unseemly of me to engage in such a thing under the circumstances?" She indicated her blacks.

Edith shrugged. "Was your brother very stiff? Or was he the sort who loved to laugh?"

Miss Perry smiled. "The latter, most assuredly. And he was very fond of the game."

"Then I think he would be very pleased. We may do it in his honor."

Miss Perry hesitated a moment longer, then nodded, an irrepressible smile forming on her lips.

Edith clasped her hands together. "Very good! We shall need flour, of course, and a knife, and then something heavy but small."

Seeming to enter into the spirit of it, Miss Perry nodded. "I shall engage to have it all brought to the coffee room. Or should it be one of the parlors?"

"A parlor, I think, provided one is available. I can't imagine Mr. Drew would wish for us to make a spectacle of ourselves in front of the other guests."

Miss Perry nodded. "True. Very well, then. I will instruct the servants on the required items, and you may inform Mr. Abram of our plans." And with that, she was off.

Edith glanced at Susan, who was busying herself with arranging everything in the bedchamber that had been repacked in their intent to leave earlier. Edith had debated bringing Susan along. Somehow she thought that eloping couples weren't terribly likely to care much for propriety. But in the end, the thought of her father catching wind of the affair had determined her to take the precaution. She was glad for it, especially given how things had turned out. "Thank you, Susan," she said with genuine feeling.

"Of course, miss," the maid said as she straightened to respond to Edith. "Would you like me to set up the game downstairs?"

"Thank you, but no. We shall manage very well, I think." She frowned. The maid looked exhausted and nervous. Where had she slept, after all? "The inn was quite full last night, as I understand it. Where did you sleep?"

Susan didn't meet her eyes, busying herself with straightening the bed covers. "In the stables, miss."

Edith's eyes widened. "The stables?"

Susan nodded, still not meeting her eyes.

"Were you not freezing, then? And wet besides?"

Susan managed a tired smile. "It is no matter."

An unexpected lump rose in Edith's throat as she thought of Susan sleeping in the half-wet straw. "I disagree. And I am terribly sorry that you were made to do that. I can't imagine you had much sleep." She glanced at the freshly-made bed and put a hand on it. "Why don't you lie down for a while? Right here."

Susan's eyes widened. "Oh, miss, I couldn't."

Edith smiled. "That is an order."

Susan nodded obediently, and the corner of her mouth trembled slightly. "Thank you, miss. It is very kind of you."

Edith pulled back the covers and patted them invitingly, then left the room, walking the short way down the corridor and pausing in front of Elias's room to glance around. It wasn't entirely proper for her to knock on his door, but it seemed silly to call for a servant to do it when she was already there, and she didn't want to disturb Susan. Her nerves she chose to ascribe to the unseemliness of what she was about to do rather than to… anything else.

She knocked softly.

"Come in."

She wavered, putting a hand on the doorknob as flashes of her dream assailed her unsolicited. For the sake of her own judiciousness, she was relieved upon waking to know that it *had* only been a dream, but there had been an undeniable feeling of disappointment along with it. In her dream, she had felt safe, encompassed in Elias's arms. Strange how something originating in her own head could have felt so very real. She could even remember how his fingers had been intertwined in hers, his warm breath grazing her neck.

She shook her head and clenched her eyes shut. It was a silly dream. She knocked again more loudly.

Footsteps. "I *said,* 'Come i—'" The door opened, and Elias stopped short, blinking. "Oh. Edith."

She mustered a smile, ignoring the untied cravat that hung around his shoulders, exposing his neck, which had traces of shaving soap. It must have been the inn's shaving soap, for it had a different scent from the rosewater from the library.

"Miss Perry and I wished to invite you to play a game of bullet pudding."

He raised his brows. "Miss Perry agreed to this?"

"Of course she agreed! Do you imagine I threatened her with a pistol?"

He shrugged. "It wouldn't surprise me overmuch." His eyes twinkled at her.

He delighted in provoking her. And, truth be told, she liked it as well. She liked a challenge, after all. That was all it was. He kept the boredom at bay.

She glared at him—unconvincingly, she guessed. "I look forward to seeing you make a fool of yourself with a face full of flour."

"I assure you I shall finish the game with a face as clean as it is now." He rubbed his jaw.

She raised a brow, unable to suppress a smile. "Clean as it is now?" Edith swiped a finger at a spot of shaving soap on his neck, realizing a moment too late the intimacy of the gesture. She felt him still and noted the arrested look in his eyes, which flitted to her mouth for the briefest moment. That small touch brought back a host of memories from the library—her hand wrapped around his neck, bringing his lips down to hers—and a desire to see if repeating the experience would be as enjoyable as it was the first time.

Stepping back, she put up her finger to display the soap, hoping she looked calmer than she felt inside.

"You missed a few spots." She turned on her heel, forcing calm, confident steps.

She *knew* she was being ridiculous, and it was all because of that silly, ill-advised kiss. She had avoided anything approaching such intimacy all these years for good reason: she had been terrified of enjoying it. If she didn't experience it, she couldn't know what she was missing.

But now she *did* know what she was missing, and it aggravated her to no end that she wanted to experience it again and again. And worst of all—and just as she had always suspected—she was no better than her parents. Her desire to kiss Elias was entirely selfish.

She wouldn't give in to such base motivations. She had always been in command of herself, and she had no intention of yielding now.

She took in a breath and entered the private parlor.

Miss Perry was in the process of making a pile of flour, frowning in concentration as she packed it into a bowl and then flipped it over in an abrupt motion. With painstaking care, she removed the bowl, revealing a mound of flour that retained the shape of the container. "Ha!" she cried in victory. Her maid, who was stitching something in the corner, startled and then went back to her work.

"This" —Miss Perry held up a small marble— "I was able to acquire from the young boy in the stable yard. I believe he assists the ostlers."

Edith shut the door behind her, then walked over to inspect the mound. "I am surprised he surrendered it to you."

Miss Perry smiled, brushing off her hands. "He was loath to part with it until I offered him tuppence—and a promise of the marble's return with another tuppence. We are all ready now. Is Mr. Abram to join us?"

"Yes, he shall be down shortly."

"I have a feeling he shall be a skilled competitor." Miss Perry pursed her lips as she slowly set the marble atop the pile, letting out a relieved breath when nothing disastrous occurred.

"Yes, I imagine so, for he hates to lose."

"Does he? Yes, I suppose I can see that. But, then again, none of us likes to lose. Have you played very many games like this with him?"

Edith thought over the time she had known Elias. There had been plenty of evenings together, for he often joined Matthew at Shipton House, but they had never done anything more exciting than playing whist. "No, but that is only because my father abhors such pastimes and always has."

"You have a long history with Mr. Abram, then? One cannot help but notice how close you are." She let out one of her soft laughs. "If you hadn't told me you were not married, I should likely have gone on believing it forever."

Edith felt a blush creeping into her cheeks and was only glad Miss Perry was too focused on putting aside the extra flour to notice.

Miss Perry looked up at her hesitantly. "I hope it is not terribly forward of me to ask, but why *aren't* you married?" She rushed on, as if to defend her asking. "I obviously am not so very well acquainted with you, but it seems a smart match."

Edith forced a laugh. "A fatal match, more likely. Elias and I never meet without coming to dagger-drawing. We are too alike. And somehow too different as well. Besides, I have no plans to marry."

Miss Perry blinked twice. "No plans to marry? Why ever not?"

Edith had always been more than happy to enlighten anyone who broached the subject on her views of marriage, but she hesitated now, reluctant for some reason to thrust her cynicism on the young woman. She smiled wryly. "My views on marriage and love would shock you, I think."

Miss Perry's brow furrowed. "What are your views?"

"Not positive, I fear." Seeing Miss Perry look nonplussed,

Edith shrugged. "I have observed it to end unhappily more often than not."

"But marriage *doesn't* end—at least not in anything but the most extreme cases."

Edith brushed at a bit of spilled flour on the table. "Yes, that is part of the problem, though, isn't it? Two unhappy people unable to escape one another."

Miss Perry's head tipped from side to side. "I suppose it *is* a problem in some cases. But in others, surely the fact that there is no end is cause for hope? If something has no end, it can always be improved and become better, don't you think?"

Edith could hardly argue with such a rosy view. The last thing Miss Perry needed was for someone to give her another reason for sadness or despair. Edith lifted a shoulder. "I imagine you are right, but the long and short of it is, I haven't ever met someone who made me wish to marry."

"Not even Mr. Abram?" Miss Perry asked incredulously. "But he is kind and amusing and very handsome and—"

"And unbearably arrogant and terribly aggravating—"

"Do I hear my virtues being extolled?" Elias entered the room with an amused smile, his eyes lingering on Edith for a moment before moving to Miss Perry. "I cannot go anywhere without her insisting upon doing so, you know."

Edith hardly knew whether she was glad or embarrassed at his timing. It was one thing to hurl insults at a man to his face and quite another to speak ill of him when he wasn't there to fight back. She hated the feeling that he had discovered any pettiness in her. She played fair, and she took pride in that.

But there was no helping it. Besides, it was better that he know there was nothing to that moment in his doorway a few minutes ago. They were as they had always been: rivals of wit. "I wouldn't want anyone to remain in ignorance, of course. But I was hardly done *extolling your virtues*, as you say." She smiled at him. "There are so very many to choose from."

"Yes. I believe such *virtues* are most easily recognized in one who also possesses them. You are very fit for the task."

Miss Perry was looking back and forth between them. "How fascinating. I am now more than ever excited at the prospect of this game, for it is apparent that you are well-matched in one another. I only hope that you don't find me aggravating, for I am quite slow, I fear." She clapped her hands together once. "Come, let us begin. Perhaps it is only the moisture in the air from all the rain, but this flour seems to be stickier than I am accustomed to, which shall make for a very thrilling game, since the mound isn't likely to fall over as easily as usual. I assume you are acquainted with the rules of play, Mr. Abram?"

He bowed, setting out a hand to welcome the knife. "May I do the honors?" He glanced at Edith, the familiar challenging gleam in his eyes, and put a hand below his face as if to display it. "Behold, ladies. A clean face" —he looked at Edith significantly— "which shall remain clean."

"What is the saying, Miss Perry?" Edith asked, moving to make way for Elias to begin the game. "Ah yes, pride goeth before the fall."

"Undoubtedly very familiar to a woman who has spent all her life falling."

They locked eyes, and she raised a brow at him. "Shall we play, or do you insist on delaying the inevitable as long as possible?"

He dipped his head and set to cutting the mound of flour.

Edith always sought victory, but for some reason, it seemed more important today than ever, as if she needed to prove her mettle not only to Elias but to herself. She *was* still in command of herself.

Chapter Nineteen

There was an intensity to Edith's play that surprised Elias and drew him in, sparking his own competitive spirit and sharpening his senses.

It was just a game. He knew that. Yet he sensed that there was something else at play for Edith, and he couldn't help responding in kind. He needed to win. He didn't know precisely why, but he needed to.

Miss Perry had been right about the flour. The grains seemed to adhere more tightly to one another, making for cleaner cuts—and stiffer competition. Miss Perry was no less determined than the other two to come off conqueror, and her strategy was to slice the smallest possible section from the flour pile, while Elias and Edith were more daring in their cuts, anxious to prove their skill.

Miss Perry's calculated and careful efforts were rewarded by the mound's collapse on her third cut, drawing irrepressible laughter from Edith and Elias. She clasped her hands behind her back and took a deep breath before plunging her nose and chin into the toppled remains, fishing for the elusive marble in its depths. She emerged twice with nothing, finding her mark on the third dive. Face caked with flour, she held up her hands in victory.

The flour was packed down again and the mound resurrected. With each cut, Elias's heart quickened pace, and he drew nearer and nearer as the mound became smaller and smaller. He watched unblinking as Edith held the knife above, shifting it around as she decided where to make the next cut. There was hardly an inch of flour left around the marble on every side, and Elias tensed as he saw her position the knife to slice away at what little remained.

The flour collapsed into a heap, and Elias cheered.

Edith whipped around. "You nudged me!"

He reared back, knowing a moment's misgiving as he realized how near he had been to her.

"Did you not see it, Miss Perry?" Edith cried.

Miss Perry bared a mouth of clenched teeth, clearly unwilling to be cast as judge.

Edith gave Elias a little shove. "Only look how near to me he is and ask yourself how easy it would have been for him to bump my arm. He is no better than a cheat."

Elias threw his head back. "Take no heed of her, Miss Perry. She is a poor loser, nothing more. Come, Edith. No more of these excuses. You must find the marble now—though it shall be much easier thanks to all of the flour I cut away for you."

Edith glared at him, her chest heaving. He didn't even attempt to suppress his grin—it would have been entirely futile.

She shook her head with eyes that promised vengeance, then turned back to her task. Lowering her face so that it hovered above the mound, she sent another spiteful sidelong glance at Elias before turning to the flour. A wavy strand of hair dropped near her mouth, and she brought up a hand. Without even thinking, Elias snatched her wrist.

Edith's head whipped around in disbelief.

Feeling some sort of explanation was warranted, Elias lifted his shoulders innocently. "No hands allowed!"

She rose so that she stood straight, and the lock of hair stubbornly stayed in place, covering one eye. "May I?" she asked in an acid tone. She wrested her wrist from his grasp and, in an exaggerated gesture, tucked the strand of hair behind her ear.

Elias's shoulders shook with silent laughter as he watched Edith's face rove about in the flour, eyes closed and brows knit in concentration. She was quick to find the marble, emerging with it tucked between her powdered lips.

"Bravo!" cried Miss Perry, who had managed to wipe away the majority of the evidence of her own time spent in the mound.

Edith took the marble from her mouth and dipped into a grand curtsy, but her gaze met Elias's as she came up. "I demand a rematch. Without you hovering over me or knocking me about."

Elias scoffed. "Knocking you about? What exaggeration is this?"

"What? Afraid you shall lose if we play another round?" She leveled her most challenging gaze at him, and he had to put a hand to his mouth to stifle a laugh.

"Hardly," he managed. "I merely can't imagine that there is much flour left for it with how much remains on your face and clothing."

She glanced down at her dress, and her mouth twisted to the side, but she was unable to suppress a twitch. She said nothing for a moment, then, before Elias realized what she was about, snatched a handful of flour and threw it at his face. "Now we are even," she said.

Elias had blinked just in time to spare his eyes, but in his surprise, he inhaled, and he coughed and coughed, doubling over. One fist covered his mouth, the other resting on his thigh.

When he was finally able to compose himself, tears were streaming down his face, and he was sure he was red as a beet. He felt Edith's hand on his back and took a moment, hands still on his thighs.

"Are you all right, Mr. Abram?" Miss Perry's voice was full of concern.

"No," he said, still hunched over as he caught his breath. He glanced at what remained of the flour, then pretended to stumble slightly, feeling Edith's hand grasp at his arm to steady him while he reached for the edge of the table to do the same. In a quick motion, he snatched whatever he could manage to gather up in his fist, rose to a stand, and tossed it at Edith, who blocked the attack with an arm in front of her face. She reached for more flour—what little remained on the table, and Miss Perry cried out and ran for the door. "Not on my dress! It is my only mourning attire!"

"Miss!" Miss Perry's maid—all but forgotten till now—hurried after her mistress. Puffs of flour hung in the air, descending slowly as the door shut behind maid and mistress.

Elias and Edith looked at each other, both standing prepared for attack. Her eyes moved to the bag of flour Miss Perry had set aside, and she made to grab it.

But Elias was too quick for her. It only took two long strides to bring him beside her, where he flung an arm at the bag, sending it sliding to the edge of the table. He snatched at her wrists, pulling them behind her and smiling down at her in victory. Their bodies pressed up against each other, chests rising and falling.

"You, madam, are without scruple!" he said, though his mouth was pulled into an irrepressible grin.

"Says the cheat!" She strove against his grasp on her wrists, and he laughed as he saw her eyes flick toward the flour again.

"Don't even think about it. I should wrestle you to the ground before you took your second step."

"Bully," she breathed, her chin raised defiantly, and her eyes blazing with energy and fire like he'd never seen them. Flecks of flour hung on the edge of her lashes and brows, and her face was sprinkled with a white mask, thicker at the nose, cheeks, and chin, fading near her hairline. There was a streak across her mouth where she had wiped at the flour with a sleeve. She was ridiculous. And yet captivating.

He took pains to calm his breathing, knowing it would drive her mad to see him calm when she was so worked up. "Let's see. Arrogant. Cheat. Bully. Just how many insults *do* you have stored up for me this evening?"

She tugged at her hands again, but he regained his strong hold on them. Her nostrils flared. "Even more than you have for me, I assure you."

He chuckled. Insults? She had him completely wrong.

She misinterpreted his reaction. "Would you care to test me, then?"

"Go on," he said, pulling her closer as she again attempted to free herself from his grasp. But this time there was less will in the attempt. Or perhaps he was merely seeing what he wanted to see, but he was not holding her wrists so tightly anymore. She could certainly have escaped if she'd had a mind to.

She looked into his eyes, and he found himself back in the library at Shipton House.

"I have already offered the three you mentioned," she said. "And unlike you, I play fairly. It is your turn. So tell me—tell me what you really think of me."

His heart thudded against his chest, and her eyes dared him to insult her. He could easily offer a list of adjectives he might have used to describe her a few days ago: haughty, cold, heartless. For some reason, he thought it might satisfy her to hear it. She was in a strange mood.

"Very well," he said. "Firstly, I think that you are not who you pretend to be."

"Oh?" She was all feigned curiosity and skepticism.

"I think that Matthew was more right about you than I believed."

She let out a small scoff. "A helpless kitten, am I?"

"And I think"—he slowly released his grip on her wrists, leaving his arm draped around her so that his hand slipped down to cover hers softly.

Her breathing stilled, an arrested look in her eyes.

"I think that you are not as anxious to leave my arms as you would have me believe."

He hardly believed his own audacity. And yet he couldn't stop there. He had come too far to turn back. He brought his other hand up and brushed at one of the thicker spots of flour on her cheek. It sprinkled onto her chest, which rose and fell against his. "I think you are beautiful, Edith Donne. Inside and out." The edge of his lip pulled up into a half-smile, a nonchalant gesture entirely at odds with the tension he felt inside. "I've cheated again, haven't I? That was four things."

Her cheeks were red under the mask of flour, her nostrils flared, but she said nothing. Elias had released her hands, and he didn't know whether she wished to embrace him or slap him. But she hadn't moved away from him. Certainly that was something.

Her eyes flicked down to his mouth, and, needing no more invitation than that, Elias dipped his head until their lips met.

It was everything her eyes had been: fire and passion and anger, as if revenge could be taken through a kiss. He pulled her into him, pressing on her hands, which still hung at the small of her waist. With his other hand, he took her cheek, anchoring her lips to his. She pushed her lips more firmly against his, as if it were a battle and she on the offensive. He responded in kind, bringing her toward him with the arm at her waist, even as he pressed her away with his lips. There was no retreat, only attack and counterattack.

And then resistance.

She pulled her arms out from under his hands and pushed away from him, their lips breaking roughly apart. She stepped back, and he blinked, bewildered at the abrupt change, his breath ragged.

"You are a knave," she said, her voice level but shaking as she wiped her red mouth with the back of her hand. She turned on her heel and made her way toward the door, which opened just as she stretched out a hand toward the doorknob.

Miss Perry appeared, her head peeking in hesitantly. "Is it safe now? I thought I heard enough silence to indicate—oh dear." She looked at the mess of scattered flour that covered the floor around Elias.

Edith said nothing, merely opening the door wide enough so that she could pass through.

"It is safe," Elias said, brushing a hand against his lips while his eyes lingered on Edith's retreating form. He hadn't any idea what to think. He had been *certain* she had yielded—even returned the embrace. Had he imagined it? Had she truly been resisting the entire time? "I should change." He dipped his head and strode from the room.

Chapter Twenty

Edith wiped at her lips again with the back of her hand, trying to erase the lingering memory on them. She had seen the alarm in Elias's eyes when she had pulled away, and the guilt at her behavior stung. She had welcomed the kiss, much as she might wish to convince herself and Elias otherwise. Being so near to him, she hadn't been able to keep their last kiss at bay. She *wanted* him to kiss her. And she had enjoyed it when he had—so much that it terrified her—the feeling of desiring him more than she had desired anything in her life.

She shut the door to her bedchamber, leaning her forehead against it and shutting her eyes. She had enjoyed it every bit as much as the first kiss they had shared. More, even. And it hadn't taken her more than a moment to realize that Elias was an essential ingredient to that enjoyment—or to hope he was taking as much pleasure in it as she was.

It was the next thought, though, which had caused her to pull away: the humiliating realization that Elias had kissed her unbidden—that she had given him no reason to think she would welcome a kiss, and yet he had done it anyway. She was a means to an end—one entry on a long list of women who had shared such moments with him.

And she couldn't abide that thought.

Susan still lay peacefully in the bed, and Edith couldn't bear to wake her. She looked at the state of her clothing and then found the handheld mirror to survey her face. She pulled her lips together to stifle an expression of dismay. She looked an utter and complete fool, flour covering her face in varying degrees of thickness, hair askew, lips slightly swollen.

She attempted to change without Susan's help, but she was so undone, so jittery, that her movements were clumsy enough to disturb the maid's sleep. Susan rubbed her eyes and rushed out of bed, clearly ashamed.

"Don't fret, Susan," Edith said, slipping out of her olive-green traveling dress. "I didn't mean to wake you."

Susan helped her into the only other dress Edith had brought—a long-sleeved pale blue muslin. She needn't have changed, though, for she had no intention of leaving her room. It would mean facing Elias, and she hadn't the first idea how to do that. She wouldn't do so until she was in the company of Miss Perry—when there was no opportunity for private discussion.

But, as it turned out, she had only been cooped up for an hour, reading the supremely boring book Susan had been able to acquire from Mr. Drew, when a soft knock sounded on her door. Miss Perry no doubt.

"Come in," Edith said.

The door remained shut.

A voice came through the door. "I merely wished to inform you that we can make our way back to Shipton House whenever you are ready."

She threw her legs over the side of the bed and hurried to the door, opening it.

Elias was already a few steps down the corridor, not waiting for her response.

"Elias," she said.

He stopped, but it was a moment before he turned, his expression impassive.

"I don't understand," she said.

"Some men from the village have been working all morning to repair the bridge. They seem to have found success, based on the reports of equipages that have passed through in the last fifteen minutes. The damage was not so great as it was first thought to be."

Home. They could go home. Edith didn't know whether to be relieved or terrified. "That is certainly unexpected. I shall have Susan prepare my things again. And hope that the bridge holds in the meantime."

He nodded with a civil smile. "Very good." He turned back toward his room, and she had to stifle the desire to call out to him again.

Elias had said any number of cutting and provoking things to her in the past, but nothing had affected her so much as the distant coolness he now showed. Was he hurt? Regretful? Annoyed?

Within half an hour, they were bidding Miss Perry goodbye as Elias helped her up into a hired chaise—something he had insisted upon paying for.

"Thank you both from the bottom of my heart," Miss Perry said, pausing in the door of the carriage. "I don't know how I should have borne these two days without you." She looked to Elias with a bit of a smile. "I am relieved—as I am sure you are—that you weren't obliged to escort me home on horseback."

"It would have been my pleasure, Miss Perry, I assure you," he said kindly, placing a soft kiss on her gloved hand. The gesture was as kind and intimate as his behavior toward Edith upstairs had been distant and aloof.

She felt the unwelcome but unmistakable stirrings of jealousy. Miss Perry was everything someone like Elias should want—everything he needed. Young, kind, optimistic. She was the perfect argument against Elias's cynical view of women. Indeed, she was everything a woman was supposed to be—everything Edith was not.

But even more than that, she was everything Edith never *could* be. For what was Edith but the worst combination of her parents? She was her father's anger and his sharp tongue; she was her mother's stubbornness; she was both of their absolute determination to have their way, no matter the cost.

Edith wasn't fit for marriage. She wasn't fit for love.

It wasn't until Miss Perry's chaise was rolling out of the muddy yard that Edith noted the horse which stood by the waiting chaise, saddled and ready for a ride.

"Do you intend to ride?" she asked Elias.

He nodded, and his affirmative response hurt somewhere in her chest.

It was silly, of course. Not only was his riding beside the chaise a wise decision—less likely to incur the wrath of her father upon their arrival—but there was no reason at all for her to wish to spend another two hours with him in a carriage. And what concern was it of hers if he wished to arrive at Shipton covered in a thick layer of mud?

This was all a ruse, she reminded herself. It's all it ever had been. And yet, somehow Edith felt like the fool at the center of it all, a victim of her own vengeful ambition, the butt of her own jest. No doubt Elias was laughing at her as well, just as he so clearly had been in the library—taunting her, pushing her to her limits.

The horrifying thought occurred to her that he might be a co-conspirator in all of this. What if he was playing her for the fool all along, convinced he could bring her to her knees?

Well, he had not brought her there. She certainly enjoyed

his company more than she was comfortable admitting, and she had enjoyed kissing him—indeed, the thought of kissing someone else held little attraction for her. But if he thought more than that, he was fooling himself.

She climbed into the chaise before Elias could come assist her, but it was only a few minutes into the journey when the chaise slowed to a stop.

Edith peered through the carriage window. They had come to a bridge—*the* bridge, no doubt. The door opened, and Elias appeared, leading his horse by the reins.

"I think we should cross on foot," he said. "To be safe."

Susan rose obediently, but Edith remained in her seat. "Surely that isn't necessary? We've passed at least five carriages, each of which must have crossed over the bridge—and one of them a heavily laden stagecoach with several people on top." It was silly for Elias's precaution to bother her, but it did. Or perhaps she just thrived on being defiant.

"Please," he said, extending his hand to her, an imploring light in his eyes which made her heart jolt.

"Your attempts at chivalry are inspiring, I'm sure, but somewhat superfluous," she said, but she stepped down all the same.

"Chivalry?" he said with a twinkling look at her. "I am merely doing whatever I can to save my own skin. I can't imagine I would fare well with your father if I arrived at Shipton House without you."

She offered no answer to this, but she couldn't help wondering how much truth there might be to his jest.

Chapter Twenty-One

The bridge was crossed over uneventfully by people and equipage alike, and the rest of the journey passed in a similar, unremarkable manner. Elias had debated what to do when they reached the bridge, but in the end, he found that having the party cross on foot was the only solution which rid him of the heart-stopping images assailing his mind of the bridge collapsing under the weight of the chaise with Edith inside.

She was an enigma, impossible to fathom, by turns hot and cold. At times, he wondered if she hadn't begun to feel something for him. But without fail, those moments were followed by one much like the one when she had shoved him away in the private parlor of the inn—a reminder that she wanted him no closer than arm's length.

It didn't surprise him, and he knew it wasn't fair to ask more of her. They had agreed clearly about the nature of this endeavor—this ridiculous and failed endeavor. The purpose had been to teach Matthew and the others their mistake. They had misjudged their victims when they had undertaken to make a May game of Edith and Elias.

Precisely when Elias had lost track of that, he couldn't say. But he certainly *had* lost track of it, allowing the lines between reality and charade to blur together, until he found himself in a fight against admitting what had truly occurred: he had fallen in love with Edith Donne.

The irony of it all was maddening, for he had fallen in love with the most potent testament he could possibly have found to what he had known for years: women were fickle creatures. Their emotions, their actions, their words were not to be trusted.

He let out a slow, steady breath as Shipton House came into sight. There would be laughter at their expense—provided Mr. Donne's temper didn't eclipse the humor. Either way, unpleasantness lay ahead as far as Elias's eyes could see.

The large, wooden door to Shipton House opened as Elias dismounted and walked to the chaise to hand Edith down.

It was Matthew who came out, a look of astonishment on his face as he hurried over. "What the devil? What are you doing here?"

Elias's head reared back as Edith stepped down. "What are we *doing* here?"

Matthew threw up his hands. "I thought you were for Scotland! No, dash it. You told me as much in that note." He looked at Edith. "You haven't got to Scotland and back in two days. What, then?"

Edith laughed, but it had a forced quality to it. "Don't be ridiculous, Matthew. It was all a jest, of course!"

Matthew stared. "A jest?" He looked to Elias, and his brows snapped together. "What the devil does she mean, Eli?"

He looked to Edith, unsure how she wished for him to handle the situation, and he saw uncertainty in her eyes—a question he didn't recognize.

She turned back to Matthew. "We know of the trick you meant to play on us. Ensuring Elias and I overheard your conversations." She raised her brows. "We thought you could use a taste of your own medicine."

Matthew scoffed, looking at her for all the world as if she were mad. "Perhaps if you'd left it at the note. But, hang it, Edith! You can't leave with a man for two days and call it a jest!"

Edith's color heightened, and her eyes flashed. "Well, if you had come after us like any half-decent brother, we might not be having this conversation. Why on earth do you think I left you a note and ensured its delivery so soon after our departure? Surely you can't think I'd be stupid enough to do so if I were truly hoping to elope?"

"Come after you? When you chose the rainiest day of the year to elope? And after I saw you kissing Eli in the library like some dashed lightskirt?"

Elias took two strides over and threw a fist into Matthew's face. Matthew stumbled back, covering his nose with a hand. He brought it away, blood on his fingers and dribbling from his nose. His eyes, blinking and watering, sought out Elias.

Elias flexed his fingers, feeling his knuckles burn. "Forgive me, but you shouldn't talk to your sister like that, Matthew."

Matthew swiped at his bloody nose with a thumb. "You're giving *me* lessons on how to treat a woman after making off with her for days on end and bringing her home with no reputation to speak of?"

Elias's jaw hardened, and he clenched his hands, feeling how the knuckles burned and bones ached on the one he'd used to punch Matthew.

"Contrary to what you believe," Edith spat, "I require no protection. Not from either of you. My reputation is just that— my own—and it is none of your concern." She pushed through them with a smoldering glare and made her way inside.

Matthew sniffed, scrunching his nose and wiping at the blood again. "I wouldn't leave. My father will no doubt wish to have a word with you."

Elias leveled an annoyed gaze at his friend. "Whether he wishes it or not, I will be requesting to have a word with *him*."

Matthew turned to follow after Edith, leaving Elias to wonder how in the wide world he was to settle the situation to everyone's satisfaction.

Chapter Twenty-Two

Edith had fully intended to speak with Elias before their arrival at Shipton House—to discuss how best to handle the inevitable explanation which would be required of them. But she had not counted on his riding beside rather than in the chaise, and Matthew had ensured that there was no opportunity for a private word once they did arrive.

Her father seemed to have been notified of their arrival, for Edith was informed after a mere five minutes in her bedchamber that she was expected in her father's study immediately.

She took in a steadying breath. The way before her was anything but clear. Based on Matthew's surprise, the family hadn't any idea that their journey had ended at The Old Dog and Pheasant. Edith and Elias had done *too* good a job at making the elopement believable.

Her family's ignorance also meant, though, that there had been no communication from Mr. Stratton, an enormous relief to Edith. Her father's wrath would be great enough without adding that blow on top.

Her cynicism told her that it was only a matter of time until Mr. Stratton made use of what he knew, but she couldn't help hoping she was wrong. Perhaps her story had satisfied him, particularly as she and Elias had given no other indication that their relationship was anything but platonic.

Not until after Stratton's departure, that is.

She slowed as she neared the door of the study, seeing Elias approaching from down the corridor.

"What are you doing?" she said.

"I am to speak with your father."

She shook her head. "It will be for the best if I speak to him first."

Elias shrugged. "I cannot simply ignore his request. More like a command than a request, really."

Edith stared at him, her stomach clenching. He had called them to come in together? "Then I suppose we must both go in, for my presence is also *requested*."

Elias nodded, his face impassive as he invited her to pass before him.

Edith's father was seated behind his desk, and he stared at them wordlessly as they took their seats across from him. The silence lengthened, but Edith knew better than to so much as move. The large vein in her father's forehead bulged, telling her that the slightest movement could spark an explosion of wrath. Edith looked to Elias to send him a silent warning, but it was too late.

"Mr. Donne, please allow me—"

Her father shot up from his seat, his hands gripping the edge of the desk. "Silence!"

Elias started in his chair, and Edith shut her eyes, blocking out the way her father's face and hands trembled, as if it might lessen the tension in the room.

"Never," he spat, "in all my years did I imagine that I would raise a good-for-nothing hoyden for a daughter."

Edith saw Elias stiffen beside her. He was unaccustomed to her father's temper. This meeting would be most unpleasant for him.

"A hoyden, I say!" her father said, looking to Edith. "Explain yourself!"

For a moment, Edith considered ironically thanking her father for his concern over her safety, but she knew it would only add fuel to the fire.

Instead, she set about explaining, as rationally as she could, what had led them to embark upon their journey and return two days later. There wasn't a chance of her father sympathizing with the reasoning provided to him. Playing a trick on someone for pure amusement was a concept entirely foreign to a man whose every decision was calculated to bring about a practical result. But the truth was the only option. Her father had no patience for anything but directness.

To her surprise, he listened without saying a word as she recounted their implausible tale.

"I assure you, Father, that we took every precaution to guard my reputation."

Elias nodded.

"If that were true, you would not have left in the first place!" Her father's face exploded in color, and he slammed a fist on the table. "And you, Mr. Abram. What have you to say for yourself? My daughter is clearly no better than a jade, but I thought better of *you*."

Elias glanced at Edith, who looked away, trying to stifle the embarrassment she felt at her father's description of her.

"I am afraid that I have no satisfactory excuse, sir, and can only assure you that I would never purposely endanger your daughter's reputation."

"Is that so? Then I suppose you are prepared to marry her, are you?"

Edith froze, gaze flying to her father. "Father!"

He leveled a furious glance at her. "What did you expect? That you would be able to waltz back here as though nothing had happened? I think not! You shall marry, of course."

She shook her head from side to side frantically. "You assured me that I was free to choose whether I wished to marry, and *I* have assured you time and again that I do *not* wish to."

"Perhaps you should have considered that *before* playing a hoyden's trick on your family! It is not at all what your aunt imagined when she left you her fortune, I assure you."

She made to rise, and Elias set a hand on hers, directing a look at her that was both pleading and full of warning. She held his eyes for a moment, then resumed her seat, trying to take in deep breaths to steady herself. Matching her father's anger would do nothing. But she would do anything to stop his forcing a marriage upon them.

"I understand your anger, Father." She willed her voice to sound calm. "Indeed, I am very sorry for the turn things took. It was folly on my part, and I accept the full blame. But there is truly no need for Elias and me to marry." She found she was leaning forward, her hands clasped as she appealed to whatever mercy might lay hidden inside her father's heart. "If you are in any doubt of the care we took, you may apply to Miss Perry, for she can attest to it—indeed, she slept in the same room—the same bed—as me."

Her father's forehead wrinkled. "And who is this Miss Perry? Where was *her* chaperon on this journey?"

Edith swallowed, feeling trapped. She looked to Elias. He was watching her with a strange look in his eye—a touch of sadness, perhaps? But his gaze moved to her father.

"If I may, sir, I think a swift marriage between us is more likely to occasion gossip than doing nothing, particularly after we took such pains to avoid any behavior that might give anyone reason to doubt our story. Would it not be better to wait and see if such a step is necessary?"

For the first time, her father hesitated. No doubt he was thinking of the repercussions of both routes, and Edith sat anxiously on the edge of her seat as he deliberated, brushing off the impulse she felt to take Elias's hand as they awaited her father's decision.

"There is something to what you say," her father said. "I am getting the necessary votes in place for the bill I hope will be voted upon when we resume in the autumn, and I cannot afford to occasion any gossip, which is certainly what would happen if it became known that my daughter had married so suddenly." He looked to Edith with a flash of annoyance. "You have put about your opinion on the subject too widely for people to accept a sudden marriage without comment, and I understand that *you*" —he indicated Elias— "have done very much the same."

Elias demonstrated only the slightest hesitation before nodding. "I'm afraid my views are also quite generally known, sir."

Her father scoffed. "As if anyone was permitted to have *opinions* on marriage!" He waved a dismissive hand. "Go! Get out of my sight before I change my mind. But mark my words! If I hear even the faintest whisper of scandal...." He trailed off threateningly.

Edith rose with as much quick calm as she could muster, hoping not to anger her father by being too slow *or* too quick. "Thank you, Father." Her voice was just as feeble as her legs felt, weak as they were with relief.

Not wishing to give her father any reason to question what there was between Elias and her, she walked quickly out of the room, releasing a shut-eyed, shuddering breath when she was safely away from her father's scrutiny.

Down the corridor, she spied Mercy and Viola, passing through the doorway into one of the parlors. Mercy turned her head before entering, though, and stopped in place. "Edith!"

She came toward her. "What happened? We saw Matthew come in with blood on his face and shirt not so long since."

Edith's mouth drew into a line, and she guided Mercy back in the direction of the parlor with a firm grasp on her slender arm. "You may well wonder—and pray to escape the same fate by *my* hand, for I assure you, I am sorely tempted!"

Viola scurried into the parlor ahead of them.

"We never dreamed you would respond to the prank in such a way," Mercy said, her eyes full of apology as she shut the door. "It was all in good fun, but things went terribly awry. I am so very sorry, Edith."

"And I as well," Viola said with a pleading look. "Had I known what the result would be, nothing would have induced me...."

Edith took in a large breath and shook her head, thinking how near a miss it all had been. They hardly knew the havoc they had wreaked, and Edith had no intent whatsoever of admitting to them what commotion and confusion their silly prank had caused her. She wouldn't let anybody know.

She summoned a reluctant smile. "I admit it *was* a good prank. And there is no lasting harm done, after all, as long as we can persuade Matthew and Elias to play nicely with one another. For his part, my father has agreed to let things lie."

Mercy heaved a sigh of relief. "Thank heaven. I imagine you would never forgive us if you and Elias were forced to marry as a result of it all."

"You can be sure of that," Edith said. "And now, if you'll excuse me, I want nothing so much as my own bed and an hour or two of sleep."

They nodded, and Edith left the room, exhaustion seeping into her bones. Now that the meeting with her father was past, she realized how much fear she had been trying to keep at bay.

Thank heaven for Elias's presence in the meeting. Without

his words, Edith might be preparing herself for the very thing she had spent her whole life avoiding.

Chapter Twenty-Three

Elias dipped his head deferentially to Mr. Donne and strode from the room, jumping slightly when Mr. Donne shut the door firmly behind him. He gazed down the corridor and saw Edith slip into the parlor with Mercy. He had known a hope that she would be waiting for him outside the study. But free from the threat of marriage to Elias, she had made the quickest escape she could manage.

He stood in the corridor for a moment, leaning his back against the wall, resisting the urge to bang his head against it again and again. He shut his eyes and let out a frustrated breath. If only he could go back to two weeks ago, before any of this had happened.

"Elias?"

He stood up straight, watching as Edith walked down the corridor toward him from the parlor, brushing a finger along her lip distractedly. She came to stand before him, and he noted for the first time how tired she looked. With a glance up and down the corridor, she took his hand.

"Thank you," she said, her voice full of genuine gratitude.

There was a haunted look in her eyes, as though she had just escaped a terrible fate, and it pierced him.

He managed a chuckle he hoped sounded casual and detached—everything he was not. "For what?"

"It was *your* words that pacified my father."

He shrugged. "Did you think I would sit idly by while he consigned us both to a future of misery?" He couldn't keep a hint of bitterness from his tone, but she seemed not to notice.

Indeed, she laughed softly, letting his hand drop. "No, of course not. But thank you all the same." There was softness in her eyes as she looked at him, and the irony of it stung. Nothing he could do or say to Edith could bring about such a softening except saving her from the terrible fate of a lifetime with him. Several cutting responses came to mind—he had trained his mind to strike too well—but even in his hurt, he couldn't bring himself to do anything that might change the way she was looking at him.

He swallowed his pain. "You are welcome."

She pressed his hand again, her gaze holding his for a moment, then dropped his hand and left.

He sighed as Edith grew further and further from him. The only one who seemed to be paying a steep price for the jest was Elias himself. He'd forfeited a friend. He'd sacrificed his pride.

And he'd lost his heart.

There was no point in staying at Shipton Hall now.

Elias fully expected dinner to be an unpleasant affair, but there seemed to be no alternative to suffering through it, for he had no desire to offend his hosts by leaving less than two hours after his arrival—particularly not when he was in such a precarious position. He would leave in the morning.

There was little doubt in his mind that the right thing to do—the expected thing—was to marry Edith.

Yes, the idea to elope had been hers. But that would hardly matter to anyone. Nor would it matter that it had all been for sport. In the eyes of Society, Edith's reputation required salvaging—and he was the one to do it.

To Edith, the idea that she needed saving would be offensive at best, and Elias wasn't under any illusion that she had changed her tune regarding the desirability of marriage.

So, he was stuck between two impossible choices: marrying an unwilling bride who would resent him for the rest of his life, or allowing the reputation of the woman he loved—to say nothing of his own reputation—to be forever tainted if their escapade ever came to light.

Edith apparently regarded the latter of the two options as preferable, a fact which hurt both Elias's pride and his heart. He was every bit the fool of a man he had always derided: besotted by a woman who cared for him not a jot. Edith was merely more honest about her disdain than most of her sex.

Perhaps she was confident, too, that their folly would never be made known. For his part, Elias was too pragmatic to believe anything of the sort. He had spent enough nights at card tables and clubs to know how easily gossip circulated, and both Miss Perry and Mr. Stratton knew of their charade.

He had no doubt Miss Perry wished them well, but even an idle word of hers regarding her stay at the inn might prove their undoing. Mr. Stratton was much less predictable, and the odds of him keeping silent about what he had witnessed seemed highly unlikely to Elias.

There *was* one bit of good news, however. Mr. Donne was not to be present at dinner. He was engaged yet again on another political errand—dining with one of the MPs in the neighboring district whose party loyalties seemed to be shifting.

Mr. Donne's absence lightened the mood considerably, and good humor abounded at half of the table, presided over by Mrs. Donne's placid unconcern and contrasted against Matthew's gravity. Elias did his best to match the tone of the others who, now that they had accepted the strange situation, seemed curious for more details.

Edith no longer looked tired and was in wondrous spirits, a sight as sweet to Elias as it was bitter. He couldn't help smiling when she smiled, even if he suspected her good mood was a result of her relief at not being obliged to marry him. So captivating was she in such spirits that he found himself letting pass the various jabs she took at him, followed as they always were with a twinkling glance.

"What is this?" Solomon turned in his seat to face Elias after one such provoking comment. "No rebuttals or objections from you? Has Edith crushed your spirit, then?"

Elias chuckled, trying to remember how to spar as everyone expected him to. "Far from it. I am merely allowing her enough rope to hang herself. Once she takes a breath, I intend to put forward the accurate version of events."

Everyone chuckled, and Edith leveled him a glance full of pretended ferocity.

"And how would *you* describe it if not bursting into a room, fairly singing 'Mrs. Cherriman' at the top of your lungs?"

He dabbed his mouth with his napkin and cleared his throat, taking up the gauntlet with as much gusto as he could muster. "Firstly, it was *your* idea to assume the guise of Mr. and Mrs. Cherriman. I was more than happy to act as a brother. Secondly, I believe you had your revenge upon me when you informed the inn that I snored"—he cleared his throat again—"as loudly as thunder, I believe you said."

Mercy's head whipped around to verify the claim, and Edith let out a scoffing laugh. "After which *you* informed the same audience how much my knees bother me on the stairs, as though I were three-and-sixty instead of three-and-twenty!"

Elias covered his laugh with a hand, remembering the way her eyes had sworn revenge at the time.

"Who *were* these people being treated to such a spectacle?" Mr. Kennett asked. "And what did they make of you? I admit to having a difficult time believing that you could convince anyone into believing you married—at least not happily so."

Elias reached for his drink, frustrated at how the comment nicked his heart. Everyone was so certain that he could never make Edith happy.

"Yes," Viola said, scooping up a spoonful of peas, "how fortunate that you didn't happen upon someone of your acquaintance."

Edith's eyes shot to Elias, and he watched her knuckles whiten gripping her fork. Her smile became more strained. "Yes, well, there was a method to the madness when I selected the inn, for everyone prefers The George to The Old Dog and Pheasant."

"Not everyone," Mrs. Donne said. "I believe John Stratton frequents The Old Dog often enough that he has horses stabled there."

There was a pause.

Edith reached for her drink. "I'm sure I couldn't say. Enough about that, though. What has been happening here for the last two days?"

While she managed to steer the conversation clear of Mr. Stratton or the inn, Edith's good humor was less genuine for the duration of the meal. When the women rose to retire to the drawing room, she caught Elias's eye, no doubt wondering how he and Matthew would fare drinking port together given Matthew's temper—and swollen lip.

"I'll join you in the drawing room," Matthew said, rising

along with the women. He didn't even look at Elias, instead stepping in with Viola as she left the room.

Edith came up to Elias, leaning in so that he had to stop breathing to avoid the vanilla that followed her everywhere. "You mustn't mind Matthew. I will see to him. He has taken it all as a personal affront, but he is too good-humored by nature to hold a grudge for long."

Elias stared at the doorway Mrs. Donne was passing through. "Perhaps. I can't say that I would blame him if he did, though."

Mrs. Donne glanced over her shoulder, her eyes lingering on them for a moment and Edith seemed to notice and took Elias's unoffered arm, tugging him forward. What was that about?

"What do you mean you wouldn't blame him?" Edith asked. "I find his behavior today to be entirely ridiculous, though I must admit that your hitting him was hardly any better."

He let out a soft chuckle. "No, you don't seem to be someone who appreciates chivalry overmuch."

"No," she admitted. "I think chivalry is usually male conceit masquerading as concern for female weakness. I don't see how I can be expected to feel gratitude for such a thing."

Elias pulled back slightly, bringing them to a stop. "You think I hit your brother for my own benefit?"

She sent him a skeptical look. "You tell *me*."

He looked down at her and frowned. "It is hardly a wonder you are so resistant to the idea of marriage if that is your concept of men and chivalry."

She shrugged. "I find that people's motivations are rarely as pure as they try to make them seem."

He smiled wryly. "Do you include yourself in that, or do you refer exclusively to mere mortals like myself?"

There was no smile as she gazed back at him. "Of course I include myself in it."

Elias had no teasing response, only questions and more questions. The more he came to know Edith, the more it became apparent to him that her wit and skepticism hid hurt. She didn't need a brother like Matthew, striving to protect her; she had built more than enough walls around herself for that.

She was a stone castle on a cliff, her imposing façade urging the retreat of passers-by, promising their defeat should they dare to venture closer. But Elias was more and more certain that, inside those commanding walls, she concealed beauty and quiet strength, gardens and labyrinths to inspire wonder and awe in whatever person was fortunate enough to catch a glimpse of them or walk their paths.

Elias wanted nothing more than to explore it all, to understand Edith so he could love her as she deserved.

But she seemed to see every man as the enemy. She seemed to see *herself* as the enemy. And Elias hadn't the first idea how to change her mind.

Chapter Twenty-Four

Edith's mother intercepted her as she walked through the door of the drawing room, directing an evaluative gaze at her. Edith had to stifle the desire to squirm under her mother's shrewd eye. She hadn't yet spoken to her directly since she and Elias had returned, and she wasn't precisely looking forward to it.

"So, you are home again," her mother said, stating the obvious in a way that gave Edith the impression it was a disappointment.

Edith nodded, summoning her most nonchalant smile. "Of course. Where else should I be?"

Her mother's eyes roved toward Elias, who was in conversation with Mr. Kennett on the other side of the room. "I admit to a hope that you had taken our last conversation to heart."

Edith felt a flash of annoyance at the heat building in her cheeks as she remembered her mother's words, her unabashed argument for Edith's marrying a man her mother viewed as *tractable*—a man to be molded according to Edith's pleasure. "You think me so capricious that I would have such a sudden change of heart and mind? That I should suddenly wish to marry?"

Her mother shrugged. She seemed ready to leave the subject alone, but Edith was too bothered. Her mother had prodded the beast, and she couldn't merely expect it to fall back asleep.

"Never have I exhibited the least inclination to marry; never have I wavered in my determination to remain single. Why would you ever assume that I should so abruptly go against my own words?"

Her mother said nothing. She merely surveyed the room under her placid gaze, goading Edith even more, provoking her with the need to defend herself against her mother's silent skepticism. Her poise could be maddening at times.

"I assure you nothing would have induced me to leave if I had known that we would not have Matthew on our heels—at the very least."

Her mother gave a soft laugh, still not looking at her. "And you might have had I not persuaded him to leave things well alone."

"What?" Edith stared.

Her mother's gaze finally turned to meet hers, the slightest raised brow and tip to her lips.

Edith shook her head. "It was the weather that prevented his coming after us."

"Was it, now?" There was no mistaking the false curiosity in her tone.

Edith was feeling out of all patience with her mother's cryptic behavior. "Was it not?"

She smiled and shook her head. "Of course, the weather would certainly have been an inconvenience, but he was quite determined to go after the two of you despite that."

"And you stopped him? Why would you do that?"

"Out of curiosity, I suppose." Her mother put out a hand

and inspected her neat nails. "When Matthew told me of the"—she paused, letting her hand drop into her lap—"intimacy he witnessed between you and Elias, I was convinced that we would do better to let you two sort things out between you."

Edith scoffed. "The intimacy he witnessed? An intimacy contrived entirely for his benefit—enough to throw him off the scent of our ruse, for he should never have come after us if he hadn't believed us to truly be eloping."

Her mother waited a moment before responding. "A very convincing contrivance, from what Matthew said."

Edith's cheeks flamed, and her mother pressed on. "I merely thought you and Elias might benefit from a bit of time to determine whether it truly *was* contrived."

Edith's nostrils flared, and an image of their kiss at the inn—the one no one else was aware of, the one that *hadn't* been contrived for anyone's benefit—flashed across her mind. She thrust it aside. "Then let me assure you on that count, Mother. It was as contrived as is Father's support for your ridiculous bill—the one doomed to fail." Her mother's jaw clenched, and Edith knew a flush of victory. "I am not so variable as you seem to think me. Now, if you will excuse me."

Edith tried to demonstrate the same poise as her mother as she left the room—why could she not have inherited *that* from her? Hearing footsteps behind her, she stopped short in the corridor.

"Edith." Elias looked at her, concern wrinkling his brow. When had he begun to look at her with those soft eyes instead of the challenging ones she had become so accustomed to? "Why have you left so soon?"

She shut her eyes and took in a large breath, letting it out slowly, and with it, the desire to censure him for following her. There was little doubt her mother had noticed. "My mother knows precisely how to infuriate me."

"What a lowering thought," he said, frowning deeply. "I thought that was *my* exclusive specialty."

She couldn't stifle a small smile.

"What has she said? Was it something about our...prank?"

Edith knew an impulse to confide in Elias—to tell him her frustrations, that it was her own mother who was responsible for their situation—but she could hardly tell him what her mother had said or why her mother had prevented Matthew's coming after them. "She thinks me foolish. That is all."

"Ah, well, I'm afraid I cannot disagree with that." He turned away and took a step, only to stop and look over his shoulder at her with the most provoking, teasing face imaginable. It did things to her heart that she was too terrified to explore.

"You are insufferable," she said without venom.

"I don't deny it." He came back to stand before her. "But I think the fault for that lies partly with you, for you bear the suffering better than anyone." His smile faded, and he took her hand.

The touch was electrifying, stopping and then starting her heart. How much of the effect was betrayed in her face? And what might her mother say if she were to witness them now? *A very convincing contrivance.*

Edith nearly pulled her hand away at the thought, but the knowledge that it might hurt Elias stopped her. Or maybe she simply enjoyed his touch too much. Neither alternative fit in with the person she thought herself.

"I shan't let you suffer for what happened, Edith. No matter how foolish you may be." His eyes smiled down into hers.

She wanted him to kiss her. She wanted it so much she struggled to breathe—she *needed* it. Strong, independent Edith wanted to wrap herself up in his assurances—in his arms.

"Thank you," she said. "You never could resist a show of chivalry." She managed a teasing smile.

"As long as it adds to my consequence," he said.

A melody on the piano sounded, muffled by the walls of the drawing room, and Edith's eyes drifted to the closed door. What must everyone in the room be thinking at their simultaneous absence?

"I think I shall retire early this evening." She looked up at Elias, gently pulling her hand away. "I am sure everyone will understand how utterly exhausted I am after spending two days in *your* company."

He took in a large breath, rising tall and puffing out his chest. "It is true that only the strongest can keep pace with my charm and wit." He patted her arm gently, as if she was a fragile creature who might fall apart at his touch. "Fear not—I shall explain to the others."

She curtsied dramatically. "I am indebted to you." When she rose, their gazes held for a moment, both of them smiling, until Edith gave a little nod. "Good night, Elias."

"Good night, Edith."

Elias felt eyes follow him from the other side of the room as he reentered. Matthew's expression was unreadable. Elias tried to ignore the guilty pangs of his conscience. Did Matthew truly believe he was merely toying with Edith's feelings and reputation?

He had a mind to go enlighten him, but the idea was dismissed as quickly as it presented itself. The last thing Elias needed was for Matthew to apply pressure to Edith to marry him, and he suspected that was exactly what would happen if Matthew discovered the truth of the matter.

Besides, Edith had assured him that she would see to Matthew. Whether she would be successful was a different matter.

"Is Edith well?"

Elias startled a bit, not having noted Viola come up beside him.

"Hmm?" he said.

"You left the room—I assumed you had done so to inquire after Edith, since she left in distress."

Distress. What a strange word to apply to Edith Donne. Only a mind as romantic as Viola's could find the word fitting.

"Ah, yes. She is simply tired."

Viola nodded. "I imagine the past few days have been quite eventful."

He looked down at her, a brow raised. "Yes, no thanks to *you*. I understand you to have been no small part of the jest played upon us."

"The jest?" Viola smiled softly, her eyes glazing over as they so often did when she was about to quote verse. "Perhaps."

"Perhaps?" he chuckled. "Come. I see you are full of poetry. You mustn't hold it in, or you might explode."

She glanced up at him with a smile. "I don't wish to offend you, of course, but I was thinking that perhaps you are" —she raised her chin as she always did when quoting verse— "'*A fool / That seest a game play'd home, the rich stake drawn, / And takest it all for jest.*'"

Elias stilled for a moment, then forced a laugh. "I am no Shakespeare devotee, but I caught the part where you called me a fool. Do you intend to say that you did *not* mean it in jest?"

She shrugged, looking at him with that knowing gaze that made him want to shift and move in avoidance. "Not everything that is begun in jest ends in jest."

His gaze found Matthew. "No, certainly there are some who find it not amusing at all." It was strange to see his friend so grave.

"Yes, I am afraid Matthew is very angry with you. And what of you? Are *you* angry? Do you wish that we had not contrived it all to begin with?"

Elias didn't answer right away. He hardly knew how to. It was the devil of a situation, the way things had unfolded. And yet, to take it all back would be to forgo everything he had experienced of Edith for the past week. Every shared enjoyment, every bit of adventure, every glimpse into what lay beyond those impenetrable walls.

Every kiss.

"At times," he said softly. "I am not angry, but I begin to think Edith the one likely to suffer the most from it all."

"Perhaps. But at least some of her suffering is needless, I think. She merely needs someone to help her see that."

Elias narrowed his eyes at Viola. He contemplated pretending ignorance at what she implied—or even fighting her on it—but there was such understanding in her eyes, so much perceptiveness. "I take your meaning quite clearly. And I do not disagree with you. But one cannot force another to accept something they are intent upon refusing."

"No, one cannot." She took in a long breath. "I stood in awe of Edith for so long, you know. I found her both terrifying and intriguing. But I think I understand her more clearly now. She is not so different from you or me." She glanced at him. "We all go to great lengths to avoid pain. We will even accept the pain we know—be it ever so severe—over the pain we don't know. Edith is merely better at masking her fear, and fear is nothing but a response to unfed hope. Edith's hope must be fed and her faith restored if her fears are to be crushed."

Elias was bereft of speech, but Viola clearly expected no response, as she gave him a soft smile and walked away. It was as though she were some sort of vessel of wisdom, staring into the very core of everyone she came by and disbursing a few choice phrases here and a few there before returning to her reading.

E*dith's hope must be fed and her faith restored if her fears are to be crushed.*

Elias was fairly certain he had fallen asleep—very near to dawn, from what he remembered—to Viola's words. He felt their truth, and yet he was at a loss for how to apply them. He gathered his belongings with a deep frown on his face, feeling nagging slivers of hesitation at his decision to leave. But what good would it do anyone for him to remain?

His eye searched the bedchamber a final time, but he knew he hadn't forgotten anything. He was delaying. Would he leave without saying goodbye to Edith? No. He was selfish enough not to entertain the idea for more than a second.

A knock sounded on the door.

"Enter."

The Donnes' footman opened the door. "Mr. Donne requests your immediate presence in the library, sir."

"Thank you. I shall go down presently." He indicated his belongings with a nod of his head. "If you could see that these are taken downstairs, I believe my carriage is waiting."

"Very good, sir." He came in and took up the valise and portmanteau, then scurried from the room.

Elias blew a breath through his lips. He'd had every intention of speaking with Mr. Donne before departing, but the fact that he was being summoned didn't precisely bode well. *If I hear even the faintest whisper of scandal...*

He strode down the corridor and then the stairs, grasping for words that would help Mr. Donne understand the complexity of the situation.

Edith was already standing in the library when he arrived, her gaze wary and full of warning as she watched Elias's entrance.

"Leaving, are you?" Mr. Donne said. His voice was level, but it seemed to tremble slightly, and the way his hands gripped the arms of his chair was anything but relaxed.

Elias cleared his throat. "Yes, sir. I have a few matters to attend to at home."

Mr. Donne's lips stretched into a smile entirely devoid of any of the sentiments the expression normally conveyed. "You come to Shipton House as a trusted guest. You make off with my daughter for two days, refuse to marry her, and now you are leaving?"

Elias's breathing quickened.

Mr. Donne's mouth pulled up into a contemptuous sneer as the color in his face shifted to pink and then red. "You shall not serve this family such a trick!"

"Father," Edith said.

"Silence!" His voice reverberated in the library, and he held up a note. "In all your attempts to evade the consequences of your actions, you both very conveniently failed to mention that your imprudent antics were observed by the man I most abhor in this entire world—a man who now threatens this family with exposure." He slammed the note down on the desk in front of him, uttering a loud oath. He looked to Edith and then Elias and back again. "You will marry by special license within the week."

"But—"

"That is final! There is nothing else to be said. You have made your bed, and now you will lie in it." He folded the note and shoved it into a drawer. "Mr. Abram, you may as well instruct the servants to have your belongings taken back to your bedchamber. I will inform you both when the license has been acquired. It should take two or three days at most." He looked to them a final time, his stern eyes daring them to argue with him, then stalked out of the room.

Elias moved his gaze slowly to Edith. Her chest heaved, and

her eyes carried a stricken look. He moved to her side. "Edith," he said softly.

Her eyes darted to him, as though she had forgotten his presence. She blinked twice, eyelashes fluttering. "What can we do?"

He frowned. "There seems to be little choice in the matter at this point."

She shook her head quickly and began pacing the floor, her fist tapping gently but rhythmically against her mouth. "There must be *something*. We must, of course, appeal to Miss Perry. Her word cannot be entirely disregarded. And the innkeeper, Mr. Drew. He can attest to the fact that propriety was strictly kept." She stopped, her gaze fixed blankly on Elias. "I must find a way to speak with Mr. Stratton, to appeal to him—beg him if necessary." She resumed her quick steps, eyes staring at the floor, a frantic energy to her movements.

Elias took her hand, preventing her from continuing her frenetic pacing. She stopped and looked at him questioningly, and he swallowed. "Are you truly so opposed to the idea of marrying me?" The question hurt even to utter.

She blinked at him. "You agree with my father?"

He lifted his shoulders. "I told you I wouldn't let you be harmed by this, did I not? If Mr. Stratton is determined to do your family injury, *this* is the way to prevent that."

She wrenched her hand from his grasp, looking at him with eyes alight in anger. "I don't care a fig for my reputation! Nor for my father's precious politics. I will *not* become a martyr for his gain."

Her words struck at his heart. *A martyr*. He clenched his jaw. "You would rather be ostracized than subject yourself to marrying me. How you flatter me, Edith!"

"And flattering you should be my primary concern?"

He threw his hands up. "Would it hurt you so very much to stop and consider how your decisions are affecting anyone but yourself? Your reputation is at stake, your father's position on the line, an act of reform that would change the lives of countless people is under threat, not to mention my honor, and yet you insist upon flying in the face of common sense so that you can protect some false illusion of freedom?"

She stepped toward him, eyes bright and cheeks colorful with emotion. "And that is your argument for marriage? Your offer to me? You throw in my face everything I most despise about marriage, suggesting we come together for the most selfish of reasons, and you expect me to jump at the opportunity?" She scoffed, her lips curled up in disgust. "Forgive me, but I don't wish to be married to someone whose motive is saving his own honor." She made to move away, but Elias grabbed her arm. She whirled around, eyes flashing him a warning.

His jaw shifted back and forth for a moment. "And *you* simply cannot conceive of a world where such a thing is but a secondary consideration, can you? Where people cannot be reduced to one, single ill motive but rather have many competing motives, some of which are pure?" He dropped her arm. "Gad, Edith. At some point, I think you have to acknowledge that you are making the world in your own image. Can your father not wish to salvage his political career *and* ensure the well-being of his daughter? Are you unwilling to entertain the notion that a man might wish to save his own honor while also desiring to protect the woman he loves?"

He may as well have slapped Edith for the stunned look on her face, but she recovered quickly. "Perhaps I cannot. And I have very good reason for that. Meanwhile *you*" —she stepped toward him and prodded him in the chest with a finger— "seem unable to fathom a world where a woman should be taken seriously. You assume that it is I who am at fault here— that my determination not to sacrifice myself on the altar of my father's ego—or yours—is somehow selfish or unreasonable?" She shook her head, glaring into his eyes, her face mere inches from his. "*None* of this is about my reputation—not really. My father would sacrifice me in a heartbeat if he felt it served his ends. And you? You insult me and confess your love in a single breath." She let out a scoff. "No, I thank you. Marriage is not for me."

She held his eyes a moment longer and then turned, striding from the room.

Chapter Twenty-Five

Edith's chest heaved, and her eyes burned as she hurried up the stairs to her bedchamber. She blinked rapidly to dispel the tears. She couldn't remember the last time she had cried. Years ago, certainly.

She tugged on the bell in her bedchamber, shutting her eyes and trying to breathe deeply before Susan arrived. She wouldn't let anyone see her in such a state. She was the daughter of Agnes Donne. Appearing unconcerned should come more naturally to her.

"Prepare the curricle," she told her maid. "And inform Matthew that I require his escort for a drive."

A few minutes later, she hurried down the stairs, praying mightily that she wouldn't encounter her father or Elias, and rushed through the front door, where the curricle was being brought around from the stables. Matthew emerged two minutes later, his brow wrinkled.

"What's this about, Edith?"

"I need you to accompany me somewhere."

He raised his brows, waiting for further enlightenment.

She walked toward the curricle, and he followed behind her. "To Ivybridge," she said.

"Ivybridge?" He shook his head, looking at her as though she was mad. "That's fifteen miles away. We would barely make it home in time for dinner."

She shut her eyes to summon elusive patience. "Fine," she said, stepping up into the curricle with as much grace as she could muster. "I shall go alone."

"Dash it, Edith! You can't go all the way to Ivybridge alone—and in an open carriage!"

She took the reins from the stable hand. "I assure you I can." Her reputation was already ruined, after all.

He swore and hopped up into the curricle beside her. "You are by far the most infuriating woman in existence. I must say, I can't really blame Elias for not wanting to marry you."

Edith pinched her lips together to keep her chin from trembling. Why the words hurt her, she didn't know. But they stung, and Matthew hardly knew how much truth they held. Whatever desire Elias had had to marry her, whatever love he imagined he held for her, she had undoubtedly cured him of it by her words in the library.

Edith set the horses to, navigating the lane that led from Shipton House to the main road as well as she could with the added annoyance of tears obscuring her vision. The stable hand had assured her the horses had just been walking, but they were resistant to Edith's efforts, a fact which hardly added to her good humor.

"You'll jerk their mouths to pieces!" Matthew protested. "Give me the reins." He put his hands out expectantly.

"Nonsense." She tried to relax her wrists more. "Besides, I don't trust you."

He kept his hands outstretched, ready to accept them. "I won't turn us around, Edith. I promise you. Just give me the reins."

She glanced at him then surrendered.

The horses moved more easily under his guidance, tossing their heads less and keeping more even footing. No doubt they had felt Edith's tension through the reins.

She sat back and folded her arms, allowing silence to fall between them for a time. She had promised herself to take up Elias's cause with Matthew, to help him see that Elias wasn't at fault. And there was hardly a better time than this, when they were forced to spend time together, with nothing but miles of road ahead.

But the last thing Edith wanted to do was defend Elias. She had pretended not to be affected by his declaration of love, but the truth was it had stunned her. She had wanted to believe it —more than she had wanted anything in a very long time—but she couldn't allow herself to.

Elias himself had said that the matter of salvaging his honor was a driving factor in his desire to marry her. And now more than ever, she struggled to believe that his motives were pure. Why should Elias be so different from everyone else she knew? Her father was all too happy to sacrifice her happiness for his political ends, and Mr. Stratton was eager to do the same. People were but pawns to one another, to be used and discarded at each one's will and convenience.

She had neither the desire to be such a pawn nor to use Elias as one.

He may have convinced himself that he loved her, but if she surrendered to the appeal of loving him and being loved, it would only be a matter of time before they both realized how incompatible they were—and that what they had believed was love was merely a desire to *be* loved.

But whatever Edith's feelings, Elias didn't deserve to be despised by Matthew for a situation not of his own making.

"You shouldn't be angry with Elias," she said tersely.

Matthew only scoffed.

"I mean it, Matthew. He has done no wrong."

"Done no wrong?" He whipped his head around briefly to look at her, his puffed lip challenging her words, then returned it to the road. "Are you truly so dim-witted?"

"Are *you*? He is your friend, Matthew. And you know me too well to believe I would ever allow myself to be taken in by a man. There is no reason for you to be upset with Elias."

"No reason! Ha! That's rich now. I'll tell you, Edith. A man doesn't forget walking in on his best friend—one with a reputation, no less—kissing his own sister." His face screwed up in frustration and disgust.

"I kissed *him,* Matthew." Edith suppressed the desire to shift under Matthew's stunned gaze.

"The devil you did!"

"I don't know what the devil has to say to it, but I *did*. So, you mustn't blame Elias."

He hesitated, his mouth opening and closing multiple times. "Be that as it may, he ran off with you, Edith! Under my very nose."

"Yes, but in *jest*. Not in earnest. You should have expected retaliation after the trick you and the others played."

"Well, your revenge fell flat," Matthew responded.

The uneven ground rumbled beneath them, and the horses' hooves kicked up clods of dirt, still moist from the rainstorms.

Matthew shook his head. "I've heard too many stories of his conquests from Eli's own lips, listened to how he speaks of women too many times to think it the least bit funny of him to go off with you."

Edith brushed aside the hurt she felt—it *shouldn't* hurt her. Elias was just like every other gentleman she knew—quick to discard women once they ceased to amuse. And yet, the thought that she might fall into the same category as any other woman Elias had had a dalliance with? It was a low blow.

"I am more than capable of taking care of myself, Matthew."

"You're not. Yes, you may look daggers at me, but it's true. You give yourself airs, Edith. You're not as strong as you pretend to be, and there's something about Elias and his scorn for women that has women falling over themselves for him. I imagine each one thinks she'll be the one to change his tune." He laughed through his nose. "Elias will never trust a woman."

"Why not?" Edith couldn't help herself. She couldn't fault anyone for their cynicism, of course, but at least she was consistent in hers: she believed the worst of *everyone*. It hardly seemed fair to acquit one sex—and one which, by and large, had not shown collective concern with their trustworthiness.

Matthew shrugged. "He's like you—doesn't precisely open himself up on the subject. But the women in his life haven't been paragons of love and concern, you know."

She didn't know.

The curricle rolled into the area in front of Ivy Cottage, the home belonging to the Perrys. It was a modest house—two stories high and a bit worse for wear, with parts of the roof in serious need of new clay tiles, and the wooden front door sitting crooked.

"Are they expecting us?" Matthew asked.

Edith shook her head. They stepped down from the curricle, and Edith smoothed out her dress as well as she could, grateful to be on steady ground after the jostling of the past two hours. She led the way to the door while Matthew stood with the horses. They needed tending to, but no servant had come to see to them.

The door opened, and a woman servant's questioning eyes were directed at Edith. "How may I help you, miss?"

"Is Miss Perry at home?"

The servant nodded.

"Will you please inform her that Miss Donne is here in company with her brother? And if you could ensure that our horses are seen to, it would be very kind and appreciated."

The servant pinched her lips together but nodded. "Very good, miss." She called out behind her, presumably for another servant, and a few moments later, a man came up beside her, listening to her instructions with several curious glances at the visitors. He relieved Matthew of the reins, and both Matthew and Edith were welcomed into the Perry home.

The interior was as modest as the exterior. The Perrys seemed to be genteel, though not wealthy enough to keep on more than a couple of servants. The house hadn't been redecorated for two decades, by all appearances. The siblings were shown into a small room that looked to be a sort of sitting room and drawing room, and the servant left to inform Miss Perry of her visitors.

"What exactly are we doing here, Edith?" Matthew asked in a low voice as the door closed behind the servant.

Edith looked around the room curiously. The air in the home had an oppressive feel, and with a jolt, Edith remembered the family's recent loss. She cringed to think how unfeeling it was to visit so soon after. She had been too concerned with her own situation to spare a thought for the Perrys and what they were experiencing.

"We are expressing our condolences for their recent loss and asking Miss Perry to lend her voice in support of Elias and me—to assure Father that propriety was strictly guarded at the inn."

Matthew looked at her significantly. She already knew what he would say: their father was unlikely to place much importance on the word of a family in such circumstances as the Perrys looked to be in.

The door opened, and Miss Perry appeared, attired in the same black dress she had been wearing at The Old Dog and Pheasant.

"Miss Donne," she said, striding over with a smile. "What an unexpected surprise." There was a bit of nervousness in the way her eyes darted around the room, but she embraced Edith warmly.

"Yes," Edith said, "I hope you will forgive me for arriving unanticipated. I'm afraid it couldn't be avoided."

"You need not apologize, I assure you. You are very welcome here." Miss Perry's eyes shifted to Matthew, and Edith provided the necessary introduction. Matthew expressed his sympathies for Miss Perry's loss, and Edith couldn't help noting the way Miss Perry looked at him with an added measure of shyness.

They took their seats, and Miss Perry called for tea to be brought, putting an absent hand to her neck once the servant left to fulfill her order.

"Your necklace!" Edith cried in surprise. "You found it."

Miss Perry's hand dropped from it hurriedly, and her ears tinged with pink. "Yes, yes. Wonderful, isn't it?"

"Indeed. Such a relief, I'm sure. I know how much it means to you."

Miss Perry nodded slowly, a stricken look in her eyes. "Yes. Yes, it means everything to me." She brought her tea to her mouth, and it trembled, causing a clanking as the cup and saucer hit against each other.

It was obvious that Miss Perry was still struggling under the weight of her brother's passing. Perhaps she wasn't able to sleep, which would account for the jittery quality to her movements. Edith had heard of grief affecting people in strange ways.

She set down her tea on the table. "I feel very ashamed to admit that the purpose of our visit isn't purely one of condolence, but I find myself in a terrible bind, and I hoped you might be able to help."

Miss Perry shifted forward on her seat, setting down her tea as well. "Of course. What can I do?"

"Perhaps you remember a gentleman who stayed at the inn

while we were there. He left quite early in the morning—just as we were searching for the necklace, I believe."

Miss Perry swallowed, and her hand clasped at the pendant as she gave a hint of a nod.

Edith pressed on, wishing she could have come once Miss Perry had had more time to recover from her initial grief. "His name is Mr. Stratton, and he and my father have long been rivals in the House of Commons. At present, they find themselves on opposite sides of a very controversial issue—one that has the potential to affect Mr. Stratton quite nearly. So concerned is he that the vote come out in his favor that he has threatened to use my reputation as leverage to ensure my father's cooperation. He believes that my time at the inn in the company of Mr. Abram is more than enough to ruin my father's credibility." She gripped the handle of her teacup, vowing not to betray how angry the situation made her. "I had hoped that you might be willing to again vouch for us?" Seeing the pallid color of Miss Perry's wide-eyed face, Edith rushed on. "It wouldn't require anything of you but to write a quick note to my father, assuring him that propriety was kept, and that you can attest to that, having been in our company almost the entirety of the time."

Miss Perry's chin trembled, and Edith sent a glance full of uncertainty at Matthew, who only gave a bemused shrug.

"I cannot!" Miss Perry said, her hand still gripping at her neck.

Edith stared, baffled by Miss Perry's reaction. She went to sit beside her. "Of course I don't wish to distress you, but...I don't understand. Does your conscience prevent you from providing such a testament?"

Miss Perry shook her head, taking her bottom lip between her teeth and directing a glance full of guilt at Edith. "It is not my conscience." She shut her eyes, and a tear slipped from underneath her lids. "I assure you that I should not have agreed to Mr. Stratton's demands under anything but the direst need!"

Edith frowned, unease making her stomach feel strange. "What do you mean? What demands?"

Miss Perry met her gaze, affliction and tears filling her eyes. "He came here—Mr. Stratton did—the day after the funeral. I recognized him from the inn, and he told my mother he had come to return something that belonged to me. You can imagine how relieved I was to see this"—she lifted the pendant from her pale chest and rubbed it between her fingers. She looked up at Edith again, her eyes pleading for understanding. "Before giving it to me, he insisted upon asking me questions. Questions about you and Mr. Abram."

Edith swallowed. "What sort of questions?"

Miss Perry looked flustered, and her eyes flitted to Matthew, as if she was worried what he thought of her too. "He wished to know whether you had truly come to the inn to see me. Whether we knew each other beforehand. He seemed to wish for more information regarding the relationship between you and Mr. Abram. I assured him that I had been with you—even slept in the same bed as you—but..."

"But what?" Edith tried to keep her voice level, but foreboding filled her.

"He pressed me on the subject—he seemed disinclined to believe that I had been with you and Mr. Abram at *all* times." Her chin trembled. "He encouraged me to think harder, and he implied that it would be very terrible indeed if my father's debts were acquired by someone less than friendly toward the family. I don't know how he knew of the debts, but"—she lifted her shoulders in a pitiful, helpless gesture. "We could barely afford to bury Robert properly."

Edith shut her eyes. She put an arm around Miss Perry, who gave a little sob.

"Please forgive me," she said.

"There is nothing to forgive, my dear," Edith said, feeling emotion rise in her throat. "I would never have had you risk your family's welfare, so don't think for a moment that I am upset with you." Anger flooded her, making her body feel hot. "Mr. Stratton will stoop to any means to obtain his ends. I am terribly sorry that you became a victim—and just as sorry that it was your meeting *me* that put you in such a position." She squeezed Miss Perry more tightly to her, glancing at Matthew, whose face was grim.

Miss Perry rested her head against Edith's shoulder, her face in her hands. "You are all goodness. I am sure I should have resisted him more—shown more courage."

"Nonsense," Edith said, her conscience panging as she thought of the extra burden she had brought upon the Perrys at an already difficult time. "You would only have angered him, putting yourself and your family at even greater risk." She rubbed Miss Perry's arm. "You mustn't worry that I shall be upset with you, but I must ask what you told him."

Miss Perry nodded, and Matthew rose to give her his handkerchief, a gesture met with a grateful smile.

"I told him," she said slowly, "that there was a short amount of time when you and Mr. Abram were alone in the private parlor—when I left to avoid becoming covered in flour." She shook her head, and Edith's cheeks flamed at the memory of the kiss they had shared during that brief time.

"I should not have left you. It was heedless of me." She took in a deep breath. "Mr. Stratton sat down at that desk" —she indicated a small escritoire that stood against the window— "and wrote something, then told me he would return Robert's necklace to me when I signed it."

Edith took in a deep breath, avoiding Matthew's eye. "What did it say?"

"It swore to my witness that you and Mr. Abram had stayed at The Old Dog and Pheasant, assuming the guise of a married couple, and that you had spent considerable time alone together, enough to cast the gravest doubts on your characters."

Edith nodded stiffly, swallowing the lump in her throat.

"It was wrong of me to sign it. I *know* you and Mr. Abram were pattern cards of propriety—"

Edith's conscience prickled with guilt, and she put up a hand to stop Miss Perry. "You mustn't blame yourself. Mr. Abram and I were foolish to do what we did. I was too intent on taking vengeance upon my brother and cousins to pay proper heed to the weather or how things might go awry." She managed a smile.

Miss Perry sniffled and lowered her head. "You must rue the day you met me!"

Edith breathed in deeply. "There is much for me to regret in my own behavior, but I *cannot* regret becoming acquainted with you." She sat up straight, trying to assume a manner that conveyed confidence. "Don't spend a moment worrying on my account—I surely shan't." It was a lie, of course. But Edith would feel like an ogre to leave Miss Perry fretting over things more than she already was.

When Miss Perry looked doubtful, Matthew chimed in. "It's true, you know. If anyone can get in and out of a scrape without being any worse for it, it's Edith. She loves a good challenge."

Miss Perry gave a watery chuckle and began to look a little less morose. Matthew spent a few minutes inquiring after her, managing to elicit a few soft laughs with his responses, and by the time they took their leave, Miss Perry was looking much better than she had at the beginning of their visit.

When they climbed into the curricle, armed with a few blueberry muffins—courtesy of the Perry family—Matthew's smile faded. He sighed as he took the reins. "What a muddle you've got yourself in, Edith."

She clasped her hands in her lap. "Yes. I know. Mr. Stratton will not be easily defeated."

"He's a blackguard, no question, to threaten a young woman like Miss Perry in the throes of mourning." He grimaced. "I must say, though, that you were devilish kind to her. Don't mean to offend you, of course, but I didn't quite expect it from you."

Edith turned her head away, hoping he wouldn't see how his perception of her character hurt. "It was dastardly of Mr. Stratton," she said, "and he certainly deserves to be hanged. But Father showed little inclination to think Miss Perry's word mattered anyway, so I suppose I am no worse off than before."

Matthew gripped her shoulder bracingly. "No, he wouldn't care much for her word, I'm afraid. Cares less about what truly happened at the inn than he does about how it will appear to others—the gossip it will generate, the stain it will be upon his character. That sort of thing." He looked at her with pity in his eyes. "I think you shall have to marry Elias after all, Edith. He may be a bit of a loose screw, but he's not so blind to reason that he won't see what his duty is. And he's a good sort of man, so I think you won't have overmuch reason to complain. I imagine he'll be just as anxious to leave you to your own devices as you'll be to leave him to his." He patted her hand. "I'll have a word with him." He turned away.

"No!"

His head whipped back around, and Edith let out a breath to calm herself.

"Don't, Matthew. I still have a few days to find another solution."

She *had* to find another solution. The thought of Elias marrying her for the sake of his own reputation had repelled her; but the thought of him doing so for the sake of *hers*? It was too humiliating, too painful to be entertained, even for a second. Being married out of self-interest was abhorrent to her; but being married out of chivalry was even worse.

Chapter Twenty-Six

Edith was not at dinner that evening, but all that was said on the matter was she had a headache and intended to take dinner in her room. The time after dinner was filled with games of whist. Elias found himself making thoughtless mistakes, and he felt Matthew's eyes on him each time. The hard light had disappeared from his gaze, though, and Elias wondered if Edith had spoken with him after all.

He bowed out of the final game, letting Viola take his place, and slipped out of the room unnoticed.

He slept in fits again, with thoughts of Edith filling both his dreams and the time awake between them. When the morning dawned brighter than any of the mornings in recent memory, the light felt too bright for Elias's tired eyes. As he stood from pulling on his boots, he ran a hand through his hair, blinking to dispel the weight that seemed to hang on his lids.

He clenched his eyes shut as he stepped toward the window. Gad, he'd said terrible things to Edith in the library. And she'd deprived him of the opportunity to apologize when she had failed to come to dinner.

No wonder she had hardly blinked when he'd said he'd loved her. How could she possibly believe it?

He didn't *really* expect her to marry him out of concern for his honor. In fact, he'd much rather she *not* do it with such a motivation. He had merely spoken out of pain—the pain of constantly having thrown in his face just how little she wished to marry him—and to what ends she was willing to go to avoid it.

It hurt him—hurt him in a humiliating way that dredged up old feelings he'd tried to lay to rest. Memories of his mother powdering her face—somehow entirely free of tears—as she prepared to go out for the night, a mere two weeks after losing a child. Not all the chastising and reasoning of Elias's father could sway her, not all of Elias's begging—not even his father's tears for little Caroline, the daughter he had prayed for for years. His mother had wished herself anywhere but with them, had found any excuse to be elsewhere, just as she had when Elias's father had died years later.

Elias repelled women. They might flirt with him and bat their eyelashes at him, but when the day of reckoning came—when he showed any hint of sincerity or any vulnerability—they were nowhere to be found.

He gazed out over the gardens of Shipton House, punctuated as they were with blots of vibrant color in the late morning light. The blots looked to be roses, and their color felt at odds with the bleakness of the future he foresaw. A gardener knelt among the bushes, his hands in the dirt of the most colorful part of the garden, where reds, pinks, and yellows dotted the rectangular bed in the center of the small boxwood labyrinth.

Elias hated feeling so somber and weighed down, and the order and vibrance of the gardens called to him. Almost without thinking, he made his way there, drawn to the color and the smell he imagined. Absently, he wound through the labyrinth, coming up against dead ends again and again. When he finally emerged into the center, the gardener looked up.

"Excuse me, sir," the man said, rising from his knees and bowing deferentially.

"No, no," Elias replied. "You needn't leave." He glanced at the pile of leaves and stems at the gardener's feet.

The gardener followed his gaze. "Just cleaning up a little. We have a few shy ones that need a bit of extra help." He smiled and indicated a few of the roses that had yet to bloom.

Elias approached them, narrowing his eyes and scanning the sea of vibrant reds around the three sealed flowers. If the gardener hadn't drawn his eyes to them, Elias would never have noticed the buds. They blended in with the leaves, only a hint of color visible at the very tips.

He looked at the nearest one, closed in a tight spade at the top of a stem whose thorns dared him to attempt a touch. The closed flower looked nothing like the full, cascading blooms around it. He reached for one of the open ones, just below the fist-sized bloom, then drew his hand away quickly. A speck of blood appeared on the tip of his finger.

"Aye," the gardener said with a smile. "They hide their claws well." He displayed his gloved hands, wiggling his fingers a bit. "It's why I wear these."

Elias chuckled and reached for one of the green buds curiously. "Why have all the others bloomed while these have not?"

The gardener surveyed the flowerbeds with a discerning eye. "Some of them need a little extra warmth and light—often they've been blocked by overgrown leaves or other flowers." He gave the pile of cut leaves a nudge with his dirty boot.

"But you can make them bloom?"

"If I've done my job, these buds will bloom every bit as bright as the others in a week—maybe two." He touched the tip of a closed bud with his gloved finger. "Once you know what the problem is, it isn't too difficult to fix it."

The sound of footsteps brought their heads around.

Edith looked back and forth between them. She wore a yellow dress that might have been intentionally selected for how well it matched some of the roses. "Do you have ambitions to become a gardener, Elias?" She was teasing him—a fact which relieved him greatly—but there was something in her demeanor that spoke unease. Was she regretting what she had said as much as he was?

"Not unless a garden full of dead plants becomes the fashion. I am glad you've come, though. I was hoping to have a word with you."

The gardener looked back and forth between them, then sprang to motion. "Well, I'm done here, so I'll be on my merry way." He gathered up his things and excused himself.

Edith watched his retreat, her fingers fiddling with the skirts of her gown. Elias hated that he had said anything that might have hurt her.

"I am sorry," he said.

Her fingers stopped, and her gaze moved toward him slowly.

He shook his head. "I would never wish you to sacrifice yourself for my honor, Edith, and I shouldn't have said the things I did." He met her gaze squarely, and his heart began to pound.

"We were both angry," she said with a lift of the shoulders.

He shook his head. "It was more than that, Edith. I suspect you don't wish to hear it again, but I cannot be silent until I am sure you understand." He swallowed, forcing himself to hold her gaze, to welcome her reaction, whatever it might be. "I love you." He smiled wryly, casting his eyes up at the sky. "Heaven help this besotted fool, but I do." He wanted to step toward her, to wrap her in his arms, and show her—to remove any doubt about how he felt.

But she stood feet away from him, rigid.

"I will not ask you to marry me to save your reputation or mine. But I would be dishonest if I did not confess that I *do* wish to marry you."

She swallowed, and her eyes flickered before she looked away. "You *think* you love me. That is all."

He took a step toward her, noting how she pulled back ever so slightly. "Can a man not know his own mind, then? Or his own heart?"

She took a full step back, and he stopped in place, frozen by her defensive action.

She wouldn't look at him, instead training her gaze on her gloved fingers, which fiddled in front of her abdomen. "Did you know that my parents fancied themselves in love when they married?"

He shook his head. He had never seen Mr. and Mrs. Donne give any indication that they were more than occupants in the same home, holding each other in civil but mutual dislike.

Edith's gaze moved to the flowers. "They did. I imagine it hasn't escaped your notice that they are hardly in love anymore."

He pressed his lips together, aware of what she was really saying. "We are not your parents, Edith."

"We are not. But we already argue as much as they do. Did you know that my sister Lydia married *her* husband for love? They have been married five years now, and they spend their time at estates in different parts of the country, her with the children, him with his mistress."

"I did not know that."

"She is miserable," she said softly.

"I am very sorry, Edith. But that need not be our story."

She finally met his gaze, her eyes steely. "And what of the women whose affections *you* have toyed with? Why should I be any different from them?"

His brows snapped together. "What?"

"Come. You are handsome, good with words, confident, and well-to-do. You speak of women with the greatest disdain. I hardly needed Matthew to tell me of your conquests—or that you have bragged about them."

He blinked. "My conquests?"

She raised her brows at him.

He rubbed his cheek harshly. When he had told his first untruth about his experience with women, he had suspected that it might come back to haunt him. But he had never imagined it would be the woman he loved confronting him about it. Gad, he had never *expected* to love a woman! "These *conquests* you speak of—they are conquests I fabricated to appease people like your brother who are forever goading me to give in to the women pretending they care the snap of their fingers for me. I did it to make them stop."

She let out a disbelieving scoff.

"You are too ready to believe anything but the truth, Edith." He stepped toward her. "I love you. *Only* you. For all you make me wish to tear my hair out at times, I love you."

She put up her hands to stop him, clenching her eyes shut. "Please. We cannot marry." Her hands dropped to her sides, and she lifted her chin, that determined look filling her gaze. "And I ask you not to speak of it to me again. You may hate me and think me the most selfish creature alive for jeopardizing your honor—and I won't even argue that with you—but I assure you it is preferable to our marrying." She swallowed. "I merely came to tell you that I paid a visit to Miss Perry yesterday."

He said nothing. He already knew her reason for going. Miss Perry was her only chance at salvaging her reputation—the one person who might save her from Elias.

"Mr. Stratton managed to find her—and threaten her—until she put into writing that both your character and mine had been ruined by our time at The Old Dog."

Elias pinched his lips into a line, wishing a fate befitting such a cur to befall Mr. Stratton. "What, then? You brave your father's ire by refusing to marry?"

Edith balled her hands into fists, looking away. "There is one more thing I can do."

"What? Your father will have the license within the next two days."

She avoided his eye. "I am going to speak with Mr. Stratton directly."

His jaw went slack.

She glanced at him. "Don't try to dissuade me. My mind is quite set. He is a villain, but even a villain has a heart somewhere inside."

"And you think yourself capable of appealing to this supposed heart of his? Gad, Edith, Mr. Stratton is the last person in the world I would wish you to grovel to, even were you capable of such a thing. The man is dangerous. You mustn't go anywhere near him."

"I am quite capable of—"

"Taking care of yourself, yes, I know. And yet, somehow we find ourselves here." He shook his head, fixing his eyes upon her intently. "Don't go, Edith."

Her nostrils flared. "I shall make no such promise."

"Then allow me to go with you."

Her brows drew together. "I hardly think that would be conducive to the purpose of the visit. I trust you not to interfere." There was no mistaking the threat in her words.

And how *could* Elias interfere? How could he thwart Edith when it would mean forcing her into marrying him?

She held his eyes for one more moment, then turned back into the labyrinth.

Chapter Twenty-Seven

❦

Edith's body quaked as she walked the familiar path through the labyrinth. She found it impossible to swallow. She put out a hand in front of her, watching it tremble, then clenched it. She had never felt less in command of herself.

She had nearly yielded in the garden. She had not been prepared for Elias to renew his declaration of love. Every reason she had carefully gathered to feel justified in her decision not to marry him had been assailed. She had only one reason to refuse him at this point, and she was certain Elias saw right to the core of it. She had made it easy enough, after all.

He saw that she was not strong—she was weak. She was fragile. She was terrified.

And she had felt so fearful of the impulse inside her—the one that told her to walk straight into his arms and admit that she returned his regard, that she had never wanted anything so much as to love him and be loved in return—that she had spoken her fears for the first time. Fears ill-masked as reasons for not marrying.

And she was such a coward that she would allow the man she loved to face Society's ill opinion rather than confront those fears. But she would rather be a coward than watch as Elias's love and her own love faded, only to be replaced with resentment or apathy. *That* she couldn't bear.

She dashed away an angry tear, trying to draw in a deep breath and finding that it shook just like her hands and legs.

Her heart urged her to return to the rose garden, and she stood just beyond the entrance to the maze, her fears and desires battling within her fiercely. But she knew the truth: she would lose no matter which won out in the end.

When Elias finally left the rose garden, he spent twice as long in the labyrinth as he had on his journey in, despite knowing the way better this time. He came upon impassible hedge after impassible hedge, but he was too numb to muster the concentration necessary to mind which turns he had already taken.

Should he leave Shipton House or stay? To leave felt cowardly—and in direct opposition to Mr. Donne, who would no doubt be returning soon with the license.

And yet, what was the point in staying? Edith was determined not to marry him, whether or not her visit to Mr. Stratton was a success. His stomach clenched at the thought of her confronting the man. He didn't know John Stratton apart from their brief encounters at The Old Dog, but Edith's and Oxley's words had been enough to get a fair idea of him. Elias knew enough men like him—men who were willing to go to any length to propel their interests forward—that it made him sick to think what Edith might endure during such an encounter. She was more likely to make Stratton angry than to persuade him against his own interests.

In a few days, it would be the second anniversary of the passing of Elias's father. He ached to have him there, to lay his predicament before him and receive his counsel. He sent a glance heavenward, wishing he could hear his father's voice one more time, his father who knew exactly what it was to deal with an intractable woman.

But the heavens were quiet—a mass of gray clouds, rolling inexorably across the sky.

He stopped in the courtyard in front of Shipton House. He didn't want to go inside—he might suffocate there. Instead, he ordered his horse to be saddled, hardly aware of the opening and closing of the front door nearby.

"Eli!" Matthew hurried toward him. "Been looking for you everywhere. I wanted to speak with you last night after dinner, but you disappeared during cards." His eyes moved to Elias's horse. "Are you going for a ride?"

Elias looked at Matthew's lip. It was less swollen than it had been yesterday, but it was still a visible reminder of the wedge between them.

"Yes, I need some fresh air."

Matthew called to the stable hand, ordering his own horse to be readied. "I shall join you. Oh, don't look at me like that! I need to talk to you."

Elias nodded, irked that his ride would no longer be a solo one yet too drained to combat Matthew over it. Apparently, he would be read a lecture. Ah well, better in the fresh air than in the oppressive indoors.

They made their way to the stables in silence, the only talk occurring between them and the servants who were preparing the horses. Elias had nothing to say. He considered apologizing for Matthew's lip, but the truth was he didn't regret it. Matthew had been insufferable for talking to Edith like he did—they had been harsh words from a man who had no idea what he was talking about.

They swung their legs over the saddles in unison and urged

their horses forward, Matthew set slightly back, making it clear that he was expecting Elias to lead the way.

"Listen, Eli," Matthew finally said as they followed the long drive away from the house. "I wanted to apologize for the way I've been acting."

Elias held up a hand to stop him.

"No," Matthew said. "Let me finish. When I found out you and Edith had run off, I was furious." He gave a wry chuckle. "I crushed her note and threw it against the wall, then had the carriage prepared so I could run after you and teach you a lesson. But I see now what was under that fury—my own terror."

Elias glanced at him, and he could see the apology in Matthew's eyes.

"I saw two people I love making the worst decision of their lives. I *knew* you and Edith would make each other miserable, and I couldn't understand how you could have persuaded yourselves otherwise."

Elias turned his head away, his heart panging at the words. Everyone but Elias seemed convinced he couldn't make Edith happy, and it hurt in places he had never felt before to hear that people thought him incapable of doing the one thing he wanted to do more than anything.

"But my mother told me to leave it be. She ordered me not to go after you, and I was mad as fire, trying to tell her what I'd seen in the library and how you were playing with Edith's heart. But she insisted." He lifted his shoulders. "And somehow she made me think that maybe you didn't have the worst of intentions, since all I could think of was the story of you and Miss Franklin and the way you led her such a pretty dance."

Elias shook his head. "I never did that, Matthew. I was merely weary of the way you and Rumford would never stop taunting me about her. I wanted it to stop, so I lied."

Matthew stared at him. "I had no idea."

Elias shrugged. It hardly mattered now.

Matthew sighed. "Well, I didn't know that. But I couldn't disregard Mother's orders, and the rain was all but pounding at that point, so I stayed home. And I began to convince myself that you meant well by Edith, strange and unexpected as your tactics were. So when I saw the chaise drive up to Shipton Hall so soon after..." He looked at Elias with a frowning brow, his mouth twisted to the side.

"I understand."

Matthew nodded, and it was silent for a moment. "I must ask, though, Eli. What *is* going on with you and Edith? I can't seem to make heads or tails of it."

Elias shot his friend a grimace. "I feel the same way."

Matthew stared at him, and Elias could feel him searching his profile, as if it held some answers. "Have you fallen in love with her?"

Elias said nothing. He didn't trust himself to.

"But you detest women! And you and Edith do nothing but fight when you're together."

Elias let out a breath through his nose. "I know."

The leaves on the trees nearby rustled in the wind as Matthew processed what he was learning. "Then I don't understand. What is the problem? Why is Edith visiting people like Miss Perry instead of marrying you?"

Elias clenched his jaw. "Because the thought of marrying me is repugnant to her."

Horse hooves on the grass were the only sound as the seconds dragged on.

"Listen, Eli. Edith isn't like other women."

Elias chuckled genuinely for the first time. "And you think this is new information to me?"

Matthew's half-smile appeared. "I suppose not. But what I mean is, I've often thought she's much like an unbroken filly."

Elias frowned, trying to follow Matthew's train of thought. "You think I must break her in order to make her marry me?"

Matthew shook his head. "No. That's the point. She's not going to respond to that kind of treatment. I don't think anyone does, in truth, but especially not Edith. She thinks everyone is trying to break her, and she needs to know that no one wants to. She doesn't want to be saddled—she wants to be free."

"Which is precisely why she refuses to marry me."

Matthew shrugged. "Maybe. Or maybe there's more to it than that. I don't know, truthfully. But I know Edith enough to tell you that she's taken things to heart that have made her the way she is, and she's become devilish good at hiding that heart. If you try to put a rope around her, she'll break the rope and run off."

"And she views my love for her as a rope?"

"I doubt she can recognize the difference. She feels a pull, she sees it as someone trying to control her—I don't think she can discern between coaxing and forcing. She's spent too many years watching my parents push and pull each other, I imagine." He sighed, looking at Elias with an understanding grimace. "Edith's got to come on her own—on her own terms."

Elias frowned, looking at the reins in his hands. "Something she has sworn never to do."

Matthew nodded. "She might never come—only she can decide that—but I can tell you with certainty that she won't do so when she feels she's being pulled."

Elias knew it. Edith was a thorny stem. She thought those thorns made her capable of dealing with people like Mr. Stratton—people determined to force her to comply with their will. But she wasn't all thorns, contrary to what she wanted people to believe, and someone like Stratton could do irreparable damage to the soft and vulnerable part of her she took pains to pretend didn't exist. Hadn't she said it herself?

Even a villain has a heart somewhere deep down. And Edith seemed to see herself as a villain.

"She intends to go see Mr. Stratton," Elias said.

Matthew's head whipped around. "What?"

"She thinks she might be able to convince him to retract his threats against your father."

Matthew swore. "She mustn't. You must stop her, Eli. He won't hesitate to use her visit against her in any way he can. The man is a blackguard."

Elias's horse tossed its head. "She warned me not to interfere—threatened me with those eyes."

"So what?"

Elias looked at Matthew with incomprehension. "We've just discussed how Edith is not to be controlled, and you tell me I must yank her rope, as it were? She'd never forgive me."

"She might not. But I guess you have to decide what's more important to you: her favor? Or her well-being?"

Elias chewed on his lip, then, realizing Matthew's eyes were on him, said only half-teasing, "Or you could do the honors. She'll forgive *you*."

Matthew seemed to consider this, tilting his head from one side to the other. "Perhaps. But she told *you* of her intention, not me. If I'm the one to stop her, she will see it as cowardice on your part, and Edith has no patience for cowards."

Elias threw his head back, a sound of consternation escaping him. "So I am to leave her well alone because she can't abide having someone exert any type of pressure upon her, yet I am to forbid her in this because if I don't, she will think me lily-livered? It makes no sense at all!"

Matthew grinned. "I daresay you'd have tired of her long since if she were so easy to comprehend. When does she mean to go?"

"I couldn't say. She only told me of her intention half an hour ago."

Matthew raised his brows, taking a tighter hold on the reins. "Knowing Edith, she's halfway to Stratton's already. Shall you stop her? Or must I?"

Elias hesitated. He couldn't see the way before him at all. He was in entirely unfamiliar territory. He could already see how Edith's eyes would flash when she realized his intention. He blew out a long breath then tugged the reins to the side without a word, guiding his horse back toward Shipton House.

Matthew followed. "You're a good man, Eli. I thought you and Edith would make the worst pair of anyone I know, but I'm beginning to think I've been wrong all along. You're the only man equipped for her vagaries. If I could shake her and bring her to her senses, I would do it."

"I'd never ask you to do something so foolhardy," Elias said with as much humor as he could muster.

He squared his shoulders and pressed on toward Shipton House.

Chapter Twenty-Eight

Edith's hands were still unsteady as she passed through the front door to the courtyard to leave for Mr. Stratton's. She told herself it was just some residual nerves from the emotional confrontation with Elias, that it had nothing to do with any fear on her part for what might occur when she arrived. She had to believe herself capable of dealing with someone like John Stratton.

She needed but persuade him that it was not in his best interests to hold Edith's reputation over her father's head in order to have his way. If his priority was his own interests, she needed to find something of more worth to him than what he thought he would gain from his current threat. What that something was, she didn't know, but she trusted that she would be able to come up with something in the half hour's carriage ride ahead of her. She had a quick mind and more experience than she ever wished for with the means men used to achieve their political ends.

The thundering of horse hooves sounded behind her, and she snapped her head around to see Elias and Matthew approaching on horseback.

They both pulled up on the reins, and Elias swung a leg over his horse, hopping down to the ground.

"What a grand entrance," she said. "You must be very proud." She had little doubt what they were there for, and the thought that they intended to stop her acted like a spur. Everyone believed they knew what was best for her.

Well, they didn't.

"You cannot go, Edith," Elias said, watching her with a set jaw and wary eyes.

"Webb," Matthew said to the groom as he dismounted, "have the horses taken back to the stables. My sister isn't going anywhere."

Edith's eyes widened, and she gritted her teeth. "Webb, do *not* listen to him. I am going to Stratton Place."

The groom hesitated, looking back and forth between Edith and Matthew as a man caught in cross-hairs.

Matthew held Edith's eyes. "Webb, take them now. That's an order."

The groom bowed, avoiding Edith's eye, and led the carriage back toward the stables.

"How dare you?" She looked to Elias. "And you! I told you not to interfere. And instead you tell Matthew?"

He looked at her impassively, the set of his jaw the only evidence that her words had hit their mark.

"Oh, Edith," Matthew said impatiently. "It doesn't matter what a man does, you *will* be angry with him. But that's beside the point. What in the devil are you thinking going to Stratton's? It's lunacy!"

"I shan't let him, or anyone" —she glared at Elias— "dictate my future."

Elias's lips drew into a thin line. "And just how do you propose to convince him against it? Did you hope that he would lay down his arms out of the goodness of his heart?"

She put her shoulders back and tipped her chin up,

annoyed that she had no good answer. "He cannot be allowed to leverage my life and reputation for his own ambition—and *certainly* not when what he is claiming is false. I did *nothing* improper at the inn."

Elias took a step forward. "You are right, of course. He is the one in the wrong. But surely you see that your arrival at Mr. Stratton's estate—an unaccompanied, single young woman—will stoke the flames of the very same doubts Mr. Stratton seeks to raise against your character. Even should you manage to wring a promise from him that he will not use his experience at The Old Dog against you—a promise worth very little, I imagine—you will have given him more ammunition against your father by your mere presence."

She swallowed, her chest rising and falling quickly. She couldn't deny the force of his argument—indeed, she had known that what she was doing was foolhardy—but neither did she feel she could simply surrender to Mr. Stratton. She was desperate.

"Come," Matthew said, walking to her side and taking her gently by the wrist. "Surely we three can come up with an alternative preferable to this one."

"What alternative, Matthew?" She wrenched her wrist from his grip, feeling her emotions build in her throat and behind her eyes.

He stared at her, looking as deficient of any ideas as she was. "We will think of something."

"There is no *time*," she said. "Father will be here with the license tomorrow—the next day with any luck—and he is determined that the wedding take place as soon as can be managed. He may well insist upon it being carried out the very next day."

She glanced at Elias, who stood a few feet away, ever impassive. It was strange to see him so quiet, so grave. She longed to return to the way things were, to the easy and electric understanding between them. She wanted challenge in his eyes, she wanted the heat of conflict, even anger—anything but the withdrawn heaviness she now saw.

She wanted to lift that heaviness, to tell him how she felt for him and assure him that she loved him so much it made her feel mad. But it would be cruel: to express her love for him yet stand firm in her refusal to marry him—to soothe him with words and then strike at his heart with her actions.

He wouldn't understand. For she couldn't marry him. She would lose her reputation before she would risk watching Elias fall out of love with her as he came to know her better. She was too passionate, too headstrong, too sharp-tongued to keep something as fragile and precious as Elias's love.

In time, their love would deteriorate. The inevitable clashes of will would nudge the love toward frustration and defensiveness, and before long, they would care more about their own self-interest than each other. She thought she could bear anything but that.

"Can I have a moment with her?"

Matthew nodded. He gave Edith one more bracing glance, full of sadness, and strode inside.

She and Elias stood in silence for a few moments. She felt Elias watching her, but she was afraid to meet his gaze. It was easier to keep her head without looking him in the eye.

"What do you want, Edith?"

It wasn't accusatory or frustrated; it was genuine, and she didn't know how to answer. What *did* she want?

She wanted what she couldn't have. She wanted the impossible. She wanted any number of contradictory things: to be free, to belong to Elias; to spit in the face of her father and Mr. Stratton, to relent; to fight, to surrender.

His brown eyes were fixed on her, watchful, begging for an answer. "If you want me to tell your father, to tell him that I refuse to marry you, I will do it if it will spare you—if it is what will make you happy. That is all I want." He let out a helpless gush of air, throwing his hands up helplessly. "I just want you to be happy."

Happy? That didn't even seem possible anymore. No matter which direction she faced, Edith saw pain.

She shook her head. "No, I don't want you to do that. I simply need some time to think. Perhaps to sleep." She was so very tired, and yet she had no time for rest or contemplation.

Elias nodded. He hesitated for a moment, searching her face with his brows drawn together, then walked toward her and slowly wrapped his arms around her so that his cheek rested on her bonnet. Her hands were tucked up under her chin, and she shut her eyes, submitting to the embrace and resting her head on his shoulder because she was tired. She was so desperately tired of fighting, and she wanted to feel safe, if only for a moment.

Elias was warmth and softness and strength, and the embrace held her together in ways she hadn't known she needed.

"It will all be all right," he whispered so softly she could hardly hear it.

She shut her eyes, trying to breathe in the words so they filled her until she believed them. "I am sorry," she said, swallowing the lump in her throat. He said nothing. He didn't ask her what she was sorry for. He only kissed her bonnet and held her.

It was minutes later—or perhaps seconds, maybe hours—when Elias next spoke, pulling away and looking down at her with a hint of a smile. "You should go rest, particularly if you don't wish to be cajoled into a reading of your cousin's poetry, for I heard her speaking of her intentions this morning."

Edith stepped back, even though she wanted him to hold her again. "Good heavens," she said with as much of a smile as she could muster. "I shall take shelter in my bedchamber at once."

They looked at each other for a moment, and she turned toward the house, knowing that every second she stayed near him weakened her resolve.

Chapter Twenty-Nine

The carriage rumbled over the uneven ground, and Elias looked with a furrowed brow at the passing countryside. Letting go of Edith physically had been one of the greatest challenges to his self-discipline he had ever encountered. He would have gladly stayed there in the courtyard forever, holding her. She was finally unfurling a few of her petals to him, finally showing him that she wasn't all stone and high walls.

But she was a tortured soul, and one embrace would not cure that.

It had been as he watched her retreating figure disappear into Shipton House that he had realized what he needed to do. He had let her go physically—now he needed to let her go in the way that would mean the most to her.

Edith needed to be set free, or she would never stop resisting. She was unhappy, and he saw her helplessness crushing her spirit. It was as Matthew had said, like watching a magnificent horse being cruelly broken. She might finally surrender, but she would never be the same again, and that prospect left Elias full of sorrow. To force Edith to marry unwillingly was to break her. He had to find a way to free her, even if it meant losing her.

The carriage turned onto the smaller lane leading to Oxley Court. Somehow, in all his years of friendship with Lord Oxley, Elias had never been there. For a moment, he forgot the weight upon him as he peered out of the carriage window toward his friend's estate.

It was every bit as imposing as Elias had expected. It matched the title it belonged to in that way—ancient and impressive, like the many Viscounts of Oxley who had lived there before. Its stone façade must have once been golden, though it was difficult to tell with the amount of gray discoloration from centuries of existence.

Elias's carriage was intercepted by a groom, and within minutes, he was awaiting Oxley's pleasure in a very grand room. If not for the tall windows that lined one edge, it would have been quite dark, encased as everything was in mahogany. The gilt-edged desk that sat before a wall of books and the chairs before it were of the same wood, the seats upholstered in a deep blue velvet.

An enormous painting of a woman hung on one end of the room. She was almost ethereal in her beauty, with flaxen hair, rosy lips and cheeks, and a regal posture. Her blue eyes watched the room, following Elias no matter where he went, as though it was her domain and he an intruder there. There was no question at all in his mind that she reigned there.

He was still looking at the painting when the door opened and Lord Oxley walked in, with his confident gait and biscuit colored pantaloons. He looked every bit the part of a viscount, with a strong jaw and dark, expressive brows that had the power to transform his aspect from alarming severity to genial good-humor.

"Abram," Oxley said with his wide grin. "Very glad to see you again so soon."

They embraced, and Oxley set to pouring Elias a glass of brandy.

"Who *is* that?" Elias pointed to the painting. He didn't know whether it was the size or the subject of the painting that drew his eyes toward it again and again.

"Ah," Oxley said. "I see you've met my mother."

Elias glanced back and forth between Oxley and the painting. He could see it now. Oxley's hair was dark rather than flaxen—and certainly not as silky as the woman's in the portrait—but there was no doubt they were related.

"Captivating, isn't she?" Oxley sat down and stretched his legs before him, crossing them at the ankles.

Terrifying, too. "What was she like?"

He shrugged. "I never knew her—at least not enough to remember her. She died giving birth to my brother when I was very young. But apparently she was somewhat of a paragon."

Neither of Oxley's parents were living, but there was no evidence that their absence affected him. Sometimes Elias felt as though he himself had lost both parents, even if it wasn't true. He rarely saw his mother, and she was hardly the picture of matronly care even when he did. From all he could tell, she forgot about him entirely most of the time.

It was with a jolt that Elias realized the anniversary of his father's death was in two days. He felt a sliver of guilt for having forgotten, even if only for a day. His mind had been so taken up with everything else.

Oxley was watching him with interest, and Elias cleared his throat.

"You seem…different." Oxley took a drink of his brandy, still watching Elias.

Elias managed a chuckle. "What do you mean?"

He raised a brow. "You haven't made a single joke at my expense since I walked in the room."

"We've only been here two minutes."

Oxley shot him a significant glance. "An eternity to go without some of Elias Abram's wit."

"I must be entering my dotage," Elias said, looking down at his glass and swirling the liquid around.

"Hardly," Oxley said. "Out with it, then. What ails you?"

Elias pursed his lips. "The truth is my mind isn't easy. It's why I'm here." He met Oxley's gaze. "I need your help, Ox, if you can give it."

"Anything. What is it?"

This was the difficult part. Oxley wasn't exactly the type to laugh at one's expense, but Elias hadn't been at all reluctant to share his views on women in the past, and he had little doubt that Oxley would see through him if he tried to hide the truth behind his visit. He cleared his throat. "When I met you at the inn, you had some conversation with John Stratton."

Oxley nodded.

Elias fixed his gaze on his friend. "I need to bring him down."

Oxley's brows flew up. "Bring him down? Why?" He readjusted in his seat. "What I mean is, I can't say that I'm opposed to it—the man is insufferable. But I never took you for the feuding type." His brows came together. "Nor did you seem to be acquainted with Stratton when we spoke with him at the inn the other day. Can't see what cause you'd have to wish for his downfall."

Elias smiled. "You complain about my becoming soft and then give me grief for wanting to take a man down?"

Oxley waved his hand. "That's different. Harmless banter." He locked his gaze on Elias. "What you're asking is different."

Elias nodded slowly. "It is." He set his glass on the table next to the settee, leaning so that his elbows rested on his knees. "Stratton is making threats. Not to me, precisely, though I'm not unaffected if he makes good on them. But I wouldn't be here if it was just me he was threatening. He's threatening Mr. Donne."

Oxley grimaced. "I can't say it surprises me. They've been at each other's throats for years, and now more than ever with this talk of changing the borough lines. But it's a moot point, in my opinion. I can't see the vote happening. At least not for some time."

"That seems to be the consensus among rational people. But Stratton doesn't seem to be rational, and neither does Donne. It's Donne's daughter whose reputation Stratton is using as leverage against him." He fiddled with his fingers and forced himself to look up and meet Oxley's eye.

Oxley's gaze took on a hint of intensity. "The one you were with at the inn?"

Elias's fingers stopped. He hadn't realized Oxley knew it was Edith who had been at the inn. He had been relieved when Oxley hadn't pressed him for information, but it seemed he hadn't needed to. "Yes. But...."

Oxley smiled. "I caught a glance of her at The Old Dog."

"I can explain," Elias said, but Oxley waved him off.

"There is no need. You know your affairs, Abram, and I've known you long enough to know you wouldn't compromise Edith Donne."

Elias pressed his lips together then sighed. "I wouldn't. And yet, if Stratton puts it about that we spent the night at The Old Dog, that will hardly matter."

Oxley drummed his fingers lightly on the desk. "Why not marry her, then? Why go after Stratton?"

Elias looked down at his hands again, debating how much to say to Oxley. He was asking for the man's help. It was better to make a clean breast of it. "Because I love her."

Oxley's fingers stopped, and he narrowed his eyes. "I don't understand."

Elias gave a wry laugh. "That's because none of it makes

sense. Believe me." He shrugged. "She doesn't want to marry me, but her father insists upon it due to the threat of Stratton. I need to remove that threat."

He tried not to wriggle under Oxley's gaze.

Oxley finally let his eyes drop, rubbing absently at a spot on his pantaloons with his thumb. "I don't know Stratton terribly well. But I've heard enough and seen enough of him to guess how he works. He and Donne have Kingsbridge in their pockets, and while I'm no great lover of Donne, I would take him over Stratton any day. Stratton doesn't show *me* his true colors —always the picture of civility when I speak with him—but I'm not as big a fool as he thinks I am. I have my suspicions about how he's managed to be reelected time and again."

Elias sat forward on his chair. "That was what I was wondering about. He threatened not only Donne but also Miss Perry from the inn—don't know if you saw her. Young woman in mourning. He wrung a statement from her condemning Edi —Miss Donne for conduct unbecoming a young woman of gentle birth."

Oxley's eyebrows snapped together. "Then I imagine the reports and rumors I have heard are true. Where there's smoke, there's bound to be fire, and Stratton seems to have a veritable blaze going." His brows rose, wrinkling his forehead. He sipped his drink. "It is my suspicion that the few voters in the borough don't vote for him out of any particular affection. I would start there."

Elias blew air through his mouth. "I had the same thoughts —it stands to reason that a man who will extort one man won't stop at the one. But what incentive will they have to come clean about things to a stranger like myself if Stratton is holding something over their heads—if he's coercing them under threat of exposure or ruin?"

Oxley put out his hands, palms facing up. "Me."

Elias waited.

"There's a reason Stratton fears me. He knows my family is strait-laced when it comes to these things. My father had no patience for the games people would play in Parliament, and he trained me the same way: to respect the responsibility of my position. Men like Stratton often have little care for anything but squeezing the last farthing out of their place in Parliament. He's taken pains not to do anything to make an enemy of me, for he knows I could have him removed from Commons if I had reason."

Elias tapped his hand on the arm of his chair, thinking. "You're a good man, Oxley. But what, then?"

He lifted his shoulders. "Use me as protection. If the voters will tell you honestly of their dealings with Stratton, I will offer them my protection—financially, if it is needed. But I suspect that Stratton will remove the threats when he discovers that the alternative is losing his seat. You need merely use my name. Tell him that you've provided me with an account of his doings." He chuckled. "To say truth, I would love to see his face when you do."

He pulled out a sheet of parchment then reached for the quill on the desk, dipping it into the nearby well. "Here are the names and addresses of a few men who might be able to enlighten you regarding Stratton's dealings." The quill scratched on the paper for a moment, before Oxley set the quill back in its stand and sanded the wet ink.

He stood, and Elias followed, feeling overwhelmed at his friend's generosity.

They walked out of the room together, making their way toward the front door, and Elias set his hat on his head, frowning. "I didn't expect you to offer yourself, Oxley, you know. I merely hoped you might point me in the right direction."

"Nonsense. You are doing me a service. If word gets about that Stratton has had to change his ways, perhaps others will follow his example. I only wish it weren't necessary."

Oxley handed him the paper, and they embraced a final time.

Elias went on his way, determined to speak to at least two of the landowners whose names Oxley had given him. Time was running short, but if he spent the night at one of the nearby inns, he could pay a visit to Stratton in the morning before returning to Shipton House. Before freeing Edith.

Chapter Thirty

Elias was not at dinner, and when Viola mercifully inquired about his absence, Matthew merely shrugged. "I am not the man's master, you know. He said something about wishing to visit his father's grave—the anniversary of his death is sometime soon, I think, but..." Matthew trailed off, his concentration shifting to the task of stabbing two stubborn peas with his fork.

The anniversary of his father's death? No wonder Elias had been so affected by Miss Perry's situation at the inn. He had enough to deal with without worrying about Edith.

She felt her mother's eyes on her and met her gaze squarely, even though her stomach felt uneasy. She had little appetite—for food or conversation—but she tried valiantly not to show it. There was a constant stream of talk, largely maintained by Viola and Matthew—but the company felt thin without Elias's presence. It was impossible not to remark his absence—he had a personality that filled a room.

When the women rose, leaving Matthew and Solomon to their port, Edith walked up beside Viola, hoping to avoid her mother, who had been watching her enough during the meal that Edith suspected she had *intentions*. Edith had no desire to discuss the situation with her mother.

"You missed the reading," Viola said, accepting Edith's arm with a bit of surprise evident in her eyes. Had Edith been too hard on Viola? Not everyone was as well equipped to deal with her abrasive manner as Elias was. She shut her eyes, annoyed at the way her mind seemed intent upon noting all the ways Elias was what she needed.

"I know. I wasn't feeling terribly well earlier, and you know how poetry affects me."

Viola looked up at her, a bit of hurt in her eyes, but Edith smiled teasingly down at her. "I'm only joking, Vi. I *would* like to hear some of your work. Do you know any of it by heart, or shall I have to wait for the next formal reading?"

Viola nodded quickly, and Edith's heart twisted at the light in Viola's eyes at her invitation.

"Come, then." She pulled Viola down onto the chaise beside her, determined to listen to the verse without giving any evidence of how she truly regarded it. "Tell me your favorite lines—that is, I imagine poets have preferences in their own work?"

Viola smiled a bit sheepishly. "I hope so because I certainly do." She sat straighter, taking in a breath and setting her hands primly in her lap.

"*When summer sun gives way to autumn chill,*
When wintery ice doth quell the daffodil,
Unchanged, my heart beats ever calm, serene.
For you, my love lives firm and evergreen."

There was silence, punctured by the conversation of Edith's mother, Mercy, and Solomon on the other side of the room.

Viola's brows drew together, searching Edith's face. "Did you dislike it terribly?" She rushed on, "I have only recently begun to try my own hand at verse, but I am afraid it is rather childish."

Edith swallowed and cleared her throat, her heart aching. "Not at all. It was quite lovely." She managed a smile. "You shall be very well served by all this wisdom when you find the gentleman worthy of your affections."

Viola smiled, dismissing Edith's comment with a shake of her head. "It is one thing to read or write poetry—it is another thing entirely to live it, I think, and you are far ahead of me in that regard."

Edith reared back. "Me?"

Viola looked at her, wariness entering her eyes, but she nodded. "I am sure you have no wish to hear it, but you are the picture of everything romantic." She touched one of the tresses that had come loose from Edith's bun. "Dark, passionate, confident." Seeming to realize how strange her gesture was, she dropped her hand. "I can quote poetry and tell you all the figures I most admire in literature, but *you* are the true romantic."

Edith laughed, shifting in her seat. "The woman who has railed against marriage nearly her entire life?"

Viola looked at Edith with her direct, guileless gaze. "Yes. I have read about many women just like you—women under whose skepticism and refusal to marry is, in fact, a determination to marry for nothing but the truest of love—and a despair of its existence. The opposite of a romantic is not someone who never marries, you know. It is someone who marries for purely practical reasons."

Edith's heart was thumping against her chest. "And what if my reasons for *not* marrying are practical ones?"

"Are they?"

Edith swallowed, regretting her own question. She looked away. "I don't know. I don't even know what I want anymore. But it hardly matters. My future is decided for me."

Viola rested a hesitant hand atop Edith's. "You refer to your father and his demand that you and Elias marry? I am very sorry, Edith. And I feel responsible."

"You?"

Viola nodded. "You would not be in this situation were it not for the idea we had of including you in the joke."

Edith shook her head, feeling her eyes prickle. "It is not your fault."

Viola didn't look convinced. "But even if you *are* forced to marry, your future is still yours."

"Still mine?" She laughed her incredulity. "How can you say so?"

Viola raised her brows and sat taller, and Edith could feel what was coming.

"'*For what is wedlock forced but a hell,
An age of discord and continual strife?
Whereas the contrary bringeth bliss,
And is a pattern of celestial peace.*'"

Edith laughed, though she couldn't help wrinkling her brow. "And that is your argument that my future still belongs to me? It sounds rather like an argument against it. '*What is wedlock forced but a hell?*' That is precisely what I embark upon. Forced wedlock."

Viola lifted her shoulders. "Unless you choose to enter into it willingly. Marriage is but one choice—an enormous one, to be sure—but so much else has yet to be decided. Your husband may have been chosen *for* you, but it remains for you to decide how you will approach your marriage to him. Shall you spend the rest of your life regretting what is already set in stone? Will you live separate lives—passing ships on a wide ocean?" She glanced falteringly at Edith, and her voice became soft and hesitant. "Or will you choose to love?"

"Love is not enough." Her eyes roved to her mother. She always looked her best when her husband was away, and tonight was no exception. "Love grows cold."

"It can, certainly. But to love is a choice, and it will always *be* a choice—a choice that must be made every day. *No one* can force you to love, and no one can keep you from it but yourself. It may seem easier or safer *not* to choose it, but I believe that that choice can ultimately lead to nothing but regret."

Mercy approached, smiling at Viola. "Your knowledge is required, Vi. Aunt Agnes insists that it was Christopher Marlowe who said *'If little labour, little are our gains,'* but I told her I was certain that it was George Herbert."

"George Herbert? No, no!" Viola shook her head emphatically. "You are both in the wrong. It was Robert Herrick."

"You are certain?" Mercy said doubtfully.

Viola looked to Edith, clearly hesitant to leave in the midst of such a conversation, yet incapable of allowing Mercy and her aunt to go on thinking something so demonstrably wrong.

"Go," Edith said, pushing Viola up to a stand with an understanding smile. "Set the world right."

Edith watched Viola walk away with Mercy, the former's hands gesturing passionately as she spoke. Edith's own smile faded as they retreated farther.

She had admittedly thought little of Viola since becoming reacquainted with her over the past two years, and she felt a pang of guilt for how she had acted toward her. She had been so convinced of her beliefs and the rightness of her position that she had looked down upon her cousin's romanticism.

But now? She would give anything for Viola's trust in humanity, her unwavering optimism.

Chapter Thirty-One

It was nearly eleven o'clock when Elias arrived at The Bull for the night, and though the evening had been productive and triumphant in many ways, his brow was heavy. It had taken all of his persuasive powers and assurances to draw out the truth from one of the two men he had visited, a Mr. Gaines. Once the man had opened up, though, the confidences poured out, obliging him to invite Elias to stay for dinner in order to explain the entirety of the circumstances.

Mr. Stratton was every bit the scoundrel Elias had supposed he might be—and more.

In the beginning of Mr. Gaines' association with him, Stratton's ambition had masqueraded as kindness. He had offered to sell some of his land to nearby yeoman farmers who were struggling after two years of below-average crop yields. Too expensive for the farmers to afford outright, the pieces of land were offered with an agreement that they would be paid over time, with interest, to Mr. Stratton.

As time went on and the farmers began to feel the weight of the interest, Stratton would offer them alternatives to paying the interest—an expressed hope by Stratton that they would support him in the upcoming election, for instance.

That hope became an expectation, and it wasn't long before Stratton expressed his great regret at being unable to forgo the interest payments any longer and, indeed, needing to increase the interest percentage, due to his own financial situation which, from all Mr. Gaines could tell, had never been better. When Gaines had asked for leniency, Stratton had found other ways for the interest to be "paid" and had made threats of reclaiming the land.

The knowledge of what type of person Stratton was caused Elias to send a prayer of gratitude to God that he and Matthew had stopped Edith from her intention of going to see him. He was far too practiced in obtaining his aims for Edith to come out of such an encounter unscathed.

After a night full of tossing and turning, evidenced by the rumpled state of the bedclothes and Elias's equally rumpled hair, he partook of a simple breakfast and went on his way. He didn't relish the encounter he was about to have. In some ways, it felt as though he was doing something very much like Stratton had been doing: forcing compliance under threat.

But Stratton needed to be stopped. Even if Edith had not been a victim of his wiles, he needed to be taken care of, just as Oxley had said. If the borough borders *were* miraculously realigned, Stratton would have an entirely new population to deceive and extort, slipping a noose over their heads before they realized what he was about.

No, it was for the best that Elias intervene.

And Edith would be free.

Stratton was all civility in welcoming Elias into the library, but there was an amused glint in his eye that hadn't escaped Elias's notice.

"I wondered if I might not receive a visit from you," Stratton said, pouring Elias a glass of brandy, which he refused.

"I confess I am surprised to hear you say that, sir," Elias said. "We are hardly acquainted, after all."

Stratton swirled his brandy, leaning back in his chair and resting his heels on the edge of his desk. "What poor sop can resist rescuing a damsel in distress?"

"Better to rescue a damsel in distress than to distress a damsel, I think."

Stratton met his gaze, and a little smile tugged up at the corner of his mouth. "They *are* more interesting in distress, though, aren't they?"

Elias wanted to throw Stratton's glass of brandy in his smug face, but he knew it was unnecessary. Elias held the winning hand, and he was determined to play it with the same cool composure Stratton oozed.

"I am here, as you have implied sir, to speak with you on the matter of Mr. Donne and his daughter."

"Does Donne know you're here?"

Elias hesitated. He didn't like to go above Donne's head, but the man would look more foolish if Elias claimed Donne *was* aware of his intervening. "No, he does not. I admittedly have little interest in whatever feud lies between you and Mr. Donne except for how it concerns Miss Donne."

Stratton clucked his tongue. "Very unfortunate, isn't it? One would think the offspring of such a paragon of virtue as Leonard Donne claims to be would have more care for her reputation. Reputation is such a fickle thing, though, isn't it?"

"Indeed, sir. You perceive the purpose of my visit quite clearly."

Stratton threw back what remained in his glass, setting it down on the desk with a clank. "I am afraid Edith's reputation lies entirely in the hands of her father. He knows his options, and it is for him to decide whether he wishes to" —he cleared his throat significantly— "jeopardize it."

Elias thought of the folded foolscap inside his waistcoat. He wanted to dangle it in front of Stratton's face and watch the arrogant smile disappear. But he resisted, taking in a breath. He would give the man an opportunity to do the right thing first.

"You know that is untrue, sir," Elias said. "*You* have the power to remove the threat, and I ask you to do so. Prove your honor as a gentleman. Resist the temptation to toy with a woman's reputation for your own gain."

Stratton's smile became more of a sneer. "You arrive at my house unexpected and uninvited, Mr. Abram, and then you insult me, expressing your doubts about my claims to the title of gentleman. Tell me, is *your* conduct the type you encourage me to adopt to prove that I am indeed a gentleman?" He tugged at the end of his coat, ensuring it covered the white wrist of his shirtsleeves. "I can't help but wonder what other evidence I might find in your life that contradicts your claim to the title," he mused.

Elias's brows drew together. "You cannot help but threaten and extort, can you? It is your first impulse."

"And yours is to insult."

Elias smiled wryly, thinking of all the times he and Edith had hurled witty insults at one another. If Edith were in the chair across the desk from him, she would throw an insult right back at him—one even more stinging than his own. "I confess it is somewhat of a pastime of mine." He leveled a serious gaze at Stratton. "This pastime of yours, though—the threats—they stop today, sir."

Stratton raised two brows in feigned curiosity. "Not only a master of insults but a foreteller of the future. Very impressive, Mr. Abram."

"Not a foreteller of the future, sir. Merely a holder of powerful information."

A wary light entered Stratton's eyes, but he said nothing, his brows still lifted.

"Your activities, sir, as a Member of Parliament are gossiped about. They are the subject of discussion among those who run in your same circles. And yet no one has made an effort to determine their veracity—until now. Reputation is, as you say, a fickle thing, and I felt you deserved that someone should disprove the defamatory rumors against you—to prove you were the gentleman and worthy candidate you have claimed yourself to be. I took that upon myself."

Stratton was still in his seat, the only movement the controlled rise and fall of his chest as his breath came through flared nostrils. "And what did you find? You have my interest."

"Far more than I—or Lord Oxley—expected."

Stratton's gaze was fixed, unblinking, upon Elias. "Lord Oxley?"

Elias nodded. "He is a friend of mine and Matthew Donne's, you know, and takes an interest in both our families."

Elias watched with satisfaction as Stratton's throat bobbed, though his face showed no hint of alarm.

"You will remove the threat from Mr. Donne and his daughter, or Lord Oxley will be obliged to make known your dealings, sir. In addition, you will cease to threaten the landowners in your borough or face the same fate—a publishing of your methods to your fellow MPs."

"You are lying."

Elias shrugged. "Would you care to hazard your future on that assumption?"

Stratton's sneer became more pronounced. "You use the same tactic on me, then, that you condemn me for?"

Elias rose from his seat. "A man must speak in the language his fellows understand. I have taken the liberty of sending Lord Oxley an account of my discoveries. If he or I receive any report that casts doubt upon your intention to function with honor in your dealings, he will have no choice but to make the contents of that letter known to your fellows in both the House of Commons and the House of Lords."

Stratton's face was taking on a red hue, and his close-fisted hands shook.

Elias inclined his head. "I trust you will forgive me for dropping in unannounced. I won't trouble you to see me out." He set his hat atop his head, stood, and left.

Chapter Thirty-Two

Elias had not returned to Shipton House the night before, a fact Edith had managed to garner from her maid as discreetly as she could. She felt empty, knowing he was gone—or perhaps she was merely hungry. She had hardly eaten at dinner again. She felt ill-at-ease, too, for her father had arrived late the night before, and she feared how he would react to the knowledge of Elias's disappearance.

A part of her was even angry with Elias for it. He and Matthew had assured her that they would find a solution together. She hadn't believed it at the time—she still didn't believe it—and yet she was bothered that neither of them had spoken of it since.

She wondered with a clenched stomach if perhaps Elias had decided to simply leave. He had mentioned that he was willing to take the brunt of her father's ire by refusing to cooperate, and it had certainly been a noble offer. But his disappearance did not accomplish that. Edith could hardly marry a man who was nowhere to be found, of course, but her father wouldn't hesitate to blame her, for he required a target for his anger.

She had to believe Elias wouldn't leave her in such a situation—and without saying goodbye.

She herself was a mess of emotion—fear, hope, anger, love—and she felt entirely incapable of predicting which of them would win out.

When the dreaded summons from her father came, with no word or sight of Elias, Edith forced herself to breathe in calmly. She hadn't any idea what she would say to her father. She supposed she could only tell the truth: she hadn't any idea of Elias's whereabouts. And while the prospect of braving her father's reaction left her feeling vulnerable and alone, she supposed it was fair. It was her fault any of this had happened, and she should be the one to bear the consequences.

Matthew stood a dozen feet away from the door to their father's study, leaning his back on the wall and chewing on his thumb. He stood straight as he saw Edith, a commiserating grimace replacing his pensive expression. He put a hand on her arm. "He'll be mad as fire that Eli's not here."

She hardly needed to be told as much. She shrugged. "There is nothing to be done."

Matthew frowned and shook his head. "I can't understand it. I didn't expect this of Eli—to abandon you at such a time." He met Edith's eyes, which, to her embarrassment, stung at his words. "He loves you, Edith. I didn't think it possible, you know, but I think I've had him wrong all this time—my own best friend." He paused. "I know you haven't asked my opinion, but I think you should marry him."

Edith felt the familiar prickling of her pride, the impulse to exert her will in opposition to what Matthew was saying.

"Just think," he continued. "For once in their lives, Mother and Father are in agreement on something, and I'm no politician, but their endeavor seems like a worthy one. But if you refuse, I can't help feeling it will all fall apart. And for what? To defy Father? To stake your independence?"

A CONSPIRATORIAL COURTING

Edith clenched her eyes shut. "Stop, Matthew. Please stop." She could feel her pulse quickening and the anger beginning to rise, and she didn't think she could stop it if it rose any further. All of her emotions were too close to the surface, covered by a thin veneer of pretended calm.

He gripped his lips together in frustration. "I know, I know. You can't abide anyone telling you what they think you should do."

"It hardly matters," she said with a bite to her tone, her gaze flitting to the windows. "I can't marry a man who's not here, can I?"

"Edith!" Her father's peremptory voice sounded from the study.

Matthew squeezed her arm a last time. "He'll come back, Edith. And when he does, I hope you'll be able to see past your pride." He walked away, and Edith stayed a moment longer.

Her pride? Did he really think this was still merely a matter of pride?

She exhaled and stepped into the study.

"Where's Abram?" her father barked.

"I haven't seen him since yesterday," she said, taking her seat.

"Given you the slip, has he?"

She didn't answer.

"Well," her father said, looking at the paper that lay in front of him on the desk. "We shall see about that. I've managed to get you a special license, and I don't intend for all my efforts to—"

He stopped as a knock sounded on the door.

"Enter."

The door opened, and Elias appeared in the doorway. His gaze seemed to skip over Edith entirely and move directly to her father.

"Ha!" her father cried. "There you are. And a good thing.

I've known you quite some time, Abram, and I never took you for a coward. I was disappointed when I thought you had made a run for it. Glad to be wrong."

"I was out on some business, sir, and have only just returned." He stepped farther into the room. "I merely wished to inform you that the threat from Mr. Stratton need no longer concern you."

Edith froze, her eyes fixed on him.

"Eh?" her father said.

Elias clasped his hands behind his back, and Edith had the feeling that he was avoiding her gaze. "I said that Mr. Stratton's threat—the one—"

Her father waved an impatient hand. "Yes, yes, I know which threat. I meant the second part."

Elias cleared his throat. "The threat is gone, sir."

It was impossible to think that Elias didn't feel her eyes boring into him, willing him to look at her. Her breaths were coming in quick, unsteady succession.

"I don't believe it," said her father. "If this is your way of escaping your duty..."

"On the contrary, sir. I felt it my duty to see to it that Mr. Stratton's heavy-handed methods were put to a stop."

Edith heard the implied insult to her father in the words—he had been ready to sacrifice his daughter rather than stand up to Mr. Stratton himself. It had required Elias to take action.

Edith's father scoffed. "And you think you've managed such a feat."

Elias inclined his head. "With the help of a friend, yes. Mr. Stratton understands that, if any word reaches either me or Lord Oxley of his attempting to extort and threaten people, he will be tried and removed from his position."

Edith abandoned attempting to force Elias to look at her and looked to her father.

A CONSPIRATORIAL COURTING

For the first time, he seemed to hesitate, his eyes flitting to a paper on his desk. "How?"

"I doubt it will come as a surprise to discover that you are not the only person Mr. Stratton has attempted to force into compliance. I was able to speak with some of his other victims, and they provided ample evidence to convict him if he is ever tried."

Her father picked up the paper in front of him, staring at it thoughtfully. The light shone through it, revealing a tax stamp in one corner and an official seal at the bottom. The special license. "How can I be certain? I went to great trouble to acquire this license, after all."

A flash of annoyance crossed Elias's face. "If my word is insufficient, Mr. Donne, I will request Lord Oxley to send his reassurances to you."

Edith's father looked searchingly at Elias for a moment then shook his head. "No. That won't be necessary. You would be a fool to concoct such a story if it were false."

Silence filled the room for a moment, with still no evidence that Elias even realized Edith was in the room.

He cleared his throat. "And now, if you will excuse me, sir, I have some family business to attend to. If you have any questions regarding the matter, you are welcome to send them to me by post. I apologize for the inconvenience this has been to you and your family."

He bowed to her father and then—finally—turned his gaze to Edith. She stood, and he held her eyes for a moment then bowed and left the room.

Edith stood transfixed, staring wide-eyed at the door Elias had disappeared through, her mind trying and failing to grasp what had just occurred.

He hadn't abandoned her to her father. He had come back. Even more than that, he had found a way—an alternative—just as he had said he would.

And now he was gone, without a word to her.

She knew an impulse—so strong that she took the first step—to chase after him. But what would she say? Her mind was reeling, and her heart even more so. With the sudden removal of the weight that had been pressing down on her—her father's demands, his political career, the Parliamentary vote; Elias's honor and wishes; her own reputation—Edith hardly knew what to feel.

"Well," her father said, rising from the desk and brushing his hands together. "That is certainly a relief. Dashed if I thought Abram had the gall to confront someone like Stratton." He walked towards the door, stopping to smile at Edith and tweak one of the wavy curls framing her face. "Free as a bird now, aren't you? Just as you wished." His face became sterner, and one of his brows rose. "And learned your lesson, too, I should hope."

She merely stared at the door and, realizing she wasn't in a state to respond to him, her father left with a little "hmph."

Chapter Thirty-Three

Elias had expected to see relief on Edith's face when he had delivered the news. Indeed, he had been so terrified of seeing that relief that he hadn't dared meet her gaze. He had felt her eyes on him the entire time he was in the study, willing him to look at her, and it had taken all his will not to give in.

But he hadn't been able to leave without one glance at her, and that brief moment had nearly broken him. There had been no relief in her face—only astonishment. Only questions. And much as he had wished to answer them, he knew he couldn't. It was left to her to make what she would of what he had done.

He'd had to leave before she could say a word—before all that he was feeling inside spilled over, undoing everything. Edith knew he loved her—he didn't need to say it again. Now he just wanted her to be happy—to be free.

Giving up Edith felt like more than losing just her, though. It felt like losing his future. He couldn't replace her. There was no one like Edith Donne.

He sighed and couldn't help glancing through the small back window of the chaise. No carriage following him. Of course not. It was silly to think Edith would do something as dramatic as chasing after him. Leave such things to Viola. It was stupidity to expect anything. He had accepted that it was all over now. But there was nothing as maddening as that little bit of hope that persisted despite all efforts to stamp it out.

He laid his head back against the squabs and shut his eyes. He hadn't slept much at The Bull. It seemed to be a trend recently, but even when he *did* manage to, he was haunted with dreams of Edith that left him feeling bereft upon waking.

It had been months since he had been to the family estate at Wooldon. It was *his* estate now, in fact, but he had insisted that his mother remain there while he spent most of his time in Town or at their smaller estate near Richmond. He had never felt like Wooldon belonged to him, and it had never felt like home since his father's passing. His mother hadn't wasted any time in demanding that all of his belongings be packed away—stuffed into one of the unused rooms where even the servants rarely ventured.

Wooldon sat within a small clearing of trees at the bottom of sloping, grassy hills. At the top of one of the hills, overlooking Wooldon on one side and the sea on the other, sat the parish church where his father and sister were buried. An unbroken line of windows stretched from one end of Wooldon's red brick façade to the other, perfectly symmetrical, but for one small wing on the south end, added shortly before Elias's father had died.

Elias tried to prepare himself for seeing his mother as the chaise drove into the small courtyard.

One of his mother's new servants met him in the courtyard. "Where is my mother?" Elias asked.

"In the morning room, I believe, sir."

Elias took in a breath, hoping it was enough to help him keep his calm. He and his mother had never got on together terribly well.

The scratching of a quill stopped as he opened the door to

the morning room, and her head turned toward him. "Elias. I hadn't any notion you intended to come." She didn't sound surprised, as one might expect a woman to sound if her son appeared unexpectedly after a long absence. She sounded like she might have if the maid had stepped in with a stack of post. Hardly interested.

"Yes," he said, still standing just beyond the door. "I wished to come home for the anniversary of Father's and Caroline's deaths."

"Ah, I see." She turned back toward her writing. Responding to invitations, no doubt. "You have always been good at remembering these things. I had quite forgotten."

Elias clenched his jaw. "Naturally," he said.

Of course she had. Her mind was taken up by too many other things—which invitations to accept and turn down, how many times one might wear a dress before beginning to occasion comment, how many couples could sit comfortably to dine at the Wooldon table without the knocking of elbows.

"I shall only be here for two or three days, I imagine, before returning to Richmond."

She sprinkled sand on the fresh ink, responding absently, "You are welcome to stay as long as you like, of course."

Yes. It was his house, after all.

He bid her good day and left the room. He couldn't help resenting her presence even more than usual. Somehow it made it feel more difficult for him to properly remember his father and sister when his mother was carrying on as if they had never even existed.

Elias sat down to dine alone. He had asked that the cook prepare his father's favorite: larded hare. His mother was finishing her toilette in preparation for the invitation she had received to dine at the Cravens' home a mile down the road.

She popped into the dining room when he was still eating the first course. "I should have thought to ask you when you first arrived, but it slipped my mind, I'm afraid. If you wish to come, I'm certain they wouldn't mind at all. They are forever asking when you will return for a visit. I imagine you could ride over behind me once you are dressed. It looks to be quite dry this evening."

He gave a polite smile. "That is very kind, but if you can please give them my regards and make my excuses, I would appreciate that." He was looking forward to an evening alone at Wooldon.

She nodded, the feather in her cap fluttering with the action, and glanced at his plate with a wrinkling of the nose. "It's been some time since I've seen *that* on a plate. I never could understand why your father loved it. Well, I am off, dear." And she was gone.

When he had finished eating, he didn't linger over his port, instead asking that the housekeeper, Mrs. Tinsley, be called for. The smile that broke onto her face at the sight of him was so familiar, surrounded though it was by extra lines, that Elias felt the first whisper of being home.

It was only after two or three minutes of chatting that Elias changed the subject. "Is everything of my father's still kept in the green room?"

She nodded. "It is."

"Thank you," he said, moving toward the stairs.

"Oh, but" —the housekeeper rushed to catch up with him — "allow me to accompany you. You shall need a key, you know."

A key? His mother kept every memory of his father and sister locked away? What, was she afraid she might accidentally stumble into the room and be forced to remember them?

"Thank you," he said.

They took the stairs then walked the full length of the corridor, turning into the smaller one that branched off at the end. Both rooms in the small corridor were unused and had been for years. During his childhood, Elias had been scared of the corridor—it was never lit with candles, and he had imagined it stretching on and on, a deep abyss with any number of terrifying creatures.

Now it housed all that remained of his father and Caroline.

Mrs. Tinsley fiddled with the keys at her waist, inspecting two or three carefully before finding the right one. "Your mother is the only other one with a key—she doesn't like to be disturbed when she comes in on Sunday mornings." She opened the door and walked in, standing so that Elias could pass through.

It took him a moment to realize she was waiting for him. He blinked and stepped into the room. "On Sunday mornings?"

She pushed the door so that it almost closed. "Yes, every Sunday morning before church. Just for half an hour or so."

Elias stared at Mrs. Tinsley, but she didn't notice. She was tugging at the holland cover that was draped over his father's favorite armchair.

"Never says a word about it," she continued, "other than to ensure the servants know that they are not allowed in this room. Though I've noticed when I come in to clean occasionally that this cover always needs adjusting, and these two items sit on this small table beside it." With a brief nod, she indicated the small doll and the pocket watch that sat on a narrow, mahogany table.

"I hadn't realized she *ever* came in here. I imagined that all of this had remained undisturbed since the last time I was here."

Mrs. Tinsley pressed her lips together in something of a grimace. "Perhaps I shouldn't have said anything. Your mother is very private."

"I shan't mention it to her." He had a feeling she would be very displeased with the housekeeper if he did. He picked up the doll. "I had forgotten about this thing. What was it Caroline called her?"

"Lady Jane," Mrs. Tinsley said with a smile. "Though her full name was Lady Jane Elizabeth Granville—"

"—of Harcourt," Elias finished with a growing smile.

Mrs. Tinsley laughed. "She wouldn't let anyone forget it."

"No, indeed." His smile faded slightly, and he looked to Mrs. Tinsley. "Why does my mother wish to be so private about coming here?"

She frowned. "Everyone handles grief in a different way, I have found. Your mother doesn't like to speak of such things, so I can only make a guess as to her reasoning. She has always abhorred displays of emotion, though, and I have wondered if perhaps she fears being overcome in the presence of others."

Elias nodded, feeling the need to swallow down his own emotions. He picked up his father's pocket watch. The little grooves of the etched design on the front and back had rubbed away in spots—his father had forever been pulling it out. Maybe he had realized his time was in shorter supply than everyone else's.

"Two years tomorrow," he said.

"And twelve years for Caroline next week." Mrs. Tinsley adjusted the doll on the table ever so slightly with a small sniff. "What I wouldn't give to see her grown into a fine young lady."

"She'd have married long since, I'm sure," Elias said with a half-smile. "She was forever forcing her toys into matrimony, wasn't she?"

Mrs. Tinsley laughed and nodded, her eyes still on the doll. "That she was." Her gaze moved to Elias, a bit of sauciness entering into her eyes. "I imagine she would have forced even you into matrimony if she were still here."

He smiled wryly, moving toward a pile of odds and ends nearby. "It's not me she'd have to force," he said softly.

"What's this now?"

He shook his head. "Nothing." He reached for a small, leather box and opened it. "Ah, father could never resist a fancy pair of sleeve buttons." This pair was white enamel with a *fleur de lis* painted in blue.

Mrs. Tinsley walked over and squinted at them. "I remember the day he decided to put them away—afraid he might come under suspicion as a revolutionary."

Elias smiled. "He always just liked the symbol, didn't he?"

It felt good to talk about Caroline and his father. They felt a bit less far away in that dusty room.

He was secretly glad to know that his mother wasn't as heartless as she had seemed for so long. Just as Mrs. Tinsley said, everyone needed to grieve in their own way. His mother's way was apparently both secret and solitary. He just wished it hadn't been.

After Caroline's death, Elias and his father had done little things to remember her—placing her dolls in her favorite spots in the house, telling stories of her amusing antics at dinner. He had forgotten how healing it had been to do such things. Rather than enhance his sorrow, it had helped him feel connected to Caroline.

When his father had passed away, though, he'd had no one to do such things with, and only when he met Miss Perry did he begin to realize how much it had affected him—or how much he had been trying to pretend it *didn't* affect him.

He wasn't so different from his mother as he had always thought.

Admitting that he was well and truly in love with Edith seemed to have opened the floodgates. Now he was feeling it all, the bitter and the sweet.

Chapter Thirty-Four

Four times Edith had reached for the bell during the course of the day, intending to ring for a carriage to be brought around, only to stop herself. Matthew had told her that Elias was at Wooldon. Tomorrow would be the anniversary of his father's death, and it seemed wrong to spring herself upon him, expecting him to reciprocate immediately after all she had put him through.

Besides, Edith had never known such self-doubt, such painful and constant deliberation. It was enough to make her wish for the past—before anyone had thought it might be amusing to play tricks on one another. They had all certainly got more than they bargained for.

But though nerves and doubt plagued Edith, she couldn't truly wish to be transported back in time even if it were a possibility. Difficult as it all had been, she had some sense that there was purpose and importance to what she had been through. Like a purifying fire, perhaps. She could only hope that, after the singeing and burning, she would come out intact.

Though she longed to yank the bell cord and set off in pursuit of Elias, she promised herself to wait. She needed time for her thoughts and emotions to settle. Everything had been so rushed for the past week—she didn't want to rush into the most important decision she would ever make.

But when the next day dawned, the desire to follow after Elias hadn't abated. Edith tried to eat the toast in front of her at the breakfast table, but her stomach flipped and churned oddly. She was aware of Mercy's eyes on her every now and again.

"Edith," Mercy finally said once her husband had risen and left to go for a ride. "You are jittery. What is it?"

She looked Mercy in the eye. Edith didn't confide in people. She didn't trust them with the truth, and she never had. But if she was going to trust her heart to Elias, that would have to change.

"Is it Elias?" Mercy asked gently.

Edith swallowed the lump in her throat and nodded, feeling her limbs tremble with fear at laying her emotions open to someone, even someone as kind as Mercy.

"You have fallen in love with him, haven't you?"

Edith shut her eyes. "I don't know, Mercy. I don't know what it is I feel for him. It may be some twisted version of hate, for all I know. But it feels like love. And if it isn't, I can't imagine what love might feel like."

Mercy smiled her understanding. "You cannot truly think you hate Elias, Edith. There is a vast difference between hate and what exists between the two of you. I have given it much thought myself, and I realized something: you are never more alive than when Elias is in the room."

Edith let out a laugh. "But what does that mean? I can assure you that, while I am more aware of his best qualities than I used to be, I have not become suddenly blind to his worst ones."

Mercy laughed. "I would be worried if you had! Love is not blind—or at least the most enduring love is not. Marrying someone, promising to love someone is merely a vow to take the good and the bad together. One cannot be expected to love or even like another person all of the time. Heaven knows there are times when I despise even myself. *But* I never give up on myself. And when I married Solomon, I promised to never give up on him, either."

Edith fiddled with the napkin on her lap. "But what if I make Elias miserable?"

Mercy grasped Edith's hands in hers. "It is not your responsibility to make him happy. It is your opportunity, rather, to love him. And the fact that you are so concerned with his happiness is the best evidence I can imagine that you do indeed love him."

Edith swallowed. "I do." She gave a watery laugh. "Much as I have tried not to, I do."

"Then stop trying *not* to and put that energy into loving him. With every bit of your soul."

Edith glanced at the bell again, and her heart raced at the thought of going. Oh, how she wanted to go!

She clamped her eyes shut. "But he is mourning, Mercy. Today is the anniversary of his father's death—hardly the time for such a declaration."

Mercy looked at her intently. "Is it not? I heard Matthew saying that Elias's mother has never been one for grief. Don't you think he might like someone beside him? And who better than the woman he loves?"

Edith thought on their conversation at The Old Dog and Pheasant: Elias's insistence that Miss Perry have the opportunity to properly mourn her brother, and his short comment about never having talked through his grief with anyone as Miss Perry was doing with them.

He *shouldn't* have to mourn alone.

In three quick steps, Edith was ringing the bell, while Mercy looked on with approbation and rose from the table.

"What can I do to help?" Mercy asked, striding over. "Shall I get your bonnet?"

Edith clasped her hands to still them, but the trembling merely traveled up her arms and down into her knees. "Yes, if you please. For I need one other thing."

"What?"

"The marriage license."

Mercy's brows flew up, and she followed Edith from the room. "Are you intending to elope in earnest this time, then?"

"I hardly know," Edith said truthfully. "I must say, the prospect is certainly appealing, for I can't imagine facing the lot of you with your self-satisfied smiles beaming up at us from the pews."

Mercy laughed and started toward the stairs. "I am the last person with ground to stand on against an elopement, so I shall respect whatever decision you make. But I assure you that I would be looking at you both with the most exquisite and genuine happiness possible if you decided not to elope."

Edith narrowed her eyes playfully then turned to the servant the bell had brought and asked that the chaise be readied immediately.

She hurried to her father's study, where the marriage license still sat upon the desk and breathed a sigh of relief that he hadn't burned it. Never had she thought to look upon her own marriage license—or to read the words with a thrill of exhilaration and nerves.

Mercy met her in the hallway, placing the bonnet upon Edith's head as they walked toward the front door.

"Send word when you know your plans, won't you?" She helped Edith into the chaise.

"Of course," Edith replied, shutting the door and leaning her body through the open window. "But Mercy?"

Mercy raised her brows questioningly.

Edith hesitated, clutching at the sill of the chaise window. "What if I am too late?"

Mercy took in a deep breath and pursed her lips. "I don't think you will be." An amused smile crept upon her lips. "Recall that but two weeks ago neither of you had any notion of love or marriage."

"And if I *am* too late, despite that?"

"If you are..." Mercy took Edith's gloved hand in hers. "Then Elias will at least know of your love—for that is no small thing, Edith, to be so loved by another person that she would willingly join herself to you for the rest of her life."

Edith nodded and leaned out to kiss Mercy on the cheek. "You are right. How very aggravating of you."

Mercy only smiled and nodded to the driver to set the horses to.

Edith gave a little wave and turned to sit forward in her seat, shutting her eyes and forcing herself to breathe. She would tell Elias she loved him, she would sit with him and celebrate the life of his father, and she would expect nothing in return from him.

She loved him, whether he could return her love or not.

Chapter Thirty-Five

The sea air whipped at Elias's hat, and he put a hand on top to keep it from floating off his head and out of the parish cemetery. He looked up at the leaves above him, fluttering in the wind, and then to the church itself. He doubted there was a more beautiful parish church in all the Southwest. Just beyond the walls of the church grounds, a small path led to the rocky coast, where waves could be heard crashing and receding. "God's own church," his father had called it.

Elias gazed down at the two headstones before him, the one as small as the person it commemorated, with years of lichen and moss creeping around its edges, and the other tall and new in comparison.

It was beautiful, in an unexpected way. His father had wanted a daughter for years, and when she had finally come, she had been taken too soon, a victim of consumption. Elias's father had never fully recovered from the loss. But here he and Caroline were, beside each other again.

The wind picked up, and Elias glanced at the deep gray skies which promised rain. He wouldn't be able to stay long before the path home became pure mud. A bit of thunder rumbled in the distance, and a carriage passed behind the drystone wall of the church grounds.

Elias pulled off his gloves and hat and bent down, putting his hat on the ground and a bare hand in the grass to stabilize himself. He reached to Caroline's gravestone, tracing the etched letters of her name. The cold, rough stone was the closest he would get to her now.

The gate to the cemetery creaked with the wind, and Elias wiped hurriedly at his eyes.

A gust of wind pushed through, blowing his hat from his side, and he stumbled a bit to rise from his bent position and hurry after it.

The hat tumbled until coming to a stop a dozen feet away. He stilled, heart stopping, when he saw what was beyond.

Edith stood just inside the gate, bonnet ribbons blowing in the wind. She held a bouquet of bright flowers in her hands. Elias was certain she had never looked more beautiful in her life, with the breeze tugging wisps of hair across her pink cheeks, and the hesitant way she stood, as if on the edge of some precipice.

"Mrs. Tinsley told me you were here, and I wondered if you might like some company."

Elias swallowed hurriedly, too afraid to try to understand what was happening. All he could manage was a nod, and she walked toward him, picking up his hat on the way and handing it to him when she reached his side. Her eyes moved to the headstones behind him, and he shut his eyes for a brief moment as the wind carried her scent around him and then away again.

She separated the flowers in her hand into two bouquets and bent down, placing one at the base of his father's gravestone and the other at the base of Caroline's, reaching for two small rocks nearby to weigh them down. Elias was only vaguely aware of what she was doing. His eyes were fixed on her face.

"What are you doing here?" He couldn't help himself, rude as the words sounded. He needed to know.

She turned toward him, meeting his gaze as she pulled in a deep breath. She reached into her pelisse and pulled out a folded paper. "I wanted to bring you this."

He set his hat down on the ground and took the paper from her, opening each corner and feeling her eyes on him.

The marriage license.

His gaze flew to hers, and he was struck by the uncertainty in her eyes, the way they searched his face nervously.

She gave a feeble laugh, indicating the paper with a nod. "Two weeks ago I would have laughed at the idea of my name on such a document—and then burnt it in the nearest grate." Her chest rose with another deep breath, and she glanced upward with a wry smile. "Today I find myself terrified that it might blow away with the wind, for it holds the dearest wish of my heart."

Elias's grip slackened on the paper, and the wind licked at it, pulling it from his hands. Edith hurried to grasp it, as did he.

She laughed, letting her hand drop. "Apparently I was justified in my fears." She held his gaze again. "Elias, I love you. I haven't the first idea how it came to happen or precisely *when* it happened, but it did. And you have watched me fight it, just as I fight everything that terrifies me." She paused. "But I don't want to fight anymore. I *am* scared" —she shut her eyes a moment and looked down— "scared of so many things: that I shall hurt you, or that you shall hurt me; that I won't know how to love you the way you deserve to be loved."

Elias could barely hear her words over the pounding in his own chest, and he quickly folded the paper back into its neat square so that he could grasp one of her hands in his.

She smiled with a watery chuckle. "Above all things, I must ensure you have the very lowest expectations of me, for I am certain that I *shall* say unkind things, that I *shall* provoke you, that I *shall* fail at times. But I am even *more* certain that I want to try—I want to love you as you are meant to be loved." She looked at him shyly. "If you will let me?"

He stared down at her, his heart thundering in his chest, and studied every detail of her face in a moment so full of unanticipated joy that it ached. He reached a hand to her face, savoring the softness of her cheek. "Do you think me so spineless that I am afraid of you?"

She smiled and looked down. "Perhaps you should be."

He slid his hand under her chin, urging it upward so that he could look into her eyes. "For some time now, I have been certain that the only life I wish to live is one by your side, Edith. There is no doubt in my mind that we will come to blows on a regular basis—always your fault, naturally." He smiled and tenderly brushed a hair from her face. "But I shouldn't wish for it any other way, if only it means I get the chance to love you for the rest of my life."

She swallowed, emitting a trembling breath, and put a hand to cover his, leaning her cheek into it. "I am terribly stubborn," she said.

"I know this. But as long as you promise to *love* me stubbornly..."

She lifted her eyes to his and gave a fervent nod. "I promise."

He wrapped his arms around her waist, holding her gaze so that she couldn't doubt his next words. "I love you now and will love you always, Edith. I will fight with you, yes. Every day, perhaps. But I will just as certainly make up with you every single time, with a promise to love you more deeply than ever."

He tilted his head and leaned toward her until his lips touched hers, sending a thrill through him at their warmth and softness. They had kissed before—unplanned kisses full of passion and attraction and anger—but this kiss was all love and promise, gentle but firm. It was the garden beyond the high, stone walls; it was the very part of Edith that he had longed to experience for himself—the part that could not be taken, only willingly given.

Her hands wrapped around his neck, pulling him more tightly toward her, and he shivered as the first raindrops fell on his hands and hair. Her hands threaded lightly through his hair, and he felt his knees threaten to give way underneath him.

She pulled away, looking up with squinted eyes as a raindrop fell on her face. Taking his hand from around her waist, she took the folded certificate from it, smiling as she tucked it back into her pelisse. "For its safety," she said.

"What, then? Are we to elope again?" he asked, secretly touched at her concern that the license not be ruined. He put out his hand, and two raindrops landed upon it. "I don't think the weather will hold."

She smiled mischievously. "You mustn't mind the clouds in the south. The worst weather always follows the coastline."

"But we *are* on the coastline."

She narrowed her eyes at him playfully. "Have a bit of courage, my love." She reached a hand to his hair, which was getting more wet by the second. "We needn't elope, but I admit that I have no wish to wait for the banns to be posted. What do you say to making use of the perfectly good wedding my father planned for us?"

He smiled, nodding at the stone church. "I would marry you in this church right now if the vicar was here."

She glanced at the church and then to the gravestones, her face becoming thoughtful. "Perhaps we *should* be married here."

Elias's gaze followed hers, and he felt emotion rise in his throat.

Their eyes met. "I should like that," he said.

She took his hand in hers, clasping it tightly. "Tell me about them."

"I have already forgotten so much." There was a small break in his voice.

She leaned her head on his shoulder. "The more you tell me, the more you will remember—and the more I can help keep those memories alive."

He planted a kiss on her bonnet, and his lips came away wet from raindrops.

"If you'd like," she said, raising her head to look at him, "we might sit down together and write things down. Then you shall always have the memories."

He nodded, and a watery chuckle escaped from him. He brushed a tear from his cheek. "Blasted raindrops."

She raised a skeptical brow.

He grimaced helplessly. "I'm afraid I tend to cry quite often, Edith."

Her mouth stretched into a smile. "If I can manage you snoring like a lion, I can surely handle your crying like a baby."

"A lion?" He pulled her along with him on the path toward the gate. "I believe you likened it to thunder last time. I seem to have made very quick progress." In a swift motion, he scooped her up into his arms, ignoring the exclamation of surprise she emitted.

"What in the world are you doing?" she cried.

He smiled down at her. "I know how your knees trouble you, Mrs. Cherriman." He leaned in to kiss her before she could protest.

Epilogue

The fire crackled in the grate of the drawing room in Edith and Elias Abram's London townhouse, causing a steamy mist to cover the bottom half of the sash windows on either side of the fireplace. Edith glanced through the window as carriages clattered and the breath of the horses pulling them puffed out in small clouds up and down the street in the January air.

"Who is it?" Elias asked, glancing up from the letter he was reading.

Edith squinted at the equipage that had come to a stop in front of their house, with its large yellow wheels and an ornate crest emblazoned on the door. The door opened, and a man attired in very precise clothing stretched across a pair of fine shoulders stepped down. He spoke a few words of instruction to the driver of the chaise before striding toward the front door of the Abram townhouse.

"It is Lord Oxley," Edith said.

"Ah, good." Elias folded up the letter and rose. "I have been waiting for news of his arrival in town. He isn't one to miss the opening of Parliament, which was this morning, I believe."

"What news from Matthew?" Edith said, glancing at herself in the reflection of the standing clock and tucking a stray hair behind her ear.

Elias chuckled, taking Edith's hand and pulling her into his arms. "He claims he's been detained at Shipton House with further business, but...."

"Is *that* how he refers to Miss Perry?" Edith said with a smile, looking up into her husband's eyes.

Elias wagged his eyebrows once, and the door opened.

"Lord Oxley," the footman announced.

Lord Oxley stepped through the doorway, a wide, straight smile lightening his dark features and softening his angular jaw. His nose was touched with pink, evidence of the frigid winter air, some of which swept with him into the room.

He raised a brow at the sight of Edith and Elias in each other's arms then laughed. "A sight I never thought to see!" He inclined his head at Edith. "Good day, Mrs. Abram. Very pleased to see you, though I can't say I'm impressed with the man you've shackled yourself to."

Edith arched a brow, looking up at Elias again. "I took pity on him."

Elias flicked her hair playfully. "You've always had a pitifully soft heart."

She rolled her eyes and kissed him on the cheek, then, feeling Lord Oxley's eyes on them, she pulled away slightly. She had become no better than Mercy and Solomon—forgetting anyone else was in the room when she was with Elias.

But Lord Oxley didn't seem bothered. "Marriage looks good on you, Abram. Never thought to say that, I admit, but I offer you my congratulations."

Lord Oxley and Elias embraced in the way that only men would: shaking hands and then yanking each other in and clapping one another on the back.

Edith surveyed the man she owed much of her current

happiness to. She hoped that, absent Elias's gesture and Lord Oxley's assistance, she would have come to see the wisdom and joy in marrying Elias, even if it wasn't of her own free will. But she was a stubborn woman, and she was simply glad that things had happened the way they had.

The men stepped back from one another, and Elias glanced at Edith. "My wife and I have both eaten our fair share of humble pie as everyone has come to know of our marriage. But I'll tell you something, Ox. Humble pie tastes very tolerable indeed when you have a wife to share it with. And now" —he made an exaggerated bow— "we gladly pass the torch to you." He rose and raised a brow. "*Get thee a wife.*"

"All in good time," Lord Oxley said, with a dismissive hand wave. "If this morning is any indication, I shall have my hands too full to think of aught else but my duties in Parliament. I came to tell you that the motion to discuss the borough issue has been postponed indefinitely. It caused quite a ruckus amongst the cause's champions in the House, as I understand."

Edith stepped toward him. "Postponed?"

Lord Oxley nodded. "It comes as little surprise to most of us. There isn't near enough support for it yet. I imagine it will be years before there will be, if ever."

Edith nodded and looked at Elias, who came to stand beside her again. "My parents will both be sorely disappointed."

He raised his brows significantly. "Stratton, on the other hand...."

Lord Oxley frowned. "Have you heard that he is up to any of his antics again?"

Elias shook his head. "No. I think the threat of you bringing action against him has been enough to keep him in line. But time will tell."

Lord Oxley nodded then looked at them with another

smile. "Well, I shan't stay any longer. I just thought I would step in as I passed on my way to St. James's."

He bid Edith goodbye, and Elias walked him to the front door, while Edith looked out of the window again, grateful to be inside.

When Elias returned, he came straight up to Edith, feigning a glare at her. "Now, madam." He pulled her into his arms. "What's this about you taking pity on me?"

She wrapped her own arms around his neck and cocked a brow, feeling that familiar thrill of being in his arms. "What of it?"

He shrugged, tugging her in toward him more tightly. "I was merely wondering what I might expect—pathetic creature that I am—from your admirable compassion?"

She laughed and ran a hand through his dark hair. "Allow me to give you a demonstration, Mr. Cherriman."

He tipped his head so his lips hovered just shy of hers. "Gladly, my lady."

THE END

Afterword

Thank you so much for reading this book. I had a wonderful time writing it, and I hope you enjoyed getting to know the characters.

I also hope you look forward to reading the upcoming books in the series to learn more in depth about some of the characters you've only heard briefly about so far.

I have done my best to be true to the time period and particulars of the day, so I apologize if I got anything wrong. I continue learning and researching while trying to craft stories that will be enjoyable to readers like you.

If you enjoyed the book, please leave a review and tell your friends! Authors like me rely on readers like you to spread the word about books you've enjoyed.

If you would like to stay in touch, please sign up for my newsletter.

Other titles by Martha Keyes

If you enjoyed this book, make sure to check out my other books:

The Donovans

Unrequited (Book .5)

The Art of Victory (Book 1)

A Confirmed Rake (Book 2)

Battling the Bluestocking (Book 3)

Tales from the Highlands Series

The Widow and the Highlander (Book 1)

The Enemy and Miss Innes (Book 2)

The Innkeeper and the Fugitive (Book 3)

The Gentleman and the Maid (Book 4)

Families of Dorset Series

Wyndcross: A Regency Romance (Book 1)

Isabel: A Regency Romance (Book 2)

Cecilia: A Regency Romance (Book 3)

Hazelhurst: A Regency Romance (Book 4)

Romance Retold Series

Redeeming Miss Marcotte (Book 1)

A Conspiratorial Courting (Book 2)

A Matchmaking Mismatch (Book 3)

Standalone Titles

Host for the Holidays (Christmas Escape Series)

Goodwill for the Gentleman (Belles of Christmas Book 2)

The Christmas Foundling (Belles of Christmas: Frost Fair Book 5)

The Highwayman's Letter (Sons of Somerset Book 5)

Of Lands High and Low

A Seaside Summer (Timeless Regency Collection)

The Road through Rushbury (Seasons of Change Book 1)

Eleanor: A Regency Romance

Acknowledgments

Suffice it to say, I would never have had the courage—or the gall—to tackle a Shakespeare retelling without my mom. I grew up hearing and performing Shakespeare, thanks to her. She spent years—seventeen, to be exact—directing the sixth grade Shakespeare play at our local elementary school, changing many lives in the process. I owe so much to her.

My husband is always kind, understanding, and quick to make writing time possible—along with all the other tasks that come with it—whenever I need.

Thank you to my children who have continued to nap so that I can find time to write. May the odds continue to be in my favor.

Thank you to my editor, Jenny Proctor, for her wonderful feedback—I'm so glad I have you!

Thank you to my critique group partners, Jess, Kasey, and Emily for helping me get the book where I wanted it. I value our friendship and your input so much! Thank you to my other beta readers for taking on the daunting task of tightening things up in the manuscript.

Thank you to my Review Team for your help and support in an often nervewracking business.

About the Author

Whitney Award-winning author Martha Keyes was born, raised, and educated in Utah—a home she loves dearly but also dearly loves to escape to travel the world. She received a BA in French Studies and a Master of Public Health, both from Brigham Young University.

Her route to becoming an author has been full of twists and turns, but she's finally settled into something she loves. Researching, daydreaming, and snacking have become full-time jobs, and she couldn't be happier about it. When she isn't writing, she is honing her photography skills, looking for travel deals, and spending time with her family.